Dessert for Three

An Egyptian Collection

By
Aida Nasr
Mariam Shouman
Fatima ElKalay

CONTENTS

To friendship and partnership,
to women who stand together to
create something, whatever it might be.

O bird, I have bewildering tales
that I wrote with tears
They are known to the sea
each wave is a page to one of its lines

Jamil Hussein El Saadi
(translated by Nesma Gewily)

FOREWORD

"My dream is to write a collection of short stories that would be a portal to Egypt."

It was a hot summer's day in Cairo. Mariam and I were sitting in the shade of a poinciana at the Shooting Club, sipping chilled karkaday and watching our children in the play area.

I heard Mariam's words clearly, but somehow my mind registered porthole instead of portal. In a flash, that is what I saw: a ship's round window looking out onto a vast, unpredictable ocean called Egypt.

"Let's do this together, Fatima!"

"You're serious?"

I'd never mentioned to Mariam before that this was my dream too, one I'd cherished for most of my life.

"Of course! Aren't two heads always better than one?"

I had to agree with that. Two voices, two different outlooks. We knew our territory so well; it was home after all. This could be so exciting and timely.

That summer I'd also been seeing a lot more of our mutual friend Aida. We'd meet up for coffee in Café Greco on Road 9 in Maadi and chat mostly about writing. I sometimes brought along works in progress on which Aida gave profound feedback. She was a good writer; I'd read her nonfiction in *Cairo Today* and *Mother & Child*, two reputable magazines in Egypt, but what I really wanted was to read her fiction. I knew she hadn't written any in a while and needed some encouragement to get back in flow.

Something was taking shape, and it felt important. If two heads were better than one, then three would be perfect. Aida had to be part of this project. I talked it over with Mariam, and she was thrilled. Then I invited Aida aboard. The ocean awaited. Three women setting sail to tell Egyptian tales.

Slowly ideas formed, our unique take on Egypt, a mixed bag of socio-economic allsorts. We gave the stories titles, our characters came to life, we read each other's work. Aida's stories were about the upper middle class, Mariam's were rural and working class, mine were somewhere in between. But even as the stories took shape, so did life. I had lost my mother and was handling first one move, then another, trying to keep my little family afloat amid change; Mariam fell pregnant with her fourth child who, it would turn out, had special needs. She moved to the United States to seek medical support. Aida struggled to keep herself and us motivated.

Time passed. The project lost some momentum. At one point, my husband asked me why I didn't take my stories and publish alone. My answer was always the same: "These stories aren't going anywhere. They belong in this collection, however long it takes."

At the time, I didn't understand why it felt so important to stick with a project that had come to a halt. But nothing in life is arbitrary, even when it seems to be. I believe some things are truly bigger than the sum of their parts and that this book is one of them. What started as a project became something of a journey that in all aspects is a story in itself. It's a story of friendship, loyalty, love and loss. In time, we changed as people and as writers, but these tales, like messages in bottles, have withstood our personal storms and survived, even when not all of us did. It's hard to be writing this foreword with one of us missing. We often dreamed of writing it together, once our voyage came to an end and our stories were complete. But some things end before others. Life is one of them.

In 2012, Mariam underwent major brain surgery. She reached out to tell us how much she hoped this collection would be published. So much time had passed since we first set sail, and we had lost our way. Mariam wanted to do a final edit before surgery, but time was tight.

Aida and I were understandably worried. It was a serious operation, and we couldn't be with her because she was still in the United States. But we put our trust in God that she was in good hands and would pull through. I occupied myself with the manuscript, putting the stories in an appealing order, checking the spelling of all transliterated words, and praying for her. Thankfully the surgery went well, but her postoperative circumstances were challenging and sometimes complicated. We waited for her recovery, hoping she would be well enough to review her stories before we looked for an editor and a publisher. But we realized it wasn't the time to talk to her about writing. All we could do was wait and pray.

In the meantime, Aida and I kept writing. We met every week, shared laughter and coffee and writing assignments. These were the best days. We got back into our creative swing, we experimented with writing craft, and felt a renewed excitement about our project. Although Mariam's progress was slow, we knew she was a fighter. Everything was going to be fine. Then quite suddenly in November 2014, just over two years after Mariam's surgery, tragedy struck in a way no one expected. Aida had a bout of terrible back pain one Friday. She asked everyone to keep her in their prayers. I don't think anyone could have predicted what was to follow. The next morning Aida passed away in her mother's arms as quietly and peacefully as she had lived. Moments before, she had been writing me a phone message, one she never got to send.

Aida's death crushed me. I didn't see it coming. We forget how fragile life really is, even though we talk about death all the time. Then something like this hits us so hard that we are left in fragments. I could not think about our collection for a long time. I could not write anything. How could I, when everything I wrote I shared with Aida? And just like that, she wasn't here anymore.

Aida was gone. Mariam's recovery was a long haul. The responsibility to keep navigating was suddenly mine alone. I knew I owed it to these beautiful women and to myself to bring our project to light, but for a long time I couldn't. It took me two and a half years to find the emotional courage to share this manuscript, by then almost thirteen years old, with my dear friend, writer and publisher Sherine Elbanhawy. While sharing the backstory with her, it hit me that this was more than just a collaborative short story collection; ours was a very human story, with as much beauty, love, grief and pain as the stories we tell. I realized that I had to include our correspondence as part of the collection.

The stories predate Facebook and social media. Some predate cell phones. There are references to the Gulf War and bird flu in Mariam's stories. Subtle hints about the January 25 revolution in 2011 show up in my stories and Aida's, but these were introduced in rewrites, because mentioning the revolution wove in naturally with existing storylines.

The last story in the collection by Aida, "Tangerine Woman", is one she wrote during our many coffee dates while waiting for Mariam's recovery. At the time, Aida was the editor of an art blog and was inspired by the artists she interviewed to write a story about an artistic couple. I feel this is the most complete and revised story left behind and believe she would be happy to see it in print.

I hope I have done my friends justice with what I've made out of this collection. It's been a long journey out at sea. Seventeen years. Finally, it is time for our vessel to be moored.

Fatima ElKalay
Cairo, July 2022

DRIFTING

From: Aida Nasr
To: Fatima ElKalay
Subject: Hello
Sent: Sep 18, 2004 at 11:26 PM

Dear Fatima,

Great to hear from you, and really sorry I missed seeing you this summer. As you know I was in London for 2 months looking for a job, but unfortunately didn't find anything. … Back in Cairo, it took a good 3 weeks to rest from the trip, which was 60 days of non-stop action from morning till night. I was also a bit disoriented from disappointment, since what I had wanted to do isn't going to happen, at least for now, and switching gears back to Cairo life was harder than I thought! But I'm better now, and the plan is to try and have a freelance life, if I can manage that financially, because I like the variety and flexibility it gives me. But we'll see what happens. One thing I learned on this trip is that you can't really control what happens in your life as much as you (or at least I!) like to think. …

Well, I hope to see you on your next visit to Cairo, whenever that will be, and in the meantime, let's keep in touch by e-mail. Take care.

Love,

Aida

From: Aida Nasr
To: Fatima ElKalay
Subject: Re: Your message
Sent: Nov 28, 2004 at 12:42 PM

Dear Fatima,

Thanks for your message It's now gotten colder in Egypt, so winter is truly here, which is good ... I like winter weather. ...

I'm still finding my way with the freelancing ... but I can't help feeling this is not quite what I want to be doing! WHAT I want to be doing is still a mystery. ...

You asked me to send my personal writings and unfortunately, I realize that I don't have any. I haven't written creatively since I started writing as a journalist. But I may try my hand at something and send it to you. In the meantime, I am attaching another review which is different from the ones you read, because I interviewed the artist. I feel it's a bit choppy, i.e., the transitions are not very smooth, but I did find the artist's point of view really interesting, so I hope I got some of it across. Anyway, I'd value your opinion.

Yes, I agree with you that publishing is a loaded issue, because authors are judged by what other people think they are (and as you said, just about everyone has an opinion about Muslim women these days.) That's why I think it takes enormous courage to publish anything, particularly fiction or poetry, but the world does need more voices out there, whether the world likes it or not! Unfortunately, the only way to avoid criticism is not to say anything at all, and that's not always an option when you have something to say, as your stories do. ...

Well, that's about it from here. Take care and let's stay in touch.

Love,

Aida

Dear Aida,

Thanks for this review. I will read it and get back to you as soon as I can. … I've been thinking about what you said about not knowing what it is exactly that you want to do. It would be impertinent of me to tell you, but perhaps I can suggest ways to help you decide for yourself. Perhaps I can best do this by relating the question 'what do I want?' to myself. Until recently, I dreamed of travelling with a sketchbook, camera and notepad: writing, sketching, and taking photos of my surroundings. I felt that I would remain incomplete, naive, immature, until I had embarked on such a journey. I know now that this must remain a journey of my dreams, and that I will probably never get the chance to be a real "travel writer."

Before I decided on the course in creative writing, I went through a lot of distance learning options … but after reading through all sorts of course outlines, I discovered one important thing: whenever I thought of a track or a career, I thought of how it would enrich me as I writer, rather than how I would benefit from it in other ways. So, I had answered my own question. What I want to do more than anything is write … I have not yet sat down with myself and explored the possible reasons for this need, but I think I have a fair idea: I am not sure if I will ever have the refined conversational skills of a socialite, but in writing there is a chance to say all the things that don't come out quite right when you're talking. What's more, I think I just might have something to say.

… I apologize for talking about myself so much here, instead of asking about what you want, but I think if you sit with yourself in the same way and ask what means the most to you, you will find the answer. I hope I have been of some help to you. … Anyway, will be in touch.

Lots of love,

Fatima

From: Mariam Shouman
To: Fatima ElKalay
Subject: Mariam's first project
Sent: Aug 11, 2005 at 2:11 PM

Hi,

I've talked to you about writing—here's my first project to encourage you. Please let me know what you think of it. I haven't even read it over again, so it's still rough, but I thought I'd send it on to you.

Mariam

From: Fatima ElKalay
To: Mariam Shouman
Subject: Re: Mariam's first project
Sent: Aug 12, 2005 at 6:08 PM

Hi Mariam,

Thanks, for this first piece. I think it should get the ball rolling for us all, insha' Allah. It captures so much of the priorities and spirit of our society. It reminded me of my own grandmother, with some exceptions. She had daughters, but she lived long enough to be dependent on sons and daughters alike.

Do you think it's a good idea if we draw up a list of possible themes/ subjects that can be covered in each of our projects? The aim is for a varied collection, so we don't want to end up writing about the same things. Just a suggestion.

Take care and keep going,

Fatima

From: Mariam Shouman
To: Fatima ElKalay
Subject: Re: My first project
Sent: Aug 12, 2005 at 9:41 PM

Hi ya Fatima,

I'm so sad that you've gone already. I just called your phone and your father-in-law answered. We just got back from the North Coast tonight.

I know the story still has a lot of work—I have to admit that I haven't read it through yet, But I thought I would try to get us going—after that day in the club, I got excited about the idea and really got to work. There are still areas that need to be developed, but sometimes it helps me to get peoples' reaction to my writing. As far as drawing up a list of themes, it's not a bad idea ... and if we share our stories as we write them, we can try not to cover too much of the same ground.

I know you've probably got a thousand things to do right now, but let's not forget this project! I think the time is right.

Take care,

Mariam

MANNEQUIN

by Fatima ElKalay

I notice him on Wednesday. He is wearing a crisp white shirt with lots of buttons, a sleek red tie, and an inky-blue jacket to match his immaculate slacks. His outfit reminds me of the nice suits I was able to afford when I was that age. I wonder what he's doing in this place, and why he has gone to so much trouble dressing, and how he'll manage in there with all those buttons. He sits in the corner next to the giant pot of dusty, plastic azaleas and looks down at his hands, bruised blue from where there must have been a cannula. Sunlight from the open window falls across his pale features and makes the sharp bones in his cheeks more pronounced. Like most of the others in the room, he says nothing.

Next to him sits the nervous, bulb-headed inpatient from Ward 33, the one with sad bug-eyes, as green as alfalfa. He is dressed in an appropriate, loose-fitting hospital gown that is so faded you can't say if it's brown or gray or blue. Markings peep out of the top of his gown, just beneath his collarbone, the plotted parameters that he needs in the big room beyond the dark doors. His companion, in the oil-smeared boiler suit, comes and goes, whispers things in his ear then trails off with his cell phone, down one of the dusty corridors, probably hoping to find a better phone signal. Next, there is the woman of indeterminate age, the one with the broomstick legs and floppy shoes that on closer inspection prove to be bedroom slippers. The older woman with the same bone structure but more flesh—probably her mother—sits beside her, as usual, offering her sips of juice from a carton. What is it today? Apple, pineapple crush, or peach and mango? The girl turns her head away no matter the flavor and pinches her lips together, making them look chalkier than they already are.

Then there's the ever-shrinking patient in the wheelchair with the wonky back wheel. Usually, wheelchair and occupant are up by the window, but today because the gentleman in the inky-blue suit sits on a folding chair in the window spot, wheelchair and occupant are right next to me. Even this close, I can't make out whether it's a man or a woman. Beyond the skull cap and gray galabiyya there is no sign of femininity or masculinity. All I can see is a tiny bald head, a thin, hairless face, and hands with dark veins that show through gauze-thin skin like electrical wires. You can't even tell from the name, "Reda," whether you have a he or a she. Sitting this close, I am at least sure of one thing: very soon it won't make a difference. Last week three people said goodbye here, two went home to their villages; the third went to his home in the heavens.

I look at the man in the inky-blue suit again. He is so perfectly motionless he might be made of plastic, like the dusty azaleas in the pot next to him. Maybe someone brought him here from the shop window at Marie Louis to display a design from the summer collection. In that case, his neat black hair is really a wig that I can knock off with my cane if I get a little closer. But then, he could still be wearing a wig even if he's real. If he is indeed a real man, and not a mannequin, I wonder what he is thinking. Perhaps he is asking himself how long it will be. Or perhaps he is wondering about a meeting he's missed at his office. Maybe he's a bank manager. Or a school principal. It doesn't really matter now, not until he doesn't have to come here anymore.

Someone sneezes, and he moves, turning his head to the window. Aha! He is real after all! I don't catch the color of his eyes because the sun is in them. I wonder if he can see Mo'izz, hunched on the boot of his taxi. Mo'izz will be peeling oily brown paper from his fried eggplant and felafel sandwich now, and biting it with the relish of those who still have an appetite. Within an hour, he will stick a cassette tape into the car player and listen to a crooning youth sing about tears and unfulfilled love. Then he will rustle his daily newspaper, belch, and smoke a Cleopatra, before dosing off to the songs of the crooning youth, snoring with joy.

"Mo'izz," I've said, "Your smells and sounds should be a little more discreet, considering where we are."

"I'm sorry, sir."

And he genuinely is, but somehow, he forgets. Or perhaps it's because the claim of the living is so much stronger than the claim of the dying.

A small boy climbs onto the seat across from me, next to the water cooler. He looks around him with wide, curious eyes, as if he is at the circus and expects someone to perform a trick. When nobody does anything, he fills a paper cup with water from the cooler and bubbles his lips through it as if he is smoking a hookah. Minutes later, he is bored. He abandons his bubbling and begins to pick at the stitches in the upholstery with a thin, burrowing finger. I want to wave my cane at him, tell him to stop, but I'm worried that the cane will come down on his head. What if I cracked his skull? That wouldn't be a nice thing for me to carry to my grave. I suppose a few more loose stitches can't make a difference. Some of the seats have veritable hernias of bulging sponge poking through the imitation leather upholstery. Just one more ugly thing here. Finger blobs of chocolate milk, car grease and green snot decorate the walls. The white tiles are stained yellow-brown, like the discolored teeth of a chain smoker. The place is only seven years old, but already worn and weary, like most of the gaunt human shadows that come through its doors, day in, day out. Anyway, we barely notice these things in this middle place, where we wait.

Swing doors on every side spew out the uniformed usuals at intervals. White uniforms and starched caps clutch clipboards, chew gum, and hop across the tiles in rubber-soled shoes; white coats over somber suits march briskly into rooms and fortify themselves behind oak desks and doors; green overalls and masks with misty spectacles wheel trolley after trolley in and out of the operating theatre; plainclothes professionals with name tags burst in and out of rooms with great urgency, while drably dressed boys bustle around with trays of syrupy-sweet tea and Turkish coffee.

A nurse in springy shoes approaches Mannequin. She blocks him from view and asks him questions. I hear his voice, full of rich, resonant syllables, but cannot discern the words. She scribbles notes and nods. Then she lifts him by the elbow and leads him to a small office, two seats away from the plastic plant. Standing up, he is taller than I expect. His back is straight and his head level, but his gait is uncomfortable, like someone wearing shoes that are too tight. I wonder where it is for him.

He walks past and looks in my direction.

"May God send you recovery, my son." His eyes, so dark and sad and mysterious, meet mine. But I still can't make out a color.

On the way home, I ask Mo'izz if he saw Mannequin coming out of the clinic.

"Saw him? Oh, did I see him! What a car! What a driver! Damn my ill-fortune!"

"Mo'izz!"

"Sorry, sir ..."

And he genuinely is.

#

On Saturday, he comes again. There is no tie, but still he wears a well-pressed shirt and beautiful silver-gray pants. He does not get the window seat today. Instead, he sits across from me on the sofa where the little boy picked at stitches on Wednesday. He rubs his bruised hands together and keeps his head down. He has no visible markings to tell the rest of us what he'll be doing in there. Reda sits by the window in the wheelchair, wrapped in a mustard-colored shawl, skin as pale as raw bone today. Where is the little man with the green bug-eyes? Perhaps he doesn't need a session today. The girl with the broomstick legs is resisting an orange drink. The woman with her gives up and walks out of the little hall, sighing deeply and dabbing her eyes with a crumpled handkerchief.

A huge woman with heavy breasts enters and squeezes herself into a tight corner, between Mannequin and the water cooler. She brings with her the reek of days' old sweat with undertones of fenugreek and naphthalene. "Aah! Aah!" The woman wails, touching the side of her breast. A dark, skinny woman with squinty eyes stands next to her, shaking her head gravely. "They gave you the evil eye, habibti!"

I look in the direction of the skinny woman and begin to nod, knowing this is enough to guarantee a conversation.

"A needle this big ..."

She holds up a bony forefinger.

"No sedative! And the orderly did it, not the doctor! I begged him, 'give her a painkiller before you take the sample', but he just stuck the needle in. And he kept shouting at her for crying."

"May God send recovery," I say.

"Ameen!"

She spreads her palms and turns her squinty eyes upwards and mumbles a prayer. I turn my own eyes to the ceiling and notice a plump, white gecko moving across the peeling paint. "Aah, aah," continues the big woman. Then she closes her eyes and rocks herself to sleep to the sound of her own moans.

Her companion talks some more.

"She's my sister-in-law, sir, but by Allah, she's a good sister-in-law. She never turned my brother against me or against our mother. Even when we had a dispute over the land that has the canal running through it, she never took sides. And when her brothers took her ducks—two hundred healthy ducks—and exchanged them for dying geese, she said 'neither ducks nor geese. I'm a well-fed lady.' She really is more of a sister than my own sister."

Mannequin hardly moves. His eyelids twitch slightly when the woman first sits down, but he does not comment, even when her fat thighs get dangerously close to his perfect, silver-gray pants. He has nothing to say about the evil eye. Or the land with the canal running through it. Or the living ducks and the dying geese.

I want to engage him in the conversation, but the gecko suddenly plops down from the ceiling onto someone's head and that causes a commotion. A moment later, Mannequin has disappeared with a nurse behind some large doors.

#

The next time I see him is Monday. His hair seems longer, but he is still clean-shaven, neatly dressed, and as perfectly quiet as ever. It's still very hard to tell the color of his eyes, partly because he keeps them down, but also because they seem to be withdrawing into the sockets. The whole bunch is here today: green bug-eyes, broomstick legs, even Reda in the wonky wheelchair. Only the heavy lady hasn't come. The nurses are scoffing about how her biopsy results are serious, and how she needs to have immediate surgery, but probably won't. Her companion said she'd take her back to the village to get a wasfa baladi from her mother-in-law's old aunt, whose traditional concoctions are far better than treatment by Cairo's greedy doctors. And the village sheikh would burn incense to drive away the evil eye from her swollen breast. That would do the trick, wouldn't it?

Mannequin shifts in his seat and looks up at me. A golden opportunity to chat! But about what? Mo'izz suddenly comes to the rescue with his crooning love songs.

"My driver makes too much noise with his music …"

He nods slowly but says nothing.

"I've told him so many times to keep it low, but it's no use, he forgets every time."

I can't get him to say anything, so I decide to ask a question.

"Do you live far from here, sir?"

"I live in Maadi."

Oh! He has the warble of woodpigeons in his voice! I must find a way to keep the conversation going.

"My uncle's house was in Maadi, son. In Degla. A villa from the twenties, but his heirs tore it down fifteen years ago for an apartment building. Are you familiar with Degla?"

"I'm in Sarayat."

"Sarayat! Ah, such a lovely place. Maadi is so far away, though. So is Dokki, where I live. But we're in the middle of nowhere here, so we're far away from everywhere, actually."

He does not feel obliged to say anything more. My observation is accurate, but I wish I had not taken the conversation to a dead end. He nods again to acknowledge my comment and falls silent.

A nurse takes me firmly by the arm, grabbing a handful of flabby flesh, and leads me to the radiology room. Damn these angels of mercy in their springy, sensible shoes! How are we supposed to socialize if they keep dragging us off?

#

It's Wednesday again. Mannequin has not brushed his hair this morning. He has shaved, but not thoroughly; there are dark, blue-black shadows of stubble on his chin. He is neatly dressed, but somehow his clothes aren't quite right. They're not their usual perfect fit today. The pants are a little baggy. The shirt flops at the shoulders like a garment that's too big for its clothes hanger. And the colors seem bland. Too beige. Maybe it's just because he is thinner and paler than when I first saw him. A week can take a lot out of you when you have to come here. It can pass like an eternity, and it's enough to transform you into someone else.

A tubby nurse comes in, one with no spring in her step and plenty of scowl in her face. She must be having a bad morning. She marches over to bug-eyes and his oil-smeared companion and begins to discuss something of urgency. Her tone is harsh and argumentative. The man tries to raise his voice, but she cuts him short.

"We have no time for this, Mister!" And in a loud enough voice for everyone to hear she presses on him him how missed sessions would not be rescheduled.

"But Madam—"

He tries to tell her how his brother is feeling very down as an inpatient, but she isn't interested.

"Khalass! That's quite enough! Don't you think I have better things to do? If he's not happy in our wards, then he should go home and be with his family. Or you should be here more often to cheer him up, but he's not allowed to make up for missed sessions and that's final."

I can't possibly listen to this and stay silent.

"What's the matter with you, lady? That's no way to treat a sick man!"

I lift my cane with a little difficulty and point it at her. My tone is edgy. She is not amused.

"And what has this got to do with you?"

She glares at me for a long moment. She has eyebrows that meet thickly across the bridge of her fat nose. I quickly survey her arms and legs and notice that she is rather hairy all over.

"We are all here for a common reason, Madam."

I wave a hand around the room.

"Show us some mercy, may Allah keep sickness away from you."

"Mercy? How have I not shown you mercy? Answer me that!"

No one says anything. She places her stubby fingers on her tubby hips and scowls at us some more.

"Do you think we have an easy job managing everyone who walks through those doors? There's a million and one tasks to do before my shift is over and there's no way we can reschedule anyone. If you miss a session then it's your own problem, not ours, do you understand?'

I am angry now. I push myself up on my withered legs, leaning on my withered cane, and protest.

"Fear Allah's retribution, Madam! We sit here day after day, waiting, waiting, waiting. We are in pain. We would rather be at home with our families. We don't know how long we have to keep coming here, and only God knows if there's any use in us being here at all. Do you think any of that is easy on us?'

She sighs impatiently and rolls her eyes.

"May God send recovery to every sick person."

The cafeteria boy comes in with a tray of refreshments and places a stout glass of dark tea in the nurse's hand. She sips from it audibly.

"But if you want to get well you must do as you're told, mustn't you? And you should remember to thank God that you are getting treatment. Some people aren't so lucky."

Another angel of mercy pokes her head through a side door and the tubby nurse marches out of our sight in a brisk, healthy flash.

Outside, Mo'izz turns on some chirpy music.

I look across to where Mannequin is sitting and realize that he isn't there. When did he get up? No one called him in. Perhaps he wandered off into the gents while we were arguing. Ah, yes, that must be it. After all, he is far too civilized to witness such a harsh exchange.

But minutes later, I spot him slipping soundlessly out of a room at the far end of the corridor. The only room with a fancy brass plaque attached to the door. A man in a smart gray suit nods pleasantly to Mannequin as he leaves, then closes the door behind him with a gentle click.

I want to ask him what he thinks of all this, but another merciful angel swoops down on him and takes him away for his session.

#

The next day I arrive a little late. Mo'izz stops by the open fruit market en route and buys all sorts of fruit for his pregnant wife Hayat and some cantaloupe for me. I am very fond of cantaloupe. The smell of it alone is nourishment. Mo'izz sometimes mashes it for me or whisks it up in a blender, but I can't seem to swallow it as well as before. Still, there's something fulfilling in a bowl of freshly diced fruit, even if I can't have any. I tell Mo'izz to park in the shade, so the fruit doesn't cook in the encroaching midday sun.

Mannequin is here today. He doesn't ever come on Thursdays. That can't be good. His clothes look only half-ironed, with creases in odd places. His hair is untidy again, sort of piled in one direction. Then I realize what's happening: his hair is beginning to shed. In an odd sort of way, it seems to me that he is somehow even more quiet. How strange that I should think this. He never says anything anyway, never has. But today he seems less here, in this place of waiting.

The girl with the broomstick legs comes in, walking unsteadily, leaning heavily on her mother. She looks in my direction and attempts a smile. Her mother smiles in support.

"God is generous!" I call out. I don't try to lift my cane; it seems to be getting heavier these days.

The mother and her daughter walk around the waiting room and wander down the corridor together. Then they appear a little while later, taking baby steps into the room for a second round.

"Bravo!" I give the girl a thumbs up.

The mother beams with joy.

I look at Mannequin. What is he thinking? Not about meetings or appointments. Suddenly my curiosity just spurts out.

"Son, what are you thinking about?"

He hears me, I know. He twitches and moves his head in my direction but doesn't reply.

"May Allah give you peace of mind."

"Ameen."

His voice is so rich and warbling.

"I'm thinking about my mother."

It is lovely to hear him talk.

"She doesn't know I come here."

"Really?"

He nods.

"I had totally recovered a year ago. But it's all … it's all back. I can't tell her—it would break her heart. So, I've made her think I'm on an assignment in Morocco. I call her on my mobile every day to tell her I'm fine and receive her daily blessing. And all the time I'm staying with a friend. I-I miss her so much."

"May God reunite you my son."

He smiles inwardly and nods with half-closed eyes.

"Yes, she's old and dying."

A nurse comes in and tells him that the doctor needs to see him. He gives her his hand and she pulls him up. He stands, half stooping, and edges his way to the doctor's office. The doctor meets him at the door and greets him with a warm handshake and a serious expression. The door closes behind them, and I am left wondering about our short conversation.

#

On Saturday, I expect to see him, but he isn't here. Perhaps he has sessions on Thursdays instead of Saturdays now. Bug-eyes arrives, wheeled in by his oil-smeared companion. The hairy nurse nods good morning to the two men and offers a small smile. Perhaps she's trying to make amends for last time.

Then a whole lot of new faces come in. Little clumps of bewildered villagers, all tangled together, talking at once so that it's hard to tell who the patients are, and who's just accompanying them. The nurses get uptight again and rush in and out of rooms, shouting at everyone, and calling out to the cafeteria boys to bring them extra tea and coffee.

A batch of fresh, young student doctors arrives as well. They chatter like birds. They carry textbooks, take notes, and look at the villagers as if they are relics on display in a museum. Then a senior doctor leads them to a side room with sliding glass doors. They stand around him and listen with beaming smiles. They nod enthusiastically to everything he says. Soon the sound of excited laughter seeps out of the room.

In the corridor, the nurses untangle the villagers. They order all newcomers to open a file in the administration department in Wing B before they can fix an appointment with the doctor, which might not be today. Someone is sobbing. Someone else is retching in a corner. Tempers flare. The peasants have come a long way and have nowhere to spend the night. The hairy nurse comes in and shouts that things are bad enough without all this commotion. Then suddenly the gentleman in the smart gray suit appears outside the important door down the corridor. The nurse falls silent. The peasants settle down little by little, until there are only muffled sobs and whispers in the background. The man speaks to the nurse in a low, terse voice, and she nods nervously.

Tasks are briskly delegated. Order is restored. There is only the shuffle of feet, the squeak of wheelchairs, and the subdued drone of those in pain.

#

On Sunday, I have to see the doctor early in the morning. It's on my schedule. A spotty nurse, who seems to me to be a girl of no more than fifteen, pinches my underarm to stand me up and lean me on my cane. On the way to the doctor's office, I see Mannequin, in a wheelchair. He is wearing a hospital gown that is so faded that you can't tell whether it is brown or gray or blue. On his head, a knitted hat sits askew and partially covers his face. The nurse sits me down, and the doctor begins to give me my update. I can't really hear what he is saying. He is talking, rather cautiously, about my last X-ray. He asks something about my appetite. He wants to know if I have anyone staying with me at home. What does it matter? I am decades and decades old. But look at Mannequin! He has aged beyond his years and mine! It's a thought that chokes me up inside.

"Don't cry, sir."

The doctor clutches my bony shoulder.

"You must have faith in God. We will do what we can for you, but there is not much point in you coming here anymore …"

What is he saying? Not come here anymore? Then who would be left to watch the dying die?

The cane seems heavier as I walk out of the doctor's office.

"Shall I get you a wheelchair?"

The spotty young nurse points to one next to the window. It has a wonky back wheel, but Reda is not sitting in it.

"Where is Reda?"

The nurse looks at the wheelchair, then down at her feet.

"May Allah rest her soul."

"Reda's a girl!"

My comment comes out a little too loud. The nurse isn't amused. She leads me to the window spot and seats me in the wheelchair.

"I will get your file and refill your prescription to take home."

Then she disappears down the corridor.

Poor Reda. I think about her sitting here, gazing out of the window in this chair. Across the car park there are trees, a haze of bluish-green against the sharp blue of the horizon. Amidst the heavy summer branches peeps the winding ribbon of road that leads to the village, far away, where Reda will be laid to rest with her ancestors.

Mannequin coughs and I look round, and his eyes, so deep in their sockets, meet mine. Whatever color they were when I first saw him in his inky-blue suit, today they are a dreary impenetrable gray. It is not a real color, and not the color I expected.

The man in the elegant suit appears at his oak door and walks across the hall to where Mannequin is sitting. The nurses seem surprised. What have they done now? He squats so his face is level with the dying man's. He hands him a letter and gently pats his knee. Mannequin reads quietly, then shakes his head.

"No. Travel, no."

The man speaks softly, but with emphasis:

"It's not something I can force you to do, son, but please consider. For my sake, please."

Mannequin looks down at the letter in his bruised hands.

"Uncle, I appreciate what you're doing, but we both know travel didn't help last time. I went for your sake. And I came here to this clinic for your sake. Now it's time to go home. I need to go home to Mother."

Doors swing on aching hinges and nameless figures gush in and out. Someone wants the important man to sign some important papers. He lingers for a moment by Mannequin's side, then returns to his office and clicks his door shut.

Outside, the summer sun shines brightly in a perfectly cloudless sky. Mo'izz sits in his taxi and plays his tragic love songs. He chomps happily at his sandwiches of fried things, lights another Cleopatra, and rustles his newspaper.

#

KARKADAY

by Aida Nasr

T he morning sun glinted insistently at the herbalist shop, but it transformed into something altogether gentler as it shone through the frosted glass windows and bathed the interior in soft, comforting light. Outside, the street was already chaotic at ten in the morning, but inside the shop, it was quiet and cool. The thick wooden door shut out all but the faintest murmurs of shouts and car horns.

Atef, the assistant, weighed out an insomnia cure for the lady who had already bought orange lentils and cumin. The smoky scent of the cumin still hung in the air.

"The weather's getting colder, and I want to make lentil soup," said Umm Ziyad to Khadiga, the owner.

It was October, and the weather wasn't cold at all, just pleasantly warm after a burning hot summer. Khadiga knew what Umm Ziyad really wanted was warmth for her heart, not her stomach. Since her children had gotten married and her crotchety old husband had died, she was scared to sleep alone in her cramped little apartment.

"I never thought I'd miss him, God have mercy on his soul," sighed Umm Ziyad.

Now the lentil soup would have to do. Ziyad and his younger sisters rarely visited their mother, or so she said. You'd think she'd be relieved she finally had some peace after caring for her husband and that brood of children all those years. What really ailed this woman, Khadiga decided, was a discontent that filled everything she did, from her shuffling walk to her whiny voice. Somehow, it felt like a bad omen that Umm Ziyad was the first customer today.

"I seek refuge with the Lord of the Daybreak ..."

Silently, Khadiga recited Quranic verses to ward off envy as Umm Ziyad looked around and said, "You're lucky to be here in this shop all day. You see so many people."

Khadiga's son Suleiman put the woman's purchases in a bag and handed it to her with a smile. "Thank you, son," she said, patting his shoulder, "I feel better just by seeing you. Assalamu 'alaikum." And with that goodbye, the door swung languidly behind her. Before it shut, they could see her making her way through the street swarming with people scurrying about like so many ants.

Khadiga leaned back in her tall wooden chair behind the counter and flicked the end of her headscarf over her shoulder. She took a sip of dark, sweet tea. She could hear her father's voice in her head, "They all have a story, Khadiga. They say they come here for hibiscus or anise or mastic to flavor their chicken, but if you listen, they all have a story they want to tell you."

Listening had been her father's strong point. He had spent over forty years in this shop, listening, until the day he died two months ago. Khadiga, on the other hand, didn't have much patience for stories about rotten teeth and bad husbands, ungrateful children, and unending problems. Why didn't these people just get on with life instead of talking and talking about it?

She surveyed the little shop with its collection of herbs and spices, mounded in brightly striped canvas sacks sitting stoutly on the floor. They had natural remedies for every kind of ailment—rheumatism, asthma, indigestion, insomnia, constipation … But most of all, the shop had always held the gentle, healing presence of her father, Suleiman Lotfy. That's what people really came here for.

She looked at the worn wooden desk in the corner where her father had always sat. She could see him there in her mind, with his neatly clipped beard, a beautiful reddish-brown when she was a girl and later a cottony-white. He was talking to people from the neighborhood, nodding patiently as they recounted their tales. Even as a grown woman, when Khadiga walked through the door and saw her father at his desk, it made her feel safe and warm, like on chilly winter nights when she was wrapped snugly in her thick cotton quilt. Now, seeing his chair empty, she felt like a bag that had been tipped over and shaken out, its contents wheeling all over the floor. She knew their customers must feel the same way.

Khadiga certainly knew everything about running the place. But could she ever emulate her father's healing essence, his spirit? That's what she was worried about. That, and her greedy uncles. They had shown up after Baba died, wanting the shop for themselves. Khadiga looked at Suleiman, her youngest son, and despite the thoughts whirling like a storm in her head, she smiled. He glanced over and gave her a mischievous grin. She picked up the phone to dial home. Abdallah, her eldest, picked up, gruff and groggy.

"Wake up. You're going to be late," she said.

"Okay, okay." He slammed down the phone.

If she didn't wake him every morning, he'd never make it to the supermarket where he delivered groceries. She never had to worry about her middle son Mohammed who woke early for his job as a refrigerator repairman's assistant. Fawzi, her husband, was still asleep, too. He owned his own taxi and kept his own hours—which meant he rarely worked anymore.

When they first got married, Khadiga realized she'd have to manage Fawzi as well as the household.

"Bring us a chicken on your way home," she'd tell him in the morning.

Or, "We need white cheese and eggs."

She soon learned that he'd drive just enough to buy whatever she asked for plus a packet of cigarettes for himself. Years ago, Fawzi had begun to skip whole days of driving his taxi. The income she brought home from the shop had been enough to support them modestly. That was fine with him.

More customers stopped in. Young Saniyya from across the road bought cinnamon sticks to boil in milk for the hot drink her mother liked. Ragab, the mechanic, came by to get anise for his wife to steep in water as a tonic for their colicky baby. Then Umm Abdo swept in.

"God gave us a grandson!" she announced happily.

"A thousand congratulations," said Khadiga, "You'll be needing moghat then."

As Atef spooned the yellowish powder into a bag on the scales, she remembered her own mother making the sweet, rich drink in their small kitchen after Suleiman was born sixteen years ago.

Gameela, their upstairs neighbor, had come to call. She had no children of her own. Khadiga's mother was just bringing out the moghat in flowery teacups on a tray when Gameela said, "Masha' Allah, you chose the right name. He looks just like his grandfather." Suleiman had the same fair complexion and reddish-brown hair everyone admired. They all wanted to kiss his pink baby cheeks.

Years later, Khadiga's mother would say, "Gameela put the evil eye on him, God cut her to pieces."

"Enough of that talk, Mama," Khadiga would reply.

#

Khadiga leaned back in her chair. She looked around the shop, now in the twinkling haze before sunset, and breathed in the herbs and spices and incense, a musty, mingled, mysterious scent that took her back to her childhood.

Just then a lady about her age walked in. They had never seen her before. She obviously was not from the neighborhood.

"Do you have hibiscus?"

"We have Sudanese for eighteen pounds a kilo and Aswani for thirty pounds a kilo. Which would you like?" said Khadiga.

"What's the difference?"

"The Aswani hibiscus makes a darker brew, a nice, deep red color from just a small handful in the water."

"That's the one I want. Half a kilo, please."

"Karkaday, Mama," said Suleiman as Atef scooped up a heap of deep purple dried hibiscus flowers. They rustled on the scale.

Suleiman smiled broadly at the customer, then took the bag of karkaday and handed it to her. She smiled back hesitantly.

"Thank you," said the lady. She paid and left, looking back curiously through the open doorway. In the moment before the door swung shut, Suleiman waved, and the lady grinned and waved back. She was walking down the street smiling as the door clicked closed.

"Karkaday" was one of three words that Suleiman could say. The others were "Mama" and "Fawzi"—for some reason, Suleiman never called him "Baba".

They closed just as the evening prayer was being called from the mosque around the corner.

#

Khadiga came out of her kitchen with a pan of fried eggs in one hand and a stack of baladi bread in the other—dinner for her family. Then she brought out an aluminum tray topped with four steaming glasses of tea and a cold glass of karkaday for Suleiman.

She looked around the table at the four men who were her life. As always, Suleiman was the center of attention. His father put eggs on his plate and asked, "How was the shop today, Suleiman?"

Khadiga watched this display of fatherly love with affection despite her usual irritation with Fawzi. Suleiman was the only person Fawzi would do anything for, at any time. Suleiman just smiled, looking at each member of his family in turn. After dinner, he yawned, gave everyone a hug and went to the room he shared with his brothers. It was tightly packed with furniture—a double bed next to a single bed separated only by a narrow passage. Suleiman always slept on the double bed.

From the kitchen as she washed the dishes, Khadiga could hear her two older sons arguing, as they had every night since they were little, about who got to sleep next to Suleiman. Abdallah always argued louder, but Mohammed usually won by default. He went to bed early and got his choice of sleeping place while Abdallah stayed out late with his friends.

Fawzi was settling on the couch to watch television when Khadiga said goodnight. She lay down in bed, thoughts whirling in her head.

#

Since Baba died, I lie awake for hours. I think mainly about Baba, but also about Fawzi and the boys, especially Suleiman. Not having Baba in the shop confused him at first. Every day he'd go to the desk and look puzzled. But one day he didn't go to the desk, and that was how I knew he understood that Baba isn't here anymore. I tried to tell him Baba went to God. I don't know if he understood that.

From the day he was born, he wasn't like his brothers. Rarely cried, smiled all the time. In a few months, he was laughing too, giggling at everyone. And he had a strange effect on the family. Fawzi wouldn't go near our older boys when they were babies. But he spent hours holding Suleiman and kissing his hands and saying "Bikh!" over and over to make him smile. When their baby brother was awake, Abdallah stopped chasing Mohammed around the apartment, and they would stand by Suleiman quietly. He'd grip their fingers in his tiny, fat baby hands.

I wanted a third boy just so I could name him after Baba. When he was born looking so much like his grandfather, I had such hopes that he'd inherit Baba's character, too—be gentle and wise.

When he was four and hadn't started talking yet, my mother and all the women of the neighborhood said not to worry. But I knew. I'm his mother. And when his seizures started, it was unquestionable, something was wrong. Poor Fawzi, so worried, driving us to all those clinics in his taxi. The public hospitals where they treat you like you're less than human. All those doctors, with their haughty, worthless words.

"There's nothing you can do, so stop tiring yourself with these questions."

"You have two other sons, so thank God for that."

What did they know?

Gameela did not put the evil eye on him. She has a kind, sincere heart. She's always genuinely happy when anyone in the neighborhood has a baby. God created Suleiman different. It was difficult to accept at first. Now I can't imagine him any other way. I do still sometimes wonder how he could have been, though. I'd never tell this to anyone, not even Fawzi, but I think Suleiman is much wiser than most people. He understands more than he can say and always makes people smile in that unusual way of his.

It's the other two I'm really agitated about. Abdallah inherited the worst qualities from both sides. Fawzi's laziness, my temper. And Mohammed, good, dependable, but too submissive. He's never stood up to Abdallah, even when they were little boys.

When I couldn't find a school to take Suleiman, I brought him to the shop with me. I think over the years, our customers came to see him as much as to see Baba. He's like his grandfather in that way. His presence soothes people, gives them some kind of peace and security. And that shop is his entire world.

The day after the burial, my uncles showed up.

"You won't be able to handle this shop all by yourself, Khadiga."

"What are you talking about? I've been running it for years with my father."

"But now that he's dead, God rest his soul, you'll need the help of men to run it."

They just can't get enough! They're in the shoe business. They don't know cumin from saffron from their own heads. Baba registered the shop in my name the week I was born, and they know it. The paperwork is all in order, the lawyer assures me.

#

Khadiga woke for the dawn prayer, did her household chores, and made more karkaday. She dumped the dried hibiscus flowers in just-boiled water, added lots of sugar—just the way Suleiman liked it—and let it steep to a ruby red. Then she strained it and put it in a glass bottle in the refrigerator to cool. Time to wake Suleiman.

He put on his beige set—beige trousers and a beige striped shirt that Khadiga buttoned for him. She always made sure he had crisp new clothes to wear, that he looked his best. They ate breakfast and made their way down the narrow, worn stairs of their building. It was a mild and gentle morning, and for the first time since her father's death, Khadiga's heart lifted a little. She linked her arm in Suleiman's as they began their walk to the shop.

As soon as they arrived, Khadiga knew something was terribly wrong, but for a few seconds couldn't grasp what it was. Suleiman was motionless beside her, eyes wide, perfectly still.

The little shop's windows had been smashed and its door torn out. The canvas bags were overturned with their contents dumped all over the floor. Khadiga's eyes quickly moved to the place where her father's desk was—and found it empty. They had even taken her tall chair. The only thing left untouched was the counter because it was bolted securely to the floor. As Khadiga took in the damage, she was almost certain she knew who had done this.

Suleiman began to cry and wail. She quickly took his hand and walked through the gaping hole where the door had been. She made her way through the debris to the phone on the counter. Her mind felt sluggish. A thought crawled across it as she dialed home, "Why hadn't they taken the phone?" After what seemed like forever, Abdallah answered.

"Give me your father now," she said over Suleiman's wailing.

Fawzi, sleepy and confused, got on the line.

"Come quickly. They've destroyed the shop."

None of the other merchants on the street had opened yet. Suleiman Lotfy Herbalists always opened before anyone else. The wait for her husband felt like the longest and loneliest of Khadiga's life. She hugged a sobbing Suleiman, staring in disbelief at the smashed ruins of her haven. The loss of her father became final, a door slammed shut in her face.

Fawzi arrived ten minutes later with Abdallah. The day that followed seemed to Khadiga to never want to end. They filed a report at the police station, and then Atef began cleaning up the mess while all the merchants on the street gathered round, muttering angrily amongst themselves. Every person on the street suspected that her uncles had done this in revenge. If they couldn't have the shop, they would make sure Khadiga didn't either.

"Thank God this is all that happened. Thank God no one was hurt," said Hagg Maged, who owned the haberdasher's.

Of course, he was right. Later, Khadiga would be grateful that she had taken home her father's vast collection of books on herbal remedies after he had died. But right now, she was calculating the damage. Thousands of pounds to replace the door, the windows, the herbs and spices. Khadiga wondered how many gold bracelets she would need to sell to raise the cash. Did she even have enough bracelets? Her father had left her very little money. The shop was his entire fortune and legacy.

Suleiman was still crying and screaming. The seizure was inevitable. Everyone crowded around concerned. When it was over and Suleiman had rested, Fawzi said, "Go home, Khadiga, and take Suleiman with you. There's nothing for you to do here. I'll make sure everything gets cleaned up."

Suleiman lay on the couch sleeping, his head in his mother's lap. Gameela appeared, worried, with glasses of fresh lemonade on a tray. After a few hours, the men returned. Abdallah argued and argued that he wanted to confront her uncles, go take a stick and beat them with it. Khadiga's head ached.

"I'll show them," he shouted.

"Don't you dare, Abdallah. It'll only make things worse and that's exactly the kind of reaction they want to provoke," countered Khadiga. It drove her crazy that he always did—or thought of doing—the most disruptive, irresponsible thing.

"Calm down, Umm Abdallah," said Fawzi firmly. "We'll find a solution."

At these words, all the exhaustion, grief and anger tumbled out of her in a torrent. "Don't call me mother of Abdallah!" she shouted, "My name is Khadiga Suleiman Lotfy. My father named me after the Prophet's wife—I'm a strong, smart businesswoman, just like her! They'll never get my father's shop. Never. All his life, that shop was for me, his only child. I'm the only one who's going to handle this. Abdallah, if you go near my uncles or even breathe in their direction, I swear I'll take off this slipper," Khadiga wiggled her foot, pointing to the slipper she was wearing, "and hit you with it in front of the whole neighborhood!"

And with that, Abdallah raged out of the apartment.

Fawzi said quietly, "Khadiga, you and Suleiman go rest for a while. We're not going to do anything more about this today."

She lay next to Suleiman on his bed for the remainder of the day, neither sleeping, nor getting up to eat the lunch or the dinner that Gameela brought down. She dragged herself out of bed at prayer times but was barely conscious of the words she was saying as she bowed and kneeled to God.

Abdallah didn't return at all that night. Fawzi called Mohammed at work, and he came home early. Again, Khadiga couldn't sleep. Instead, she stayed up, silently cursing her uncles.

#

They can go to hell—sixty thousand hells. They'll never get the shop.

Baba never finished school because he had to drop out to work and help support his parents and the same ingrates who did this. Years as a chauffeur in Kuwait, sending money back, while those three set up their shoe business. When he returned, he put all his savings into our tiny shop. He built it from nothing, just some knowledge of herbs he'd learned from books. His brothers and their sons make a hundred times more money from shoes than we ever did from herbs and spices, yet they want the shop. Pure greed and vindictiveness. Baba, the handsome, sensitive man, so intelligent and well respected. Compared to him, my uncles are beasts.

All he had was the shop and me, his only child. Now they want to destroy us both. But they'll never do that. I won't let them. Can you hear me, Baba? I won't let them.

#

After a terrible, sleepless night, Khadiga sat bleary-eyed and dizzy on the sitting room couch. Suleiman hadn't slept much either. He was fidgety and irritable, flitting around the room and fiddling with things on tables, throwing them on the floor.

"Stop that, Suleiman," Khadiga said tiredly.

She wanted to throw things, too. She felt like screaming. But she was too exhausted to do anything except sit in a daze and wonder how it had come to this. The shop smashed by people who didn't even understand what it was, or how it healed people. All Baba's work destroyed. How was she ever going to repair the damage? She had to confront her uncles somehow, even though she had forbidden Abdallah to do so. As the day dragged on, she felt utterly defeated. She spent another restless, sleepless night.

#

Early the next morning, the doorbell rang. It was Khadiga's mother. She had wisely appeared for only a few minutes in the direct aftermath of the attack. She knew her daughter's temper well and that talking to her when she was in a state like that was no good at all.

Now she said, "Khadiga, your father built that shop over the forty years of your life. He earned his money honestly and helped so many people. There's no way God will let all his effort go to waste."

"Strengthen your faith, Khadiga. There's a way out of every disaster. The Prophet, peace and blessings be upon him, said that you should ask God for something with the full belief that your prayer will be answered. So, pray to Him to save the shop. I prayed for you all night. Insha' Allah, the shop will be restored and even better than before."

It was the only time in Khadiga's life that her mother had said anything she thought was good advice. Her mother had a meek personality that was the exact opposite of her daughter's. Her passivity drove Khadiga almost as crazy as her eldest son's reckless stupidity. But today, thank God, she made sense.

After the noon prayer, Khadiga sat on the prayer rug in her bedroom and asked God to revive the shop and her father's dream for all of them, but especially for Suleiman so he could heal people's hearts as his grandfather had. Then she got up, and from the large collection of spices on her own kitchen shelf, she mixed up al-mufrih, a tonic to make you happy, learned from her father. She tipped a teaspoon of the mixture into a glass and set water to boil on the stove.

After the anger, confusion, and despair of the last two days, Khadiga felt strangely calm. She decided that she would be grateful. She thanked God for the love of her parents, for her children, her good neighbors, even for Fawzi, who had proven that he could come through in an emergency and act like a real man. Slowly, she began to feel that the shop would survive. Even Suleiman had calmed down. She poured him a glass of cold karkaday from the bottle in the fridge and settled next to him on the couch with some steaming happiness tonic for herself.

\#

By evening, the whole neighborhood had come through for Hagg Suleiman and his beloved daughter Khadiga. Every single one had sought comfort and advice in the friendly little shop. They wouldn't let it be broken and die.

Just before sunset, Fawzi took Khadiga to the shop. She was dumbfounded. Ramy, the glass fitter, had put in new frosted glass windows. Khaled, the carpenter, had made a new door. Over the windows and door, they had installed wrought iron in a flowery design. The shop was protected now. Hagg Maged, the elderly man who owned the haberdasher's, had put his own worn wooden desk where her father's used to be. The merchants on the whole street had paid for the materials. And no one would take any money for their workmanship. Khadiga insisted on paying for it all, but they refused.

It's the blessings of my parents' prayers for me my whole life that made this happen, she thought.

"Don't worry, we'll always help you protect the shop," said Hagg Maged.

Just as her mother had predicted, Khadiga's fortunes had changed. She picked up the phone and dialed the familiar number of their main supplier, a man as old as her father had been, and told him what had happened. He had everything she needed to modestly restock the shop.

"Don't worry about money. Pay me when you can," he said.

She finally pressed him to take a down payment, "Thank you, Hagg Ibrahim. I don't know how to thank you."

"For what? I'm proud you're carrying on your father's work. He raised you well. And don't let the spite of greedy, jealous people upset you. The shop will be fine, insha' Allah."

And with that pronouncement from her father's old friend, something clicked into place in Khadiga's mind. She knew she could never fill the shop with her father's essence, but she could fill it with her own, and with Suleiman's. As for her other sons, she realized she had never thought much of them, expecting one to be a troublemaker, and the other to be weak. So that's exactly how they had turned out. She wished she had a cure for what ailed them. Suleiman, she secretly believed to be wise and strong, and so he had become just that.

Late that night, Abdallah finally came home. Khadiga could tell by the way her husband's eyebrows were set that he was furious. Their eldest son had disappeared at the worst possible moment, proving what his parents already knew. He was irresponsible and selfish, not the kind of person who would be a good husband and father someday.

Suleiman must have been angry, too, because he ignored his brother completely. The rest of the family said nothing. They knew that being ignored by Suleiman was the worst punishment of all. That night, Khadiga did not hear her older boys arguing about who would sleep next to Suleiman. Abdallah had lost that particular argument for a long time to come. As she lay awake next to a snoring Fawzi, Khadiga thought of the shop.

#

When I was still a little girl with two thick braids down my back, I thought we should have remedies in our shop to cure what really ailed people. Things like greed, envy, selfishness, laziness, stinginess, anger, and so on.

When I told Baba, he laughed until his cheeks got even redder than usual. Then he said, "I wish we had herbs to cure those things, Khadiga, but we don't. The most we can do is give people something for their high blood pressure and listen to their problems. That makes them feel a bit better. But only people can cure what ails their own hearts and minds, with God's help of course. If there was a cure for greed and envy, my dear, no one would have any problems."

#

In the morning, Khadiga said to Mohammed, "After you come home from work, join us at the shop. I want you to start learning how things are done there."

She linked arms with Suleiman and when they got to the shop, she showed him that everything had been fixed.

"Hagg Ibrahim will send us all the things we need today, dear."

Suleiman gave her a very wide smile, his first since the shop had been smashed, as if he had been expecting this all along. He went to the desk that replaced his grandfather's and sat down. In that moment, Khadiga felt that somehow, he had known the little shop would be mended and healed. Now she suspected that her agitated reaction had caused Suleiman's. She thought to herself, I'll try not to always expect the worst.

They spent the morning receiving well-wishers from the neighborhood. When Umm Ziyad showed up to lament their misfortune in her whiny voice, Khadiga shut her up immediately.

"Thank God, the shop is fine."

The herbs and spices arrived that afternoon, and Atef placed the canvas sacks in rows along one wall. Suleiman examined and sniffed the contents of each sack until he found the karkaday, happily running his fingers through the small, rustling hibiscus flowers.

The next day, Khadiga and Fawzi went to visit one of her uncles, unannounced. Just a few days earlier, she had imagined hitting the offenders with her slipper, over and over, cursing and screaming.

Now she found herself very calm. She told them the shop had been vandalized, that she couldn't imagine who would do such a thing. But it had been fixed with the help of the whole neighborhood. They vowed to protect it no matter what.

"I filed a police report. I want whoever did this to get what he deserves, no more, no less. Thank you for your offer to help with the shop, but I won't be needing anything. As you know, the shop was Baba's whole life, and I'm the only one who knows how to run it the way he did. As for you, I suggest you stick to selling shoes and slippers. That's what you're good at," she said coolly.

That night, Khadiga slept as soon as her head touched the pillow.

#

I had the most amazing dream last night. I saw my beautiful Suleiman in a green garden. All around him were people I didn't know, singing and laughing and dancing. They looked at my son as though he were a very important person.

In a clear voice, he said to them, "I'm Hagg Suleiman Lotfy's grandson." And they all cheered and waved.

#

Al-Mufrih (Happiness Tonic)

30 g ground dried basil
25 g cloves
25 g ground cinnamon
25 g ground ginger
100 g ground cardamom pods

Mix all the ingredients. Put a teaspoon of the mixture in a glass. Pour boiling water over it and stir. Sweeten to taste.

#

MOTHER OF MEN

by Mariam Shouman

E man knocked softly on the wooden door. "Who is it?" came a querulous voice.

"I'm from the health unit down the road. They sent me to give you a shot," Eman replied. She knew that most home-cares were a bit crotchety.

"Oh, come in then. The door's open," the voice replied.

As Eman stepped into the apartment, taking care to leave the door slightly open—she was careful the first time she went anywhere new—she was struck by the darkness and the mustiness. The sun was bright and welcome on that winter morning, burning off the chill outside, but the damp cold of the apartment was closely shuttered against it. "Assalamu 'alaikum, ya hagga." Eman called out the traditional greeting as she stepped into the square, windowless room that served as a sitting room. She followed the voice returning her greeting back into the bedroom, which opened off the entrance. The room was dark, lit only by a little lamp that glowed next to the bed, throwing a yellow light on the old woman hunched on the bed. She had obviously been napping but had gotten up in a hurry and was modestly trying to pull her galabiyya over her knees.

"It's so dark in here, ya hagga. Can I open the shutters for you? The sun will warm up the room," Eman said, as she stepped toward the tightly shuttered windows.

"Oh, leave them closed. If you open them, I'll only have to worry about who will close them for me," the woman gestured feebly. "I can't open or close them anymore, so they are only opened when the girl comes to clean every week."

Eman paused, but then continued, "I'll close them before I leave, don't worry. I'll need the light to give you your injection." As she flung open the shutters, light poured into the bedroom, leaving the old woman blinking furiously. "You don't move around much, do you?" Eman asked.

"I can just manage the bathroom, which is right next to this room. I had them move the refrigerator in here so I wouldn't have to go to the kitchen anymore." She waved a translucent hand in the direction of the refrigerator in the corner of the room.

Eman moved to the bedside, "Roll up your sleeve, ya hagga, and I'll give you your shot," she said as she got her tools ready. To distract her patient, she added cheerily, "I'm Eman. What's your name, ya hagga?" Eman always called her patients "hagga", a term of respect that implied that they had made the Hajj pilgrimage to Mecca.

"My name?" she gave a short laugh. "I think I may have forgotten my real name. In the village they called me 'Umm Dastit Regala.'"

Eman laughed in surprise, "What kind of a name is that? Your oldest son's name is 'Dastit Regala'?"

"Ya habibti, ya Eman, I was the envy of my entire village because I gave birth to a dozen boys—not a single girl in the lot! And I raised them all to adulthood. Now they are all men," she reflected with pride. "After I'd had the first three or four, the whole village would wait for news of the baby to see if it was a boy or if a girl had come along to break my good luck streak."

"Where are they all now? You should have lots of grandchildren by now to fill your house," Eman asked, concentrating on giving the old woman her injection, the slippery skin loose in Eman's fingers.

"That's the question, isn't it?" she answered, her tone bittersweet. "They built this building—each one of them has an apartment here, all shut up tight as tombs."

"All of them gone? Where are they, ya Umm Dastit Regala?" Eman asked.

"Before their father died ten years ago, each one found work abroad. First, Mohammed went to Saudi Arabia, then Mahmoud went to Kuwait … and then one by one they left," she remembered. "The last one to leave—Karim—is the one who broke my heart. He was the youngest, the one dearest to me. Never believe that the eldest is the closest—a mother grows in understanding as her children grow up. The first child, she tries to control; by the time she's raised a dozen, she wants a companion, a friend. He used to sneak up behind me while I did my chores and give me a fright. I never laughed with the others like I laughed with Karim. And now he's a doctor off in America, and it's been seven years since I've seen him."

Eman swabbed the old woman's arm with cotton, "But they call you, don't they? And make sure you have everything you need?

The old woman gestured limply to the black phone that rested next to her pillow, the cord stretched across the bed, "Each of them calls every week and they take turns sending money. I'm never without money. And the ones in the Gulf come to Egypt every year, or every other year, and open the house for a few weeks in the summer. But other than that, I am alone."

Eman thought of her own children: three girls. Her husband was pushing for number four, invoking the argument that they would stand together as they grew older, helping one another—but really, he was hoping for a boy. "And do they see each other? Surely some of them live in the same place …"

"Not one. Oh, they see each other here in Cairo when they come, but only for a glass of tea or a meal. Each one has his own problems. They all came home to get married and then whisked their brides off to foreign lands. The grandchildren I imagined filling the house, I hardly know," she sighed.

As Eman slid the needle into the loose skin, the old woman exhaled slightly, so lost in her emotional pain that a needle prick was nothing.

"You know what I regret most of all, ya Eman?" she asked, cocking her head to peer at the young nurse.

"What's that, ya hagga?" Eman inquired.

"That I never had a daughter," the old woman shook her head. "Everyone made it seem like such a miracle that I'd had a dozen boys … no one bothered to mention what a comfort a daughter is to a woman as she grows old. A mother passes on all her secrets to her daughter …

she entrusts her with the family heirlooms and history. My daughters-in-law have no patience for me and my secrets. You know, the last time they were here, they cleaned out my china cabinet and threw away the only piece I had left of my wedding china. It was a teapot with a pink rose on it—it had a chip, but it reminded me of days gone by. Karim is the one who chipped it one day when his grandfather came to tea. He tried to pour for his giddo by himself, and the lid fell off. I cried to see my beautiful pot with a chip in it, but as the years went by, I came to love it more for the chip because it reminded me of Karim. Now I'll never see it again."

"Never mind, ya hagga …" Eman murmured as she patted her on the shoulder. Why did this woman's story affect her so, she wondered as she put her things away and prepared to leave. She walked over to the shutters, "Shall I close them for you, ya hagga? The sun is so cheerful and bright."

"Yes, my dear, close them tight. The sun is bright right now, but the cold will be bitter on my old bones tonight if you leave them open," the old woman replied. She fumbled under her pillow and came out with her pocketbook. "How much for the visit, my dear? And when will you come again?"

"Don't worry about it …" Eman began.

"No, I have money; my sons have let me want for nothing," the old woman pulled out a wad of bills. "I think the man on the phone said it would cost five pounds, is that right?" She shuffled through the notes and found both a five- and a fifty-pound note. "Which one is a five, my dear? I can't see very well anymore."

Eman gently plucked the five from her hand. "Do you pay for many things, ya hagga? Be careful that no one cheats you of your money."

"Only the groceries and the girl who comes to clean … and the electricity bill when the collector comes around. Everyone is honest here. No one would cheat an old woman, would they?" she cocked her gray head.

"Let me help you, ya hagga," Eman took the wad of bills and straightened them. She separated out the fifties and hundreds and put them in a separate pocket. "Don't get them out unless you need them. At least that way, you won't lose too much, okay?"

"I'll do that," she nodded. "Do you have to leave now? I like to talk to you."

"I'll come back in a week. You're supposed to have a shot every week. Is this time of day good for you?" she asked.

"Anytime is fine. One minute is much like another for me."

"Assalamu 'alaikum," Eman said as she turned to go.

"Wa 'alaikum assalam," the old woman murmured as she leaned her head upon her cane, perched on the side of her bed, staring after the young woman who had brightened her day momentarily.

#

As the week wore on, Eman found herself fretting over the old mother of a dozen sons. She bustled around her own mother, who lived with her, trying her best to do whatever she wanted. The image of a dozen sons, all gone their separate ways haunted her in a way she couldn't explain. She knew it was all part of what intellectuals called the "brain drain," where the best of Egypt's young sought work abroad. They gave their best years to a country that was not their own and then returned with pension plans to find a country much changed from what they remembered.

But it was the fact of twelve sons that overwhelmed her. Eman herself would never forget the disappointment on her husband's and her mother-in-law's faces when her first and second little girls were born … or even worse, how no one came to visit after her third baby girl. According to Umm Dastit Regala, boys weren't everything.

#

The day dawned on Eman's next visit to the old woman. As she strode through the dusty alleys leading to the apartment, Eman happened upon a man peddling fresh felafel sandwiches and bought two.

As she knocked on the door, she wondered what kept the villains away. A poor old woman with no one to look after her, who had to leave the door unlocked so that her few visitors could get in.

The feeble voice called from deep in the apartment, "Who is it?"

"It's me, Eman the nurse, ya hagga, ya Umm Dastit Regala," Eman called cheerfully.

"Come in, come in, my dear," the old woman urged.

As Eman bustled about the room, the old woman barely murmured an objection as she swung the shutters open, "Don't worry, I'll close them before I leave," Eman reassured her.

"Before your shot, let's have breakfast, what do you say?" Eman asked, spreading the plastic sandwich sack on the bedside table and laying one sandwich in front of the old woman and one out for herself. "I even brought some pickles!"

The old woman looked unexpectedly timid, "I haven't had felafel in ages…"

"Go on, help yourself," Eman urged. As they sat in quiet companionship, Eman asked, "Tell me, ya hagga, what was it like to have twelve sons?"

"In the village, everyone envied me. My husband would get a sheikh to come and read Quran after each birth, so that the babies wouldn't die. Each one of them wore a blue bead until the day they left Egypt—to ward off the evil eye," she laughed, "My mother-in-law even wanted me to name one of them 'Khaysha', as if to be called 'burlap sack' would keep envy from touching him … I wouldn't hear of it though!"

As she finished the last of her sandwich, she gave a little cough, "Could you bring me a drink of water, if you don't mind?"

Eman went to the refrigerator and swung open the door. It was a very neat fridge, as fridges go. The top shelf held yogurt—six tubs—the second shelf held a sack of flat baladi bread, the third shelf held a plastic container of white cheese and a bowl of cucumbers. The door was lined with water bottles. Eman chose one and brought it to the old woman. "I have the girl fill them for me every week when she comes. One for each day of the week."

"Wouldn't you like a cup of tea, after your meal?" Eman asked.

"Tea … yes, I'd like that," she answered. "You'll find tea in the kitchen, I think," and she waved vaguely off to the right.

Eman walked gingerly through the house. It was immaculately clean, the windows all shuttered tight, but it lacked the air of a house where anyone lived. The burgundy dust covers on the chairs and couches were smooth, unruffled by the everyday movement of life, well-worn but not recently.

The kitchen, the center of any house, was dead quiet and completely unused. The floor was clean swept, the window tightly shut. Eman picked a cupboard and gently tugged its door open. Neat rows of glasses stood at attention. In the next cupboard over, unused plates sat awaiting long unseen customers. The last one held tea, sugar, and dried mint. Eman found the teapot, swished water through it and then filled it half full. She found matches on the shelf over the stove, but when she tried to light it, she had no luck. She tried all the knobs, lighting match after match and touching them to the burner. No flame sprang to life. Then she remembered the gas cylinder—people often closed the valve when they were gone for long periods of time. Once she'd taken care of that, she easily lit the stove. While the water boiled, she set out the glasses for tea—half a spoonful of tea and a little mint in each one. "How many spoons of sugar, ya hagga?" she called. When no answer came, she stepped back into the bedroom. The old woman had fallen asleep, perched on the side of her bed, her cane in her hands and her head resting on them. Gently, so as not to surprise her, she laid her hand on the old woman's shoulder, "Do you still want tea, or would you rather have a nap?" she asked.

With a start, the old woman raised her head. "Who …?" And then comprehension dawned in her eyes. "Oh yes, Eman. I had forgotten you were here. I must have dozed off. How much sugar, you say? I don't know … maybe two?"

Eman went into the kitchen and came back with two steaming glasses on a small stainless-steel tray. As she set it down, the old woman sighed, "I remember what it was like to drink tea in the afternoon with my husband and sons. For a while, I had thirteen men in my house to keep me busy. I knew how each one liked his tea … how each one wanted his eggs … Karim drank his with four spoons of sugar and always accused me of not stirring it enough. He would hold it up to the light to see the color and the clarity of the tea."

As she reminisced, the phone rang, breaking the quiet mood. Eman moved to the window to give the old woman privacy. Right outside the window, life was teeming—overflowing even. The junk peddler wandered through the dusty winding streets calling, "Rubabikya! Rubabikya! Old washing machines! Used clothing!" The prickly pear salesman had set his pushcart in the shade of a spreading Poinciana tree with its bright canopy of red flowers and tiny green leaves, billowing in the breeze. He was slicing open the prickly fruit and expertly cutting away the needles before popping the orange flesh into a plastic bag. The children gathered around him, clamoring for the juiciest, plumpest fruit for their fifty piasters. An old woman sat on a black plastic sack to protect her clothes from the dust of the street where she squatted all day long, swatting away flies from her basket of burlap-covered blocks of cottage cheese. The bustle of the street contrasted starkly with the stillness of the apartment.

"Yes, she still comes every week and cleans the apartment," the old woman nodded her head, waving her hand aimlessly. "Last week she made okra and molokhiyya and a big pot of rice, a chicken, and some meat."

After a pause during which she listened, grimacing, she said impatiently, "Out of season? How do I know … maybe she bought frozen. Everything's available these days at the supermarket."

"I'm fine, ya Karim. I don't have any news. I'm an old woman, living alone. How are you? Tell me about the children," she said.

For about five minutes, the woman listened avidly, interjecting an occasional laugh or comment, and then bid a fond goodbye and hung up, wiping a tear from her eye.

For a moment, she sat in absolute silence, looking at the phone, as if it could bring her son physically to her, then she looked around the room, starting when her eyes fell on Eman. "Come drink your tea," she invited. "Why did you let it get cold? That was my youngest son, calling from America. He worries about me."

Eman sat across from the old woman and sipped her tea, making small talk.

As she stood at the door, taking her leave, she asked, "Do you need anything, ya hagga? If you want any groceries or food, I could buy them for you next time I'm on my way here …"

"You heard me telling Karim that the girl was cooking for me … She used to, you know. But I got so tired of eating my dinner cold, I decided to stick to meals that are meant to be eaten out of the fridge. Food doesn't mean much to me, anyway. Today's felafel sandwich is probably the best meal I've had since the summer when my children were here—because of the company, not anything else. Don't you worry about me. My body runs fine on white cheese and yogurt," she smiled, as she waved goodbye.

#

The next morning as Eman cooked her family's lunch before going out to work, she spied a small plastic box in the cupboard. The smell of peas and carrots simmering in a rich tomato sauce, interspersed with chunks of meat was inviting to say the least. On impulse, Eman pulled the box out of the cupboard, spooned rice and vegetables into it and closed it, wrapping it tightly in a sheet of newspaper and putting it into a plastic bag before she could change her mind. She hurriedly got dressed and rushed out of the house, trying to make up for the half hour it would take her to go visit the old woman.

As she knocked on the door, she momentarily worried that the old woman would reject her offer as charity but couldn't turn back. From inside the dark apartment, the feeble voice called, "Who is it? Oh, come in, whoever you are."

The old woman had just sat up on the edge of her bed as Eman entered her bedroom, "Eman," she said, "Is it time for my shot again?"

"No, no, ya hagga. I was just coming down your street on my way to work, and thought I'd pop in and check on you. Do you need anything?"

"No, my dear, but please stop by anytime you like," the old woman's face brightened. "Sit down for a moment."

"How about a cup of tea?" Eman asked.

"I'd love one … you reminded me of the taste of tea last time. I'd almost forgotten it."

As Eman turned to go into the kitchen, she laid her package on the little table next to the old woman, "I was cooking peas this morning and thought you might tell me if they tasted all right or if they were missing something. Let me get you a spoon." Before the woman could answer, Eman went into the kitchen and came back with a spoon. She opened the plastic bag, took out the box and laid it in front of her. "Taste it while I make the tea," she entreated.

As the appetizing smell wafted from the box, the old woman nodded, "Well, maybe just a bite, to help you adjust your seasoning."

Eman left her in peace to enjoy her meal, stepping into the kitchen to make the tea. When she came out with two glasses of tea, the woman was wiping her mouth with a tissue. "The peas were very tender and nice—they must be in season now," she commented.

"But what about the seasoning? Was it all right or was something missing? My husband always likes his food just right," Eman said, although her husband hadn't complained about her cooking since she was a new bride.

"I think it was just right," she said, "I always used to like to put a bit of lamb fat in my cooking, but I know people say that's not healthy these days. Before I stopped cooking, Karim used to tell me my cooking was too heavy—but he couldn't resist it!"

Eman put the tea glasses on the tray and quickly took them into the kitchen and washed them. "I have to go now, ya hagga. Do you need anything?"

"No, ya binti, thank you. May God keep you for me, my daughter."

#

From that day forward, Eman found her feet taking her to the old woman's apartment whenever she had an extra minute or a tasty morsel to drop off. As their friendship grew, Eman stopped mentioning her little gifts of food. She merely laid them on the table as she stepped into the kitchen to make tea. The old woman never mentioned them either, but she obviously enjoyed every morsel.

One day, as summer drew near, they were enjoying a slice of the first watermelon of the season. The old woman wiped a bit of juice from her lips, leaned back, and said, "You know, ya Eman, you have shown me the joy of having a daughter. Anyone who denies that a daughter is a pleasure and a comfort, must have only sons," she laughed. "My son Karim has a daughter … may God protect her. I hope she takes care of him in his old age."

Eman blushed in embarrassed pleasure and looked away, "Anything you need, ya hagga, I'll try to do for you."

"I know, I know, ya binti," the old woman nodded. "Bring me that box over there—the wooden one inlaid with mother-of-pearl, under the window."

Eman crossed to the window and got the box, laying it carefully in the woman's hands.

She opened it, nodding to herself, "I want to give you something but please don't turn it down," she murmured as she fished through the box. "If I had had a daughter, my gold would have gone to her … I'd like you to have a little piece—something to remember me by. Thank God, I have granddaughters. I don't like the thought of my daughters-in-law wearing my jewelry. After they threw away my teapot, I haven't been able to stomach them. Aha! Here it is," she exclaimed in satisfaction, holding up a gold heart-shaped pendant, inlaid with blue. "It's only a little thing—you couldn't sell it for more than a hundred pounds … but I'd like you to take it. It was the first piece of gold jewelry I was given as a baby. My mother gave it to me, and right before she died, she told me that her mother had given it to her."

Eman took the little pendant in her hand, gazing at it as if it were the most precious thing she'd ever seen. "I've never been given anything quite so special, ya hagga. But you should keep this for your children and their children."

"I'd rather you have it. The rest is for them. When I die, they'll get it all. But I want to give this to you—I want someone to have it who knows its history and what it meant to me. I don't imagine I'll ever see my grandchildren again in this world, so I'll never have a chance to tell them its story. And when you grow old, tell the story to your daughter and pass it on to her before you die."

"Tell me, ya hagga. What is the story of this pendant?" Eman asked, as she put the rest of the jewelry back in its box.

"My grandmother married young … a large landowner who could afford the best for her. She became pregnant immediately and had a perfect baby girl—my mother. But after childbirth, she caught a fever that left her infertile. My grandfather was outraged. How could he only have a daughter to pass his land on to? But my grandmother's father had specified in the marriage contract that his daughter would accept no co-wives. My grandmother was set to become a rich woman from the money she would inherit from her father, so my grandfather didn't want to divorce her. He chafed under the restriction for some years and finally decided that having sons outweighed everything else. He divorced my grandmother and managed to trick her out of all the gold from her dowry and everything he had given her during their life together except for this one token piece. After my grandmother went home to her father's house, her ex-husband took four wives and shortly had a gaggle of sons, but he never got any joy out of them. The wives fought tooth and nail and goaded their sons to steal from their father to ensure their futures. But in the end, they were good for nothing and squandered the lot. My grandfather died without so much as an acre of land to his name to leave to his precious sons."

"And what about your grandmother? What happened to her?" Eman asked.

"Her father knew her value and gave her a place of honor in his household. Her mother had died when she was young, and he gave her the running of the household. She raised my mother in her father's house and made an excellent marriage for her. My father was a kind, educated man who knew the value of a good wife. She gave my mother this pendant on her wedding day and told her the story of her marriage. She warned her against the fickleness of fortune, and my mother gave me the same warning on my own wedding day. I thought my future was secure when I had a dozen sons … and I guess it was, after a fashion. I never wanted for food or drink or shelter. But now my heart aches for the daughter I never had." The old woman nodded her head a few times after finishing her story, the tale fading away rather than ending. "I'm a bit tired, my dear. I think I'd better rest awhile. But keep the pendant safe until you can give it to your daughter with the same warning."

Without another word, the old woman sank back on her pillows and closed her eyes. Eman pulled the sheet up around her shoulders and sat, uncertain what to do. Something about the old woman told Eman that she was nearing her end. She sat with her for another half hour in silence and then kissed her lightly on the head, the needs of her own children and husband dragging her away.

#

The next morning, Eman rose early and made her way down the old woman's winding street. When she knocked on the door and received no answer, part of her was not surprised.

As she opened the door of the house, its silence hit her anew. In the bedroom, stretched out on the bed, just as Eman had left her, was the old woman. Before Eman laid her hand upon her chest, she knew that life had fled. The woman's lonely existence was over.

As Eman sat, resting her head on her arms on the side of the old woman's bed, wondering what to do, the phone rang, breaking the stillness. Eman hesitated before answering but reasoned that she must tell someone from the old woman's family, and here was a perfect opportunity.

"Assalamu 'alaikum," Eman answered, her voice cracking as she gave the standard greeting.

"Who is this?" the deep male voice asked, suddenly concerned. "Where's my mother?"

"My name is Eman. I'm a nurse who gives el-hagga her shots. When I came this morning, I found her ... I'm sorry, may God provide you with solace."

His sob made it clear that he understood what she meant to say. "I'll be there as soon as I can ... I'll catch the first plane." It was obvious that he was grasping for a plan. "I'm sorry to impose, but could you ask the cleaning girl—I think her name is Hosniyya—to take care of her and make the arrangements."

"I'll do what I can myself ... don't worry. But if you or one of your brothers could come soon ... they won't issue the papers without the closest relatives. I'm sorry for the question, but who am I speaking with?"

"Oh, I'm sorry, I'm her youngest son ..."

"Karim. She spoke of you often."

"I will call my brothers, and one of us will be there immediately. Thank you."

Eman sat in silence for a few minutes and considered what she had to do. The first thing was to find a woman to wash the body ...

\#

Eman was dressed all in black. The condolence-giving after the funeral was almost over for the night. She sighed as she looked around the little apartment, so changed from the silent place where the woman had spent the end of her days. Her grandchildren argued in the back bedroom, their mothers hushing them periodically. Her sons sat in attendance—all twelve of them solemnly accepting the condolences of all their acquaintances. Eman picked up a tray full of Arabic coffee cups, carried it to the kitchen and began to wash them when one of the tall sons walked in. "You are Eman, aren't you?"

She lowered her eyes modestly, concentrating on her washing. "Yes, I am Eman. And you must be Mr. Karim."

"I want to thank you for taking care of my mother so well. I wish I could have been the one to do it."

"I did nothing, really. She was a very kind woman. She would have loved to see your children."

"Yes, I wish she had. I have a girl and a boy—Aisha and Ahmad," he pulled a photograph out of his pocket, showing a smiling family sitting around a kitchen table with a pretty blue teapot in the middle. "Aisha is my eldest."

"The teapot reminds me of a story that your mother told me about you pouring tea for your grandfather."

"That's the same teapot. I like for it to always be in plain sight. It reminds me of how fallible a person can be and helps me accept my children's accidents."

"Your mother thought one of her daughters-in-law had thrown it away."

"Really? I never thought she'd notice that it was gone. It was after she'd stopped moving around the apartment. I should have asked her for it."

"She wouldn't have said no."

Eman thought for a moment and gave back the photo. Karim turned to leave. "What was your mother's name, by the way?"

"You don't know?" he asked in surprise.

"She called herself 'Umm Dastit Regala.'"

Karim smiled, "Her claim to fame ... her mother named her Aisha."

#

A LIFELINE

From: Aida Nasr
To: Fatima ElKalay
Subject: Latest news
Sent: Oct 9, 2005 at 2:48 PM

Dear Fatima,

Thanks so much for your last e-mail and glad you found my previous message useful. It's nice to be of help. I'll send you any more motivational/inspirational things I come across. Sorry I disappeared for so long ... I had a busy week before Ramadan and then it started, and my sleeping schedule went out the window. I was so tired I couldn't believe it and didn't come near the computer!

Today is the first day I'm feeling a bit normal.

I hope you had a good omra. Thanks for remembering me in your prayers. I'm glad the stories arrived ... I had my doubts, but I guess Egyptian express mail does deliver after all. That's good to know! ... I saw Mariam the week before Ramadan and she told me about the idea of sending each other our stories to encourage each other and maybe even putting together a collection of our stories and I think that's a great idea. She's already sent me one of hers which I'm going to print out and read.

Anyway, I've got to close now, but will be in touch soon ...

Take care,

Aida

From: Fatima ElKalay
To: Aida Nasr
Subject: Re: My critique
Sent: April 23, 2006 at 6:36 PM

Dear Aida,

Thanks for this; you are positive as ever! … I am working on a story about a maid who is seducing the narrator's husband. I didn't really mean for it to develop that way and may try to steer it in another direction! I can't quite figure out why odd things come up in my stories without me intending them. Could it be that I am not very organized? I really do feel my stories and characters write themselves sometimes (as I said in my critique), and I wonder if everyone in my life must do exactly as they please? Am I just too democratic, even with my art?

… Please let me know if you need anything from here. I still have a good couple of months, so do let me know.

Keep in touch!

Lots of love,

Fatima

From: Aida Nasr
To: Fatima ElKalay
Subject: Your message
Sent: April 27, 2006 at 12:00 AM

Dear Fatima,

Thanks for your e-mail. Your new story sounds very interesting and it will be interesting to see which direction you take with it. …

Well, I am proofreading a book which is taking up what little concentration I have at the moment! I am also supposed to be writing an article about homeopathy and a book review, but I can't seem to concentrate on doing more than one thing at a time. I want to be more productive but am really feeling quite the opposite.

Hope I can get more motivated soon!

Anyway, I am scribbling short story ideas in my new (pink) notebook, in between the proofreading, so that's a start. I don't really have set plotlines, just a beginning of a conversation or a description of a person … not sure where it will all lead but must take the plunge.

I read somewhere recently that one writer always asks herself, "what's in the box?," when she writes a story, and that is a way of visualizing what the reader will come away from the story with. So I am definitely not sure "what's in the box" yet, but it's an interesting way of looking at it …

Take care and will be in touch,

Love,

Aida

From: Aida Nasr
To: Mariam Shouman, Fatima ElKalay
Subject: My first story
Sent: June 6, 2007 at 7:40 PM

Dear girls,

Well, I'm really excited … here is my first story, finished! You never thought it would happen, did you? It was hard work, but actually a lot of fun once I got started ... Please tell me what you think. I'll get started on another story right away, insha' Allah. I'm going to have to work hard to catch up with the both of you!

Can't wait to see you both soon. Fatima, we have missed you so much!

Take care,

Aida

From: Mariam Shouman
To: Aida Nasr, Fatima ElKalay
Subect: RE: My first story
Sent: June 6, 2007 at 9:17 PM

Mabrouk! Mabrouk! Can't wait to read it!

From: Aida Nasr
To: Mariam Shouman, Fatima ElKalay
Subject: Dessert for Three, second story
Sent: July 20, 2007 at 8:15 PM

Hi girls,

Hope you are both well. Here is my second story.

Please let me know what you think … particularly if the characters are developed enough and also the main theme. I don't want it to be trite!

I already have the idea for my third story, which will be set in a spice shop (attar), so I'll get going on that next week. Can't wait to read your next stories and hope to see you soon ...

Love,

Aida

From: Mariam Shouman
To: Aida Nasr, Fatima ElKalay
Subject: Dessert for Three, second story
Sent: July 25, 2007 at 10:14 AM

Aida!

I loved it!!!

This one has a real flow and that sense of taking a slice out of Egyptian life and examining it. Great job!!!

Now me and Fatima have to get to work!

Mariam

LES BOUTONS

by Fatima ElKalay

The little shop off the square was not as my grandmother had described it. It was not painted a warm apricot and the sight of it did not make your heart leap. There were no baladi roses on its front ledge, no cats napping on its steps. It didn't have a polished cedar door with a big brass knocker, or a green and white awning draped over its windows. Instead, it was a sad little place, hunched and unloved. Most of the shop window was boarded up with plywood. The single pane that remained had not been washed in many seasons, and from a distance, looked as if coated with the woolly gray fluff that comes out of a vacuum cleaner. The bottom edge of the door had rotted away, no doubt from decades of tossing water across the threshold to cool the entrance at midday. The outer wall was encrusted in dirt, its bricks crumbling like breadsticks, its paint long gone. Someone had sprayed slogans of patriotism and protest in red and black across the façade.

What was this shop still doing here? Others from the same generation had succumbed long ago to the gift shops and travel agents, street cafés and sprawling office blocks so typical of downtown.

But you see, I went there only for the old man. Every month or two I would drop by, drink his clove tea, and leave a curl of banknotes in the jar on the counter. That's the way it's been ever since I made a promise.

#

I took a deep breath and stepped into the shop. There was more of the gray, woolly stuff to assault me from every corner. It strayed up my nostrils, formed a layer on my eyes and clothes, and got in my mouth. The old man must have good lungs to be able to breathe in here. I tried to visualize it a cleaner place. Had there really been a grand chandelier gracing this ceiling? Now it was just two neon light bulbs cradled in a huge flat dish, hanging precariously on thin wires and speckled with black polka dots— a mass grave for generations of flies. The boarded-up windows allowed little daylight into the shop, imbuing it with a sad dreariness. The paint had peeled away from the walls in dozens of tight curls—the kind children are always tempted to pick at. Hanging on one wall was a very old painting of King Farouk in a striking wooden frame that looked out of place against the flaking paint. Though ingrained with dirt, it was clearly a treasure, hand-carved, gold-leafed. The first time I saw it I wondered if it had been there in my grandmother's day, and if she had admired it the way I now did. But back then, there must have been other things in the shop to enchant a young girl more than the wood that framed the head of the monarch.

If I were a customer, I'd find nothing inviting here; it was a haberdashery of very sparse sorts. Rows of cobwebbed shelves displayed many jars, all empty. These were quite pretty, but not for sale. There were more jars on the counter, filled with an assortment of buttons, all jumbled together, all grimy. Dusty velvet trays displayed zippers, spools of colored thread, three packs of sewing needles (made in Germany), scissors, knitting wool—mostly in brown and black—and five faded measuring tapes. In one corner of the shop, there were two rickety kitchen chairs and a small step ladder. In another, an antique bureau in dark redwood, dirty and badly scarred, with a small gas ring on top, and tea things on a tray. At the back, there were odds and ends in a dusty, indiscernible heap: tattered books, a broken hat stand, and what looked like bits of a grandfather clock. That was it.

"Assalamu 'alaikum," I said to the man seated behind the counter. His face was buried in a newspaper, his spindly fingers clamped to the pages.

He looked up startled, then smiled in recognition.

"Wa 'alaikum assalam!"

The first time I had come here I had gotten very lost. All I had to go on were a scrawled address, a letter, and the first of many curls of banknotes. The underground had whisked me to the other end of Cairo to find an unknown man in an unknown little shop.

"Could you tell me the way to Les Boutons?" I asked every third person I met.

That seemed to have been a difficult question. The name of the street had changed three times in half a century, and this was Cairo, where no one ever wanted to appear as if they didn't have an answer.

"Ah yes, next to the fire station straight ahead, then as far left as you can go, then a sharp right."

"Oh no, not Les Boutons, that's up next to the old Catholic middle school, four stops from here; you'd better take a bus, Miss."

"No, no, no, you are thinking of the yarn shop that used to be a fishmonger. Miss, you'd better ask the florist; there isn't a spot he hasn't delivered flowers to."

I covered every inch of the neighborhood. The florist brought me closer than any of the others, not because he had delivered flowers there, nor because he knew the old man, but because he remembered one of his old customers mentioning the story of the little shop …

The old man looked at me reproachfully "All this time, little Soraya? It's been months … I thought you had forgotten me."

He always spoke my name in a soft half-whisper.

"I'm sorry, I've been away."

"Ah …"

Silence fell, but not the uncomfortable kind. I watched him as he folded his newspaper, the skin on his hands loose and brown. He'd grown thinner than last time and more stooped, and had lost yet another tooth. But the dark gray semi-circle of hair oiled to his scalp was still the same, and as far as I could recall, he was wearing the same olive pants and oversized shirt, marbled gray with ingrained dirt, that I had last seen him in.

#

Sometimes I pick up my paintbrush and capture my grandmother's memory of him. I paint him with deeply dimpled cheeks, a slim moustache, hair dark and parted down the middle. I see him in neat blue overalls, carefully stacking boxes on the top shelf, conscientiously checking for the slightest grain of dust, his head almost touching the creamy-white ceiling. In that moment I am her, watching him step down the ladder, his head two handspans above mine, his eyes warm and twinkling.

"Let me show you the pearl and silver buttons, my lady. For a princess's gown."

Then he takes my hand and leads me to the oak cabinet where the special pieces are kept.

"Would you like some tea?"

His frail voice cut into the memory and brought me back to the present.

"Oh, of course! That's why I'm here!"

He laughed in delight.

"'Ammo Hamza's clove tea, right?"

"Nobody else makes a perfect cup, sir!"

He nodded in approval, and hobbled away to put the kettle on. It was true that the old man made a perfect cup of tea. Even if I hadn't made my grandmother a promise, I think the tea would still have been something worth coming back for. But that was not all I looked forward to. 'Ammo Hamza kept me curious: how he spoke, the things he knew about life and the world, even his silences were captivating. And somehow, he could always tap into my thoughts. As if he had known me all my life.

"So, what's new?"

"Oh, not much. I have a little more rheumatism now, but I'm still as fit as old men come. Plus ça change, plus c'est la même chose."

His French always startled me. So fluent and flawless, as if he had been raised in the court of Versailles on the lap of Marie Antoinette. Funnily enough, he sounded more natural when speaking French than Arabic. I questioned him about this, but he vaguely implied that he had mingled with some fine folk as a young lad, though he wouldn't elaborate. You could never get anything out of the old man that he didn't want to say. In a flash, he would feign deafness, or pretend to have wandered off, or grumpily complain that I was taxing an old man's memory.

"And how are things, 'Ammo?"

He paused and looked up at me thoughtfully.

"Things are good. Reda cooks my dinners, the Sobhi twins pick me up and drop me off every day. I go for walks on the corniche at the weekend, rheumatism permitting. Hamdy helps me bathe and does my laundry (not very well, I may add). Life couldn't be better. Allah is merciful."

"And you wouldn't consider—"

"Never! This is the way it will be for the rest of my days. Things always turn out for the best."

He always interrupted at this point—regardless of what I was about to ask—and gave that same answer. It broke my heart because I realized that he was echoing the words in my grandmother's letter:

> *My Hamza,*
>
> *Things always turn out for the best. It might seem a pointless thing to say after all this time, but despite all events, life has been good, al-hamdulillah. Still, I have never forgiven myself for bringing so much sorrow into our lives. I have often wondered how you have been all these years. I think it's only fair that you know that I never wanted anything more than to be with you forever. Please forgive me if you can.*
>
> *Hamza, this letter will be delivered by my granddaughter. I wish I could be with her, but I don't get around much anymore. I know you might protest, but I am sending you what is rightly yours. Please accept it from me and know that it is well overdue. My granddaughter will see to it that you receive it as instructed. I cannot rest without you accepting this small token.*
>
> *All that is left to say is that my heart abounds with memories of you; this is the way it will be for the rest of my days.*
>
> *Eternally loving,*
> *Soraya*

Through a veil of tears, he had commented that it was not her handwriting, and I had explained that she dictated it to me because in those last days she was too weak to write herself. To my surprise, he quietly took the banknotes and put them in a jar on the counter. He did not try to count them, nor did he protest in any way, as my grandmother had said he might. Even though he and his shop appeared very much in need of the money, he seemed oddly disinterested in it. I wondered if he counted it when he was alone. But each time I returned, the curls of banknotes looked undisturbed in the jar. What a strange little man! With every visit, he seemed less the person my grandmother had depicted.

The kettle boiled on his little gas ring.

"Now tell me your news, child."

"This and that."

But I couldn't find anything of significance to say, except for one thing. I wondered how he would take it.

"I'm getting married."

He was pouring dark gold tea into tall drinking glasses.

"Oh."

The silence was uncomfortable.

"So, it's definite this time?"

He measured the sugar and dropped in cloves, his fingers trembling as he stirred. The cloves swirled in the glasses, like figure skaters performing their final pirouette. I looked at him for a long time, soaking in the warm sadness of his eyes.

"I'm sorry, 'Ammo Hamza, I didn't want to—"

"It's alright child. I am just a foolish old man. Drink your tea. 'Ammo Hamza's tea is not much good when it grows cold."

He lowered his eyes to his glass, as if searching for something. Then perhaps to appear that he had found what he was looking for, he dipped a spoon into the glass and took out a sodden clove. Holding it up to the light, he turned it over and over.

"So very small and frail," he said in a whisper, half to himself.

I drained my glass and rose.

"You must come again—very soon. Bring him with you. I would love to see the man who won your heart."

"Yes, of course ..."

The old man's request was to be honored. I would see to that. Three weeks later I returned with a rather perplexed fiancé at my side.

"Tell me again ... what's the purpose of this visit?"

He paused outside the shop to tie a shoelace, glancing at a grimy poster on the wall of a young man making a V sign at the camera.

"It's a long story, darling. Consider it a good deed, you know, visiting a lonely old man."

The interior was its usual fluff-gray self, but now there were more dead flies in the light fixture. The old man hobbled toward us, slower than last time.

"Three weeks!" He scolded.

"I'm sorry, 'Ammo, I've been so busy."

"Ah yes, busy ... that's right, you have a wedding coming up. Let me make you both some tea. If I'd known you were coming today, I would have prepared some rose sharbat, but you never said when you would return."

"Tea would be perfect 'Ammo," I said. "We are both very fond of tea."

There was silence. The old man looked at the young one for a long time. There was nothing in his gaze to give away his feelings. He just watched him as if he was an egg boiling on the stove. The young man sipped at his drink, swallowed.

"Nice tea."

"I am glad you like it, son. When is the big day?"

His eyes were on me.

"Next month. We are waiting for the autumn. It seems a nice time of year to move on to the next stage in our life."

I smiled and reached out to take my fiancé's hand.

"I love the colors of autumn, very inspirational for my paintings, and Karim is a photojournalist, so we're planning to trek across Europe. It's sort of a honeymoon and business trip wrapped up in one. We want to travel by train from city to city."

"Train … ah yes … train. Be sure to reach your destination."

He closed his eyes, mumbling the words to himself. How strange. He sounded a lot like Teta, just before she died: 'Soraya, the train … the train … must reach a destination.' I never found out what she meant, or which Soraya she was addressing—me, or herself. Perhaps 'Ammo would know.

He opened his eyes.

"I see you're excited about this marriage thing, little Soraya."

"Yes."

"And are you excited, son?"

"I–er, yes. I have never been to Europe before, or married!"

He giggled, amused by this observation, but the old man did not find it funny.

"Nor have I, not exactly. I'm too old to do either, now. May you be blessed for it, then."

An awkwardness filled the air. The tea was finished, and we rose to leave, but there was still something I had to say. The old man sensed this and asked a question very much on target.

"So, when do you get back from Europe?"

"Well, 'Ammo Hamza, the truth is, we're … we're not coming back. Karim has a new job based in London. It's rather long term, and he has a sister there, so we're emigrating."

He did not look up from his glass. His brown cheeks were flushed.

"You won't stay to rebuild Egypt? I didn't imagine you would. But I can't blame you, really. Some people may be disappointed, but that's their problem, n'est-ce pas?"

He rose from his seat, not really expecting any answers.

"You must come to see me before the wedding, then. I will have a little something for you."

"Oh 'Ammo, you've got to come to our wedding! Look, I brought you an invitation."

He gave a strangled sound, something between a laugh and a cough.

"Shame on you! I can't possibly attend. I am getting too old for such frivolity. Besides, look at me. I am bent over double." His eyes searched my face in a rather unsettling way.

"Please … please do me the honor of coming back before the wedding." Then, looking sidelong at my fiancé, he added, "If the gentleman is too busy, perhaps you can return alone …"

I took the hint, and two weeks later, one day before the wedding, I stood in front of the door of the little shop, alone. I took a deep breath; this was to be my last lungful of gray dust before leaving.

"My child!" He put his arm around my shoulder and sat me down.

"I knew you would not let me die without seeing you one more time. Tea?"

"Please."

I put my hand in my pocket. The banknotes were there, and a fold of tissues.

"Ahh," he said. "Very refreshing, this clove tea. Have you noticed that I put only two cloves in each glass? That way, when you stir, they dance together, though quite often their dance is apart …"

His voice trailed off as it often did, so that you never knew whether he expected you to comment on his observations or not. To be safe, I nodded in acknowledgement and then tactfully changed the subject.

"So how did you like my fiancé?"

He sighed.

"He'll have to do, I suppose, mais l'habit ne fait pas le moine. Whatever happened to the surgeon?"

"Oh, you still remember. We disagreed and went our separate ways."

"You mean it was too challenging for you, so you backed out."

"'Ammo—"

"Just like your grandmother. You share more than her name—she never was one for confrontations. But you know, it was harder in those days, putting up a fight for something you really wanted, harder for the young men, too."

"My fiancé is a great person really. His family is so supportive, and they really approve of the match."

He sighed. "Sounds familiar. Perhaps things haven't changed much in sixty years. Well, you will make a stunning bride, I can tell you that. You're so like her. Same skin, same eyes."

His words brought down my tears.

"Don't cry," he whispered, "It makes you look … unbearably beautiful, my Soraya, and it breaks an old man's heart."

He gently touched my cheek.

"Drink your tea, my love. You'll be missing it soon. Remember I said I'd have something for you? It's actually a couple of things. Wait here."

He unlocked a drawer in the bureau and took out an envelope. Then he took a deep breath and very slowly handed it to me.

"This is for you."

I smiled in delight

"A wedding gift, 'Ammo?"

Inside the envelope was a carefully folded check. I unfolded it, expecting a modest token, and could not believe what I was seeing.

"Five hundred thousand dollars!" My God, 'Ammo! Did you win something?"

He gave a sad little chuckle.

"My beloved child, I have never won anything in my life, except perhaps your grandmother's heart."

I frowned in bewilderment and touched the letters on the check. 'Ammo was not one for practical jokes. Could it be that in all this time I was dealing with some old scrooge? Is that why he never spent any of the money in the jar? Or perhaps he was a cleverly disguised crook? My mind did somersaults trying to find meaning in the piece of paper I had in my hand.

The old man patted me gently on the shoulder.

"It's okay, child. You never really knew, did you? What did you think?"

I swallowed hard.

"Teta said you were the love of her life. She said you couldn't be together because of—family differences. I knew that you loved her deeply, it was all over your face, and in every gesture you made from the first time I saw you. I came away with the impression that you were a man of, well, less fortunate circumstances, which explained why she made me promise to visit you with money. She never actually said what it was for, but I assumed it was an act of charity, from a woman who once loved you. And when I saw you and the shop for the first time, it looked like you both needed every penny of it. But now with this check, now I don't understand anything."

He shook his head. He didn't seem to be listening.

"What would a young nobleman know about buttons? Nothing! I'd never even done up my own buttons or combed my own hair. This place and everything about it, was born of her inspiration.

"An autumn afternoon; my sister, frail in her wheelchair beneath the sycamore tree; Father sipping clove tea, rolling out his garbled politics; all of us together, catching the last warmth of the day. Then a girl walks across the lawn of our estate, a dainty girl, with a bolt of fabric and a jar of buttons. I'd never seen her before, nor anyone so beautiful.

I gestured to the butler.

'The seamstress's daughter. Moved in this week. Her name is Soraya.'

She must have heard her name, because she looked round, squinting in the sunlight. It made her look as if she was smiling at me, so I smiled back and she blushed.

'What's in your jar? Bonbons?' I was never one to miss an opportunity to tease the staff.

She turned to face me, the sun framing her delicate figure, her cheeks glistening, the tiny locks of hair that had escaped her bun made coppery by the afternoon light.

'Boutons, Monsieur,' she said in her very best French. 'De Montmartre.'

'Ah! Français like an aristocrat!' I said with a laugh. She lowered her gaze.

'Oh no, sir, forgive me. I just repeat what I hear.'

Just then, a hoopoe called out nearby.

'Well, perhaps you can repeat the cry of that hud-hud?' I asked.

"She looked confused. She must have thought I was calling her out for using the language of the elite, but I was just trying to be playful.

'I think you should let the girl get on with her work,' Father said, glaring, his teacup poised mid-air. He knew right then. She bowed and turned away, rolling the fabric out for my sister to admire.

"A small exchange, but it was done. I couldn't get her out of mind. I wanted to see her again, convincing myself I just wanted her to know how good her French was, and that I wasn't mocking her that day. An excuse, of course. Back then many young noblemen did as they pleased, as long as there were no attachments, no aftermath. But not me. My father didn't raise me that way. He was a man of principle. He warned me, many times. But of course, I didn't listen. I sought her out any way I could.

"She resisted—like any girl employed in a pasha's household, she knew her place. She could never be a noblewoman, and the whole idea of meddling with the aristocracy terrified her. But I assured her of my intentions.

'Don't be afraid, my darling,' I told her. If you can't climb up, I'll climb down.'

"And just like that, I bought this shop. Les Boutons—French and buttons, our first meeting immortalized right here."

His eyes swept across the dingy room with tenderness, lingering at the decaying door. It was the kind of look you have when you expect someone to walk in any minute.

"Not long after, my sister died. My grief would have consumed me if it wasn't for Soraya, but it was harder on Father. He cut himself off from everyone for a long time, so he was somewhat oblivious to our deepening relationship."

He paced the room, shifting back and forth, more like an impatient leopard than an old, old man. I had never seen him so agile, or so talkative.

"This shop became a place of solace for me, and as Soraya pulled me into her world, I experienced happiness in the simpler things: fresh bread off a donkey cart, haggling over green peppers, the vibrancy of a village carnival, sticky sweet potatoes, straight off the coals. No cutlery, no napkins, no tea in fine china in a pompous Louis Qunize drawing room.

"She introduced me to real people. They remained my faithful friends for the rest of their lives, their children now my caregivers. News reached my family, of course, and we soon had a series of break-ins here. It was very unnerving for her, and there was not a day that passed without her wanting to back out, but I was determined. I took the next step: I married her."

I covered my mouth with my hand to stifle a shriek. Teta had never told me anything about marriage, but then considering what I was hearing now, she'd told me nothing at all.

"In secret?"

He jumped at my interruption.

"No," he said with some irritation, "not in secret, but nobody came. Not from my family, nor from hers. Just a few of her friends, and a few of mine. Mines were the ones who betrayed us."

He stopped to face me, his eyes looking straight through mine.

"She was so beautiful in her peach and white gown. More beautiful than any noblewoman. We took the vows and secretly boarded my father's train to Upper Egypt, or so we thought. I had everything planned, a luxurious train trip to wherever we pleased. I was tempted to have a boisterous street celebration in Sayyedna al-Hussein, but I wanted to show her I'd spare her nothing. I had a full staff of maids, cooks, butlers to do her bidding. Everyone in attendance was to know she was my lady. 'Oh Hamza, this is too much!' she exclaimed.

"We never reached our destination. I should have known. Twenty-five minutes out of Cairo and the train was intercepted by the king's guards. We hadn't even finished our first course. We were dragged off, your grandmother apprehended like a criminal. The marriage wasn't even consummated. It was a huge scandal. My father disowned me, as expected. It was very hard on me because I genuinely loved and respected him. Your grandmother's mother was put to shame and accused of taking advantage of my family's graciousness. Three generations of seamstresses had been employed in our household; none had brought such disgrace to the family. The old seamstress, my would-be mother-in-law, had a massive stroke and died soon after. That broke your grandmother completely."

There was a long pause. His eyes glistened with the first tears. When he spoke again, there was a tremor in his voice.

"I was willing to fight everyone, but she wouldn't do it. Do you think perhaps women are more practical in matters of love than men?"

He looked down at his hands, balled into wrinkled fists.

"She came here, in heavy mourning over her mother, and asked me to terminate the marriage. It was just on paper, she said, and she was still a virgin. I could ask my father to help resolve the matter peaceably. She said her mother had always told her that the pasha was an honorable man unlike most of the decadent aristocracy. I pleaded with her not to, we could prove them all wrong, but she refused. So, I gave her my word that she would have her wish.

"Heartbroken, I approached the pasha. She was right, of course. He was still very bitter at being disgraced, but he welcomed her request. He could have easily seen to the divorce and left her in the gutter, but that was not the way of my father. As a gesture of magnanimity, he arranged for a distant relative of ours—of lower birth, of course—to be introduced to my Soraya. I don't remember his name (or perhaps I choose to forget), but he was a clerk at a government office, and any girl of your grandmother's social standing would have been more than honored to have him as a husband. There was even a handsome settlement, to make sure they had an excellent start in life. She resigned herself to the match and told my father that she was very grateful, but I think deep inside she felt broken. She had had her honor restored but had lost her heart."

He turned his face upward to the light fixture with its many dead flies, and the ceiling beyond it, rippled with grimy flakes of paint.

"It was the same for me. I made my peace with my father, but I would not go back to his estate. I couldn't; my heart belonged in this little shop. I bought a tiny one-room apartment nearby and with the support of my new-found friends, came here every day for years. Oh, there were strange years before the revolution when I did some unusual things: desert trekking, living with hermits in the Himalayas, fighting and funding obscure tribal wars in Central Africa, but I always came back here. There was always someone to keep the shop running, but it soon fell into disrepair. In a way this was good, because with the elegant furnishings gone, most people forgot who I really was. My threadbare existence in other lands helped me ignore what a hovel this place was gradually becoming. It was never really a business, you see; I've never done a stroke of work in my life, child, so in that sense I've remained true to my slothful aristocratic origins."

He sniffed and smiled a little at this last thought.

"My father continued to rebuke me for my lifestyle, but he did not disown me a second time. I suppose you can only do something like that once, then it's meaningless. Besides, I was his only child, and deep down, I always wondered if perhaps he saw in me a part of him that had been stifled by convention. He never said it, but I do believe he felt a little guilty about the way things turned out with your grandmother. When Nasser's revolution toppled the aristocracy, I expected my father to be devastated over losing land and titles. It was a severe blow to most courtiers, after all. But he seemed unruffled by events. He was very sick at the time; I thought that explained his disinterest. But after he died, I was stunned to learn that he'd had enough foresight to plan many years ahead and transfer most of our vast fortune to banks in Switzerland. What a shrewd old gentleman! I suddenly had even more to spend, and nothing I wanted to spend it on, so I resumed my escapades across the world like an aimless tramp."

He sighed and closed his eyes. He wasn't crying any more.

"I never saw your grandmother again after she came to the shop that last time to ask me to let her go. I went to the ends of the earth but could not wander across Cairo to see the light of my life. Haven't you ever asked yourself why I jump every time you walk in here? I relive that last goodbye every time I see you."

"'Ammo, what about the—"

"—money she asked you to deliver? Oh little Soraya, have you even been listening? I keep saying your grandmother was a true noblewoman. She wanted to pay back the settlement she received at the beginning of her marriage to your grandfather. She could not accept charity."

I did not know whether I was seeing the old man for the first time, or whether his mind had unravelled.

"'Ammo Hamza, sir. This is all very … remarkable."

There was an edge of doubt to my words, and he sensed it. The whole story was too fabulous. In all probability there was no bank account either. Once again, he read my thoughts.

"There is one other thing I want you to have."

He dragged the step ladder under the picture of the king, and on shaky, ninety-year-old legs climbed it, seeking my hand to help him balance. For a moment, I thought he was going to give me the beautiful frame I had long admired, but then he pushed it aside to reveal a little box embedded in the wall. His long, spindly fingers tugged it free. It was covered in white dust, which he wiped away with his shirtsleeve to reveal tarnished silver.

"The check is real, dear granddaughter, as real as my love for Soraya ever was; so are the contents of this box. Open it when you are alone. Not now. Please, not now. Goodbye, little Soraya. It is getting late and you have a wedding tomorrow and a life waiting to be lived. I don't suppose we shall see each other again."

He hugged me and hurried me out of the shop. If there were unanswered questions on my mind they would have to remain so. At the doorstep I turned and asked him for his blessing.

"Things always turn out for the best."

"Goodbye, 'Ammo Hamza."

#

In a peach and white wedding dress, I sat at the edge of my bed. The hairdresser was standing outside the bedroom door, anxious to pin up my hair, but she would have to wait. My eyes were raw and red and rimmed with tears. I had in my hand 'Ammo Hamza's staggering check. The little silver box was in my lap, open. Inside, were some amazing things. There were the deeds to the shop, and a document, signed and countersigned, stating that in the event of his death, the shop, and a number of properties in Switzerland, would be mine. There was also another document, very, very old, declaring the dissolution of the marriage of Hamza and Soraya. There was a set of beautiful pearl and silver buttons, a wedding band with the words "Hamza and Soraya forever" engraved inside the rim, and lots and lots of banknotes, all rolled into one.

But I wasn't crying because of these things. I was crying because of a faded brown and white photograph, right at the bottom of the box. It was a photograph of a pretty little shop with smooth walls, and a polished wooden door with a shiny doorknob. A striped awning stretched over the sparkling front windows. There were roses on the front ledge and two plump cats napping on the doorstep.

And standing in the foreground was a radiant young couple wrapped in each other's arms.

#

LILACS

by Aida Nasr

Lying in the soft springtime grass, Injy looked up through the lacy curtain of weeping willow leaves. With its delicate, drooping branches, the willow tree in her backyard reminded her of a woman with long, flowing hair. From beneath its protective shade, it always seemed as if the tree was reaching down to hug her.

It was her favorite spot to play, because she could watch Mama flit back and forth behind the kitchen window. As she cooked, Mama kept an eye on Injy, and Injy caught flashes of Mama's long, brown ponytail swinging by the window as she worked. The lilac bush's delicate flowers moved gently in the breeze, and a lawnmower buzzed in the background, low and steady. Injy's best friend, Janey, had just run home to dinner.

The girls had lain on their backs in the grass, looking at the clear wash of blue sky that reminded Injy of her watercolor set. The fat clouds sat so low you could almost reach out and pull them down like cotton candy.

"That one looks like a ship," said Janey.

"That one's a heart," said Injy.

Occasionally, they rolled over to pluck dandelions and blow their soft fuzz onto the grass. When they looked skyward again, the clouds had drifted and changed shape.

Injy wiggled her bare toes in the cool, tickling grass. It was her favorite time of day. That pause before Mama called her to dinner. The kitchen window opened. "Injy, honey, dinnertime," called Mama's sing-song voice. She knew that inside, Mama was now calling her big brother and little sister and Papa.

Injy skipped to the back door. Before going in, she ran her fingers through the purple burst of lilac blossoms by the house. Their sweet, heady scent filled the air and followed her for a moment as she stepped into the kitchen and the warm smells of Mama's cooking.

#

Twenty-five years later

Injy sat on the dark balcony in her cotton nightgown, eating a mango with her fingers. It was after midnight on an oppressively hot Cairo summer night, but in the north-facing balcony there was a gentle breeze. No one on the street could see her. The light was off, and the tall, old tree reached over the balcony wall and protected her from view. Even at this hour, she could occasionally hear people shouting in the distance and cars whizzing down the main street not far from her apartment.

The mango was sweet and tart, its rubbery skin slippery in her fingers as she roughly cut off pieces with a small, sharp knife. She bit into the glistening flesh, juice running down her hands. The children were asleep, and Amin was working late, so she ate contentedly. Amin hated mangos, couldn't even stand their smell, a fact that had startled her when they were first married. He had opened their shiny new refrigerator and looked inside the brown bag from the greengrocer's as if it contained hand grenades.

"What Egyptian doesn't like mangos?" Injy had demanded petulantly. "We've known each other since we were ten, Amin. How come you never told me you hated mangos?" Her reaction was out of proportion, but Injy couldn't help herself.

When she had arrived in Egypt all those years ago, a scared and uprooted ten-year-old, she couldn't seem to cope with anything. Not the heat. Not the huge extended family jammed into her grandmother's sofas and chairs and babbling in a language she didn't understand, nor the orange-blossom-scented glass bottles of water in her grandmother's refrigerator. To Injy, they just tasted like perfume.

But mangos were one of the few Egyptian things she had gotten from the start. Mangos eaten on her grandmother's balcony on those first summer nights in Egypt, with the radio crooning softly and juice running down her fingers. And now Amin, with his witty Arabic and natural way with people: Amin didn't like mangos? It felt unfair somehow, like a betrayal. She couldn't help but argue, even though she knew she was being unreasonable.

"What are you talking about, Injy? I'm sure I must have said at some point that I hated mangos. Anyway, what's the problem? Everybody doesn't like something," Amin had shot back.

It was their first real argument, silly and pointless, since meeting in Miss Zeinab's fifth primary class. But for the first year of their marriage, Injy never bought or ate a mango, so as not to upset him. All these years later, he still teased her about their mango fight. And she secretly delighted in eating mangos because she knew it irritated him ever so slightly. But she still made sure to eat them when he wasn't there.

#

Injy took the bowl to the kitchen, threw the stones and skins in the garbage, and washed her hands of the sticky juice. She smelled her fingers. A faint mango scent still clung to them.

Going to her bedroom, she looked around restlessly. Sleep? No, she was exhausted but strangely alert. Compelled to the wardrobe, she scanned its contents. The patchwork bag on the top shelf called to her. She gently lifted it down and sat on the bed to look at the sad scattering of objects inside. Taking out a tiny bottle, Injy carefully twisted its top, and breathed in its scent. The perfume had evaporated over the years, and the bottle was half empty now. But the scent of lilacs was sweet and strong. She put the bottle back.

Now she knew exactly what she wanted from the bag. She took out a sturdy wooden box, put the bag back in the wardrobe and returned to the bed. Leaning back on her pillows, she flipped open the lid. Tiny dividers, miniatures of the kind in a filing cabinet, waved like little flags out of a sea of tightly packed paper.

She always went to "Cakes & Cookies" first and pulled out the big wad of recipes. "Banana Bread" announced the first, grease-splotched card with quaint drawings of mixing bowls and wooden spoons dancing around slanting lines of cursive writing. Injy shuffled through the pile, delighting in the whimsical names: snickerdoodles, cinnamon jumbles, chocolate crinkles, gingerbread men, sugar cookies, red velvet cake.

Putting the recipes back, she flicked through the box idly until her fingers stopped at something unfamiliar tucked near the back. She pulled out a neat square and unfolded it carefully. It was a faded page torn from a newspaper. Injy sat upright in bed.

Mama smiled out at her from a photo she had never seen before. She quickly examined every detail of the picture so closely she could see the little black dots that clustered to form the whole image. Mama was standing in the kitchen of Injy's childhood wearing her white blouse with the wide collar. Her long ponytail rested on one shoulder. She looked so young. Injy looked for the date on the newspaper page, and after a few fumbled calculations, established that Mama was five years younger in this photograph than Injy was now.

She quickly scanned the text. "Mrs. Farid Antar of 10 Maplewood Lane is an accomplished cook in our community, particularly well-known for her delightful baking," trumpeted the newspaper happily. "Her neighbor, Mrs. Robert Fullman of 12 Maplewood Lane confirms, 'Darla Mae's brownies and banana bread are a joy. Everyone in the neighborhood loves them, especially the children.'"

Injy could feel her heart beating fast and sweat beading at the back of her neck. She swept her hair over one shoulder and then realized that she had just mirrored one of Mama's gestures. She felt dizzy, disoriented. In her bedroom in Cairo, out of nowhere, Mama suddenly reappeared as if nothing had ever happened: her sweet smile, her favorite blouse, her kitchen, and Janey's mother praising her banana bread.

Injy's forehead tightened and ached as she forced her eyes away from Mama's face to the rest of the article. "Mrs. Antar has generously shared her most treasured recipes from around the world with our *Chronicle* readers. Since Mrs. Antar's husband is originally from Egypt, she has learned several lovely dishes from that country, which she enjoys preparing for her family, including her mother-in-law's delightful rice pudding with rose water."

Rose water! It would be the rice pudding with the rose water, wouldn't it? Injy fumed. Nena had to lace everything with that essence of perfume. Where on earth did Mama get rose water in New Hampshire in 1979?

#

When Amin got home, he found Injy asleep at an awkward angle on the pile of pillows with the newspaper page and the little box on her lap. The tears had dried, but he could tell she'd been crying. He picked up the page and looked at the photo, puzzled, until he read the beginning of the article. Carefully, he put it back on her lap and nudged her shoulder.

"Injy? You fell asleep."

It usually irritated her beyond belief that Amin woke her to tell her that she'd been sleeping. But tonight, she was too drained to care.

"What happened? Where did you find this?" He nodded toward the clipping.

"In my Mama's recipe box, which I've looked through hundreds of times before. Can you believe this, Amin? How did I never see it? And why did I find it now? Is she trying to tell me something? Her birthday's next week, you know."

Amin looked at her intently. She rarely noticed his expression these days, but now she saw that his eyes were warm and concerned. Suddenly she could see him on the playground during recess all those years ago.

"What's wrong, Injy?" he had asked her in fluent English with a faint British accent. "Why are you always so quiet? Why don't you play with the other children?" He had had exactly the same look of intense concentration in his ten-year-old eyes as he did at the moment. It was amazing how people never changed in certain ways, and how they changed inexplicably in others.

"My mother died, and my father moved us to Cairo to live with my grandmother," she had blurted out, feeling guilty as she said it. No one at her grandmother's ever talked about Mama. "And I don't understand what anyone's saying on the playground. They're all speaking in Arabic. I want to go home," she had cried.

Amin had looked startled, but even as a boy he rallied quickly. "I'm very sorry your mother died. Now I know why you're so sad. Come on, I'll show you where my sisters are playing with their friends. They speak English very well."

#

Now Amin said gently, "It's strange that you found this article at this point in time. Your mother looks so pretty and kind in this photo; I wish I had known her. But there's nothing we can do about it now, so let's go to sleep and think about it tomorrow, okay?"

She knew he had to wake up in a few hours to get ready for work, and truly there was nothing to do. But she couldn't believe how effortlessly he wrapped things up. "Why didn't you just let me sleep then? Why wake me up to ask me about something you have no intention of talking about?"

"Injy, I know you're upset, but what can we do now? That article's been sitting in that box for years. Are a few more hours going to make a difference?"

"Yes, Amin. It makes a difference to me. I want to know why I found this now. I want you to care that I want to know."

"I do care, love." He looked weary. She suddenly felt sorry she'd said it.

"Do you understand that I do care, Injy? I just want to discuss this when we're both rested and thinking clearly. That's all. And I do have to wake up early to go to work. That's also a priority. For both of us, I would think."

"Okay, you're right. We'll talk about it tomorrow insha' Allah." It came out more harshly than she wanted. She was silent as he put the article and box on her nightstand, changed into his pajamas, clicked off the light.

"Good night, Jouja." He used her childhood nickname. "Things will be better tomorrow, insha' Allah."

"I hope so. Good night, Amin."

He settled onto his side facing away from her and was asleep in a few seconds. She tossed for ages, then fell into a restless, unsettled slumber with strange dreams. In the morning, she remembered a very clear image of her mother walking into their old kitchen. "Mama, I've missed you so much," Injy wanted to say. But she could only watch as her mother opened the refrigerator and took out a mixing bowl.

#

As she dragged herself groggily out of bed the next morning, Injy saw the article on her nightstand. She wanted to read it again, but there wasn't any time. She had to get Amin's breakfast ready. Where was he? Then she saw the clock. She had overslept. He was gone. Guilt hung over her as she dressed, but she didn't want to call him. She just wanted to get on with her day.

"Yes, I want you to deliver an order, please. Give me one medium-sized watermelon, a kilo of bananas, and a kilo of mangos." She wanted fresh coriander but, in her tiredness, she couldn't find the Arabic word for it. After struggling for a few seconds, she said, "Thank you, that's all, and don't be late." After she put the phone down, she thought hard. Karaffs? No, that was celery. Kuzbara, that was it! Barely time for a cup of tea, before errands with Sarah and Ali to get their school notebooks and book bags.

The phone was ringing insistently as they walked into the apartment at the end of a long, hot, exhausting day in Cairo's traffic jams. "How are you, habibti? I called a while ago, but you weren't home," said Amin's mother. Expectant pause.

Injy sighed to herself. She had never gotten used to this custom of hinting at things rather than saying them outright. Yes, I know we weren't home, she wanted to say.

Instead, "We were getting the children's school things, ya Tante." This was the information her mother-in-law really wanted.

"So early? School isn't starting for weeks!" Injy's habit of planning ahead was something of a joke to both her and Amin's families. The huge crowds in the stores in the few days before anything important happened were exactly why she always did her shopping early.

Ignoring this last comment, she said, "Sarah is very happy with her school bag this year, ya Tante. Here, she'll tell you all about it," and handed the phone to her daughter as she went to start lunch.

When the kids had eaten and were off in the apartment somewhere, Injy settled on the balcony with a cup of tea. It was breezy and lovely here just before sunset. The old tree reached over the wall. When she first married, it bloomed in brilliant clusters of orange flowers. Now it only produced a few scattered blossoms. In this breeze, the tree's delicate, feathery leaves fluttered like a flock of green birds.

#

When Amin returned from work, he handed Injy a small package wrapped in shiny silver paper. In her mind, she ran through the short list of occasions when he ever got her a present, but it wasn't her birthday or Mother's Day. Puzzled, she tore away the wrapping to find a shiny picture frame covered with ornate flowers and leaves. She noticed the tiny stamp on the back that said it was silver.

"I thought we'd put your mom's photo from the article in it," he said. "What do you think?"

Injy felt a strange rush of adrenaline combined with a kind of breathless surprise that he cared enough to have gone out after a long day at work to buy her this frame. She would have chosen a simpler design, but she knew the ornamentation and the silver meant that he was honoring her mother, acknowledging how important this was to her.

"Wait a minute," she said, and disappeared to their bedroom.

She lifted the patchwork bag from the wardrobe shelf and took something out of it. In the living room, she handed Amin a photo of Mama leaning against the willow tree. The once bright colors were muted now. "I can put this picture in it. It fits almost perfectly." She took the photo back from him and measured its size against the silver frame.

"This is very odd, Injy." He was looking at her with consternation. "You have a photo of your mom? Why didn't you ever put it with the photos of the rest of our family?" He looked toward the living room shelf. "We've been married for twelve years, known each other forever, and I've never once seen a photo of your mom. Where was it all this time? I just assumed you never had one."

"I had it in a bag where I kept a few of Mama's things when we moved to Egypt. I didn't get to keep many of her things."

"Why do you keep it in a bag and not out here, where we can see it?"

She searched for an answer. "I don't know. When we came to Cairo and moved in with Nena, no one ever mentioned Mama again, not even Papa. It was almost as if she had never existed. Like the first ten years of my life never happened. I just got used to keeping Mama to myself. I never thought to put her picture out."

"Well, you must put her photo out there now, Jouja." He said this kindly, but with a tone of confident finality she imagined him using with his staff at the office.

He was right, of course. Life seemed so simple when Amin dealt with things. She should have put her mother's photo out long ago. But when had he developed this tone? Where was the friendly, easygoing boy she had met at school?

To Amin she said simply, "The frame's beautiful. Thank you so much, habibi."

"You're very welcome, my dear. My pleasure," he said and loosened his tie to go change.

Injy lingered on the couch looking at Mama's photo and thinking of how she had come to have the patchwork bag and the things inside of it.

#

It was our next-door neighbor, an elderly lady, who took me aside after Mama died and told me to keep a few of her things. I can't even remember her name now. I just remember that she and her husband always took a slow, shuffling walk around the neighborhood each evening, with their elbows linked and heads bent together, silent but connected.

It was after the funeral. A few of the neighbors were over at our house. Janey was there, and her mother. I remember I had a surreal, detached feeling. As if I were watching myself in a dream.

"My mother died when I was about your age, Injy," said the old lady. "I want you to keep a few of your mother's things to remember her by … clothes, a picture. Go around the house and find things that make you think of her. Later, when you're grown, you'll be grateful. They'll bring you some comfort. Do it now, dear."

She said this quietly, gently, but with some urgency. I understood without her saying so that no one had told her this when she was a girl. And she wished they had. I remember thinking, what would remind me of Mama?

#

The next morning as he was choosing a suit for work, Amin noticed the faded, slumped bag on Injy's side of the wardrobe. He had glanced at it many times before, always assumed it held some small items of Injy's, stockings perhaps. Now he instinctively knew that this was the bag that held her mother's things. He looked toward their bedroom door, slightly ajar. Injy was in the kitchen cooking his breakfast and he could smell the savory aroma of an omelet wafting its way in.

He considered the bag briefly, then took it down and opened it. He pulled out a small child's painting of purple flowers on a background of sky blue. Amin searched his mind for a long moment trying to place where he had seen this painting before. Then he remembered. He quickly put the painting in the bag, and the bag back on the shelf. Why had she kept that painting all these years, he wondered. Wasn't she supposed to have given it to her Nena?

#

It was the last lesson of the day in Miss Zeinab's fifth primary. Amin looked at the desk next to his. Injy was bent over her painting with her head tilted, thick brown braids swung to one side. On a light blue background, she was adding delicate strokes of purple. She wasn't smiling, she rarely did. But instead of the pale, pinched face he normally saw, she looked peaceful and dreamy, almost happy.

He wondered what she was thinking. Had she understood Miss Zeinab when she explained what these paintings were for? Injy's Arabic still wasn't good, so he couldn't be sure. Should he tell her? The shrill ring of the school bell broke into his thoughts, and the classroom became a jumble of scrambling feet and book bags and chattering voices. The students surged in one unruly mass through the door to the school buses.

Miss Zeinab was tidying up her desk at the front of the class when Amin tapped her arm. She bent down to listen, nodding. Amin went to the door and turned to watch Injy, who was slowly gathering her paints into her bag. She always waited until the rush was over before leaving.

"Injy, habibti," said Miss Zeinab, who had appeared over the little girl's shoulder. Speaking slowly and clearly, she said, "Your painting is very beautiful. When you finish it, you can give it to your grandmother. She'd like that very much." The teacher gave her shoulders a little squeeze.

Injy seemed to think about this and then said, "Okay, Miss Zeinab."

#

The school bus screeched to a lurching stop, propelling Injy, her brother, and her sister down the steps and through the door. The children walked down the small Heliopolis street lined with low apartment buildings and shady trees to climb the one flight up to their grandmother's apartment. As usual, the front door was open. Nena was sitting in her customary armchair with a low table in front of her, shelling peas. She always seemed to be preparing piles of food: shaping meatballs or trimming okra or rolling vine leaves around dollops of herby rice.

"Assalamu 'alaikum." The three children chorused the greeting they had been taught by their father.

Nena looked up briefly. "Wa 'alaikum assalam. Go change your clothes and wash your faces, children. We'll have lunch when your father gets home." She said this every day after school. By now the children understood the Arabic words.

Injy and her sister went to the room where they shared a massive, lumpy bed. The air was musty, the shutters only letting in a strip of afternoon light that slanted across the room. Injy opened her school bag and looked at her painting.

Miss Zeinab had explained that they were making these for Mother's Day. This she had understood. When Amin tapped the teacher on the arm, she could guess what he was saying. Their friendship was unspoken, but she knew he was always looking out for her. The few times he was absent from school she felt lost, like a little rowboat adrift on a choppy sea.

Injy sat on the bed thinking about what Miss Zeinab had told her after the bell. She thought of Nena in her housedress with the kerchief knotted at the top of her head, hunched and doughy as she shuffled from the old humming refrigerator to the dining table, putting out their breakfast before the school bus came. An enamel bowl of boiled eggs, a block of salty white cheese, baladi bread cut into half-moons, a small, lonely bowl of honey.

Then she thought of Mama's pancakes, warm and pillowy, dripping with maple syrup. Injy looked at the painting again. These were Mama's lilacs. She could never give them to Nena. When her sister left the room, Injy reached under the bed and dragged out a small suitcase. She unzipped it, took out a faded cloth bag, and put her Mama's painting inside.

"Children, your father's home," called Nena. "Come eat lunch."

#

Soon, Injy started getting off the school bus one stop early and spending every afternoon with Amin and his three sisters.

"So lovely to see you, dear," Amin's grandmother would say in her British accent, looking up from her knitting as the children ran through the front door.

"Hello, Nan," Injy would say and skip over to give the old lady a kiss on the cheek. Injy found out that Nan was from London and had married Amin's grandfather while he was in England studying to be an architect. Then she moved with him to Cairo. He had died long ago. Now Nan lived with her eldest son and his family.

Amin's home had become Injy's haven. She dreaded returning to the tired, worn apartment where Nena was always peeling vegetables, waiting for Papa to come home as if nothing could happen without him, not even lunch. Amin's apartment was bright and noisy, with doors being flung open, people calling to each other, and the sound of children's laughter everywhere.

"Children, where are you? Welcome, Injy, dear. Girls, have you offered Injy something to drink? Amin, get your school bag off the floor!"

Amin's mother swept through the front door in a skirt suit with an elaborate gold brooch on her lapel and a matching turban-style wrap on her head. She arrived from her job at the Ministry of Culture just after the children returned from school and always shouted good-natured orders at everyone. Then she kissed them all on the cheek.

She was the whirlwind who tore through the house and took all the glory. But it was Nan who made the children their sandwiches for school, ironed their uniforms, read stories before bedtime, and cooked their meals. Amin's favorite dessert was Nan's apple crumble, warm out of the oven with a drizzle of cream on top. You could smell the cinnamon all over the house when it was baking, hugging you like soft sunshine.

Because Nan was always in the background quietly knitting or sipping a cup of tea, it took Injy years to realize that Amin had been raised by his English grandmother. It was a link they shared, these foreign women who loved them, with their gentle ways and sweet-smelling desserts.

#

First, there was the willow tree and the backyard, Mama and Janey. And then there was Nena's apartment, the school, and Amin, my anchor. That first year in Egypt is hazy now. I mainly remember Nena on her balcony in the early morning, waving as we boarded the school bus, my brother's stony silence, and my baby sister's scared face.

I loved going to Amin's house after school, then walking home laughing. I don't know what I would have done without him and his sisters.

We finished school, then university. He went to work at his family's architecture firm. Then he told me he wanted to marry me. I immediately agreed and then felt scared. What exactly was I doing, marrying young, staying in Egypt? But at that point, I couldn't imagine my life without him.

#

When she was sixteen, Injy decided to make banana bread from the card in the recipe box. Balancing a mixing bowl at the edge of the tiny countertop in Nena's dim, cramped kitchen, Injy carefully measured flour and sugar in a glass, because Nena didn't own a measuring cup. Then she set the oven dial halfway and hoped for the best. The temperature markings, if they had ever existed, had long since faded.

She stood in the kitchen for an hour while the banana bread baked to make sure it wouldn't burn. When she finally took it out of the oven and cut off a piece, it had that lovely, delicate banana flavor she remembered, that moist, springy texture. It must be beginner's luck, she thought, proudly.

Nena wrinkled her nose when she tasted it. "You forgot to add the sugar. It's too soft. It needs more time in the oven," she added in disgust.

"No, it's supposed to taste like that," insisted Injy.

"Well, no one will eat it," said Nena authoritatively.

#

First, she was the new, freckle-faced girl with the braids who sat next to me at school. Then the playmate who was always at our place, almost like a fourth sister. I'd walk her back to her Nena's each afternoon while we talked about everything and nothing. I don't remember exactly when I knew she was the one I wanted to marry. It just seemed so natural, so simple.

Where has that feeling gone? Lately, I never know what's behind her looks or her silences. Work is demanding. But the truth is I stay at the office late every night because I dread going home. It feels like she's so far away, I'd have to swim across a whole sea to reach her.

#

At work, Amin couldn't stop thinking about the bag in the wardrobe and the painting of purple flowers he had found that morning. While he fielded incessant phone calls and troublesome employees, the purple flowers wove their way through his thoughts.

Ever since that day on the playground when Injy told him that her mother had died, Amin had always prided himself in knowing how to make her feel safe. He was the one she confided in, or so he had thought. Suddenly he wondered if he knew her at all. What other secrets was she hiding? That photo of her mother by the tree, and now the painting kept all these years, disturbed him in a way he couldn't define. Hidden away, never shown to him or the children.

Tomorrow was the end of the work week. What if they could get away as a family, drive to the North Coast for the weekend, somewhere relaxing by the sea? He had to do something. This was all he could think of.

One call to a friend who managed a hotel on the Mediterranean and Amin had achieved the impossible: last-minute reservations on the last weekend of summer. He immediately picked up the phone again to tell his wife.

#

The drive out of Cairo had been tiring and tense, as masses of cars crawled out of the hot, snarled city on the weekend trek toward the sea. But at dawn, on the balcony of their hotel room, Injy felt calm in a way she had forgotten was possible. Huge clouds glowed soft pink in a sky of faint blue. Then a moment of complete stillness, heavenly peace, as the sun rose. She wrapped her cotton shawl tighter against the faint chill in the air, so welcome in the summer. Waves rolled onto the beach in sloshes of white foam. A soft Mediterranean breeze blew gently through the palm trees and her hair.

She'd forgotten how it felt to be serene, so submerged had she been in the endless details of her life. The home to run, the family to feed, the phone to answer, the same callers always with the same comments, the endless traffic, the exhausting errands.

She couldn't even remember the last time she had looked at clouds in the sky like when she and Janey were kids. Were there even clouds in Cairo or just a haze of pollution? Injy realized she didn't know. Was this the life she had imagined or wanted for herself? What had she wanted once upon a time?

The sliding door opened and Amin, in t-shirt and pajama bottoms, stepped onto the balcony. He never woke this early, so she knew he was worried about her. Mama's silent presence and smiling face from the recently revealed photographs still hung between them, creating a strange, unspoken limbo.

"What are you doing out here so early, Jouja?" He pulled a bamboo chair up to hers and put his arm around her shoulder. It felt warm and solid against her thin shawl.

"Just thinking and watching the sunrise. I can't remember the last time I saw clouds like this."

"You've been so quiet lately. Remember Miss Zeinab's class? I haven't seen you this quiet since then." It was his way of saying he knew she was thinking of her mother.

"Ever since I found that article about Mama, I've been wondering what my life would have been like if she hadn't died and we hadn't moved here. I know it's pointless, but I can't stop thinking about it."

"It's not pointless. Losing your mom at such an early age is a terrible thing. What worries me is that you have all her stuff hidden away and that you never talk about her."

He always got straight to the point. She didn't know what to say.

"Stop hiding your mom's things, Injy." His voice was plaintive. "Start talking about her. Tell our kids about your mom and what sorts of things you did when you were growing up, like I tell them about my family."

The children loved their father's stories about the crazy, chaotic household of his childhood. Injy thought about this. What would she tell Sarah and Ali about growing up with Mama? About the smell of sugar cookies baking or banana bread fresh out of the oven? Would they understand when she told them about rainstorms and grass, lilacs and dandelions, candy hearts with "Be Mine" written on them for Valentine's Day? Mud pies and worms, peanut butter and jelly? Mary had a little lamb? What kind of memories were they forming of their own childhood, of her and Amin, right now? When they were younger, she had heard her kids chanting an Arabic children's rhyme with their cousins, something about a kilo of bamia. It made her inexplicably sad that she didn't know what they were saying.

He was still waiting for her answer.

104

"I honestly wouldn't know what to tell them, Amin. I wouldn't know where to begin." And then suddenly, "If something happened to me right now, would you talk to the kids about me? Or would you stay silent and hope they'd forget me, get on with your life as best you could?"

"Injy, don't say things like that, ever. And of course, I would talk about you."

She sighed deeply.

"Nobody meant to hurt you, just the opposite. By not talking about your mom, they were trying to protect you. That's how a lot of people still are. But you're grown now, and you can do what you want. Keeping quiet about her isn't doing you or us any good." Then in a quieter and more quizzical tone, "And why don't you make some of your mom's recipes? From that box. That doesn't make any sense to me at all."

"Because her recipes are completely out of context here, Amin. When we first came to Egypt, you couldn't even find a lot of the ingredients. Even when you could make a recipe, nobody ever liked it. One time I made Mama's banana bread and Nena acted as though it was an inedible disaster. All she ever wanted to make was that awful rice pudding with the rose water and that dry, mealy yoghurt cake."

He laughed. "Honestly, Injy, can you hear yourself? Are you serious? What sort of special context do you need to make banana bread? Are you going to base your existence on whether people like or understand the desserts you bake?"

"Now you're making me feel silly, Amin."

"You are being silly. I hated the rice pudding with the rose water, too, but it was what your Nena knew how to make, what she probably learned from her own mother."

She sighed again.

"Give her some credit, Injy. It's not easy taking in three children who have been transplanted from America when you don't speak their language, can't cook the food they're used to, and certainly will never replace their mother. She definitely knew that, and it couldn't have been easy for her."

She hated it when Amin made more sense out of her own life than she did. But that was why she had married him, wasn't it?

They were both silent now, drifting in their own thoughts about each other.

#

That afternoon, Injy and Amin lay on their sun loungers as their children played on the beach. He reached over and squeezed her hand.

"What are you thinking, love?"

"I was just thinking I never went to the seaside or the ocean with Mama. Our vacations were always by a lake. I think she would have liked it here." She looked more peaceful than he could remember seeing her.

He ventured, "Did you swim in the lake?"

"I can't remember exactly, but I think so. Yes, we did. The water was freezing, even in summer. Nothing like this." She gestured to the Mediterranean.

They both looked toward their kids playing near the shore. Sarah screamed happily as Ali ran after her.

Amin was holding her hand firmly. "We used to go to Agami every summer, as you know, and my mom always managed to get sand in our sandwiches. Something of a family joke. Did your mom cook for you at the lake?" he asked.

"Yes, she did. We stayed in a little cabin with a kitchenette. She made pancakes every morning with real maple syrup. And really good sandwiches for lunch." She smiled at the memory of Mama's sandwiches and also of her mother-in-law's. Amin's mother wasn't known for her culinary skills.

"I bet her sandwiches were miles better than my mom's," he laughed. "I'm really glad you inherited your mom's talent in cooking. If you cooked anything like my mother, we would have starved by now."

"Most of my recipes are from your grandmother, Amin."

"Really? I never knew that." He looked genuinely surprised.

"Before we got married, secret cooking lessons. Nan's idea. It sounded old-fashioned, but I'm glad I listened. She was right."

"Was she right? I love your cooking, Injy, but I have to tell you that even if you only made me boiled rice every day, I'd still want to come home to you." He looked like he had surprised himself by saying this.

She smiled and kissed his cheek. "You're so sweet, Amin. And I would never make you boiled rice. What would Nan have said?"

Ali and Sarah came running, wet and happy. They seemed confused to see their parents looking happy, too.

"What were you talking about, Papi?" asked Sarah.

"Your grandmothers and their cooking, love."

"Were they good cooks, Papi?"

"Some of them were, love," Amin and Ingy laughed.

Injy lingered on the beach as the last sunbathers were collecting their things. Amin had just taken the kids to go shower and change for dinner. She watched a couple walking together along the shore, leaning into each other gently. She looked at the clouds, back-lit with a soft pink glow. She wondered what shapes she could find in these clouds. They were going home tomorrow. For the first time in a long time, she felt rested.

#

As the neighbors murmured in the living room after the funeral, Injy snuck away to Mama and Papa's room, empty and still. She shut the door quietly and turned to face the room. What would make her think of Mama? She walked tentatively to the dresser, scattered with perfume bottles, a pot of hand cream, Mama's ivory hairbrush. Photos were stuck in the corners of the mirror: one of Mama and Papa, one of the three children, and one of Mama by the willow tree. Injy quickly took this last one down and put it in the pocket of her dress.

Her heart was beating fast. She felt as if she were stealing, but the urgency in the old neighbor's voice pushed her on. In the dresser drawer, Injy found the wide, silky headband Mama wore on special occasions, when she left her long hair down. Injy took this too.

What else? Her eyes searched the dresser top and stopped at a small, dainty bottle. "Scent of Lilacs" said the label in old-fashioned script. Injy carefully twisted open the top. The sweet flowers underneath Mama's kitchen window hit her in full force, taking her breath away. She quickly closed the bottle, making sure the lid was on tight, and slipped it into her pocket.

Injy turned to look at the neatly made bed and the nightstand on Mama's side, with its small lamp and half-full glass of water, just as Mama had left it. She crossed the room and sat on Mama's side of the bed to slide open the nightstand drawer. There was a paper from the hospital on top, typed and official. Injy folded it to slip in her pocket. What else, what else? She didn't want the worn paperback novel or the pens.

In the closet, Injy pushed hangers slowly to one side. She stopped at the white blouse with the big collar and the loose sleeves. Injy wanted this blouse badly, but how would she take it without anyone seeing? It wouldn't fit in the pocket of her dress. She sat on the closet floor, surrounded by Mama's clothes and her scent. She wanted Mama back just as she had been, in the kitchen and by the willow tree. In the end, she stood up and reluctantly left the blouse behind on its hanger, closing the closet door.

Taking a last look at the room, she went to join the others. They might go looking for her if she stayed away too long. In the living room, people talked in hushed tones. Every so often, Injy reached into her pocket to make sure Mama's things were still safe.

That night, as her little sister slept, Injy snuck out of bed and tip-toed in the dark, feeling her way slowly down the stairs to the kitchen. She had already decided what she wanted from here. Clicking open a cupboard, she felt for Mama's recipe box. Then she saw the outline of Mama's patchwork bag. She quickly took the box and the bag back upstairs.

#

It was after midnight in Cairo, and Injy leaned back on her pillows. Her back ached and her feet hurt, but her head was clear and light. After the children had gone to bed, she'd spent hours baking sugar cookies from Mama's recipe, cutting the dough with an upturned glass because she didn't have a cookie cutter, and sprinkling them with sugar like Mama used to do. When she took them out of the oven, their sweet vanilla scent swirled around her. A huge pile of cookies now filled a bowl on the kitchen counter. The children would be pleased. They loved anything sweet.

She didn't hear Amin until he lay down next to her, still in his suit and tie.

"I see you've been baking," he said. "I tried one. They're good."

"Thanks, habibi. They're sugar cookies for Mama's birthday."

"I see."

"How did it go today? Did you get the contract?" she asked.

"Yes, we did," said Amin happily, and then spontaneously took her hand and kissed it. "You've been eating mangos again," he said with mock sternness and a hint of irritation.

Injy looked at him closely. He seemed so tired and relieved somehow. And she said, "Yes, habibi, I have."

#

'AMM AHMAD

by Mariam Shouman

The sun filtered down through the gray buildings onto his face. The first gaggle of schoolgirls in their pink button-down shirts and navy skirts rumbled by. The street vendors had arrived, hollering to announce their wares—fresh mint and lemons and crisp green lettuce. All sure signs of morning … so he rolled out of the gray blankets that he had wrapped securely around him all night, his weary bones creaking and aching, belying his 45 years. Sleeping on the thin cardboard next to the busy street had aged him prematurely. The cold of the cement seeped into his blood and bones and each month it seemed harder to rise. He shook his blankets out and draped them on the gray brick wall between the two buildings to dry the early morning damp.

He shambled to the faucet sticking out of the wall of the apartment building. As he rinsed his mouth and splashed water on his face, he murmured the words of the morning doa'a, an extra little prayer invoking God's mercy that came spontaneously to his lips. Ever since he had heard it recited on the Quran station on the radio all those years ago, he hadn't missed a morning. Feeling a bit better, he returned to his cardboard bed and used it to pray upon. Then he picked it up so no one would step on it, leaned it against the building, and gathered his bucket and rag to start his daily routine of washing the cars of the residents of the apartments looming above him. He had noticed that one was parked farther away than usual and under a tree and cursed its owners because he knew it would be smattered with bird droppings and caked with extra mud. As he walked past the little metal sandwich stall on wheels, he dug into his pocket to find fifty piasters, which he offered to the young man standing behind the glass pane. "Sabah el-fol! Morning of sweet-scented blossoms to you! I'll have white cheese, today, ya Mohammed."

The young man offered him his sandwich and dropped a meager handful of pickled turnips and carrots into his hand. "Sabah el-ishta! Morning of thick white cream to you! A little something extra to make the sandwich tastier, ya 'Amm Ahmad! May God give you strength! It's a cold morning to be about your business."

"Al-hamdulillah, yabni, al-hamdulillah!" He exclaimed heartily, "I'm so grateful to God I can make an honest living!"

At the nearby café patronized only by men who came to smoke their bubbly water pipes and have a glass of strong mint tea or tiny cup of sweetened, bitter Turkish coffee, 'Amm Ahmad lingered to exchange a few words with Hagg Sayed. One of the young waiters slipped him a piping hot glass of tea free of charge—a charade both took great pleasure in, even though they enacted it every day with the full approval of the shop owner. The young man whispered with a wink, "Warm your hands; they'll make you your fortune some day!" Steaming hot and invigorating—sugary and strong enough to help him start another day.

Sweet smoke clouded the air in the coffeehouse as the old men played backgammon, alternately slamming down their playing pieces and taking long drafts of smoke from the bubbling water pipes next to them. The sound of the television droned on and on in the background. No football matches today to make everyone cheer and quarrel good-naturedly. Just news and more dreary news. All about Iraq and the war that everyone had known was coming and no one wanted to believe could happen.

"What do you think Bush is playing at?" one old man asked. The man sitting in front of him merely shrugged his shoulders and clicked his backgammon piece into position, capturing an enemy playing piece.

"He wants Iraqi oil, of course," another answered from a nearby table. "Everyone knows that. He wouldn't bother with Iraq if there wasn't any oil. He wants to control the oil fields. If Saddam was just an ordinary dictator, Bush would never have bothered with him."

"I say it's an Israeli plot," a young man looked up from his college book long enough to interject. "The Israelis want the Arabs to be in a state of unrest so that they'll have a pretext for all their weapons, and they want the Americans to stay too busy elsewhere to pay attention to what they are doing in Palestine."

'Amm Ahmad nodded equally vigorously in response to both theories, the TV screen capturing his attention. He didn't know why the United States had invaded Iraq, but all he could think of was how much the eyes of those little Iraqi children lying in hospital beds with bandages wrapped around their heads and missing limbs reminded him of his brother's son back in the country. His brother's wife struggled to scrounge food for him after she'd lost her husband to cancer. Every time he saw Youssef, his eyes looked bigger … but maybe his face was getting smaller. At the end of the month he'd send him the few pounds he'd managed to save.

#

'Amm Ahmad dried his damp hands on his long galabiyya; he'd almost finished his rounds. Just one more car to go. As he crossed the busy street to where it was parked, he noticed that someone had thrown away some large pieces of glass. They were broken around the edges, but he could get a few pounds for them. What a lucky beginning to the day.

His tea long drunk and his sandwich but a memory, 'Amm Ahmad was busy wiping down an aging white Mercedes, his back to the busy traffic on Pyramids Street, when a black Jeep swerved out of its lane and lifted him away from the white car and into oncoming traffic.

His helpless body was thrown high into the air and, as he landed, his outstretched hand was quickly and neatly severed by the jagged glass protruding from the garbage bin. It landed, fingers perfectly cupped to heaven, on the hood of the shining white Mercedes.

The black Jeep skidded to a halt just in time, avoiding the heavy sin of murder by a hair's breadth. As soon as the car came to a stop, the inevitable crowd surged around it. They flung the car door open and a blond beauty emerged, distraught and fearful. "What happened? Is he all right?" she spoke in a whisper, clutching her cell phone and frantically pressing buttons as her eyes roamed over the aggressive crowd.

"No, ya sitt hanem, he'll probably never be all right again, lady," one galabiyya-clad member of the crowd proclaimed.

The crowd began to close in on the panic-stricken young woman. She nervously tugged her jacket closed, as if to protect herself from the waves of animosity rising from the ragged mob around her. She pressed her cell phone to her cheek, and waited for an answer to this unanswerable dilemma. After an interminable six rings, the calm, collected voice on the other side answered. "Papi, something terrible has happened …," she began.

"Something terrible is right, ya Papi!" a lemon vendor jeered, flipping his burlap sack over his shoulder. The faces surrounding the blond concentrated and reflected their everyday resentment into a high pitch of hatred. 'Amm Ahmad groaned in the background.

"Please, put him in my car. I will take him to the hospital," the girl called out, appealing to anyone who might be willing to help. "I'll take care of him," she whispered, her breath coming fast in anxiety, then her voice trailed off, "Oh how can I ever put it right?"

#

At the hospital, the blond paced back and forth through the dirty green hallways. More than one nurse offered her a chair, gesturing to the grubby benches that lined the walls but even at the height of her anxiety, she could not bring herself to sit on the grimy seats. Every five minutes, she would cross to the nurse to ask about the man's condition. A squat, fleshy man sat behind the accounting desk, watching her pace with a smug smile. When the news finally came that the man would live, that all that was lost was his hand, she drew a deep breath and approached the accounting desk. "I'd like to pay his bill and leave enough for any expenses he'll have. How much will it be?" The little man's eyes shifted from his piles of paper, touching on the diamond ring and the designer bracelet. She anxiously clutched her purse, opening it to pull out the bills.

Offhandedly, he waved his hand to the boy who crouched on a stool nearby in front of the rudimentary kitchen, "Get me a coffee; you know how I like my sugar," he bellowed. Slowly he turned back to his ledger, scrawling something under a column of figures. "Now," he finally directed his attention at her in a calculated leer, "What do you want?"

"I'd like to pay his bill … the man that … was hit," she said. "And put enough of a down payment to cover any other expenses he'll have."

"It won't be cheap, you know. But I guess you can afford it," he scribbled furiously. "I'd say 500 pounds would cover it."

Without hesitation, she pulled the bills out of her bag and counted out 500 more. "I'd like you to give him these … to help him get a business started, something to help him make a living."

The clerk's eyes lit up at the tidy sum, "Why certainly, Miss. May God bless you," sweeping the bills into his desk drawer while he busily started to mentally spend them.

As she turned to leave, he cleared his throat, "You can't leave until the police come, Miss. You'll be charged for this, I'm sure. Who knows, he might still die."

She snapped her purse closed and looked at her watch, fighting back tears. With the clerk's little speech, the room's attention had focused upon her again. How much longer would it be before she could leave this grimy box that had turned into a prison? Surely nothing really bad could happen to her.

When her father swept into the waiting room, he was preceded by a wave of anticipation. Everyone immediately recognized that he was a figure accustomed to obedience and respect. His three-piece designer suit sang of newness. His shoes glistened. The fact that he had come for her was more than obvious—the aura of privilege engulfed them both. She ran to him and he enfolded her in his protective arms. "Don't worry, Gigi, we'll be out of here in a minute," he spoke in a voice that carried through the room, as he scanned for the required figure. "Wait in the car, Gigi," he directed, as he headed for the manager's office.

Without a backward look, she turned on her heel and left the dingy hospital, telling herself that she had done all that she could and been as generous as anyone could expect. Right before she pulled her legs into the Jeep, it occurred to her that she should have taken the man's name and address so that she could send someone to inquire after him later, but the surging crowds at the entrance to the public hospital were as potent as an impenetrable wall to her. She slammed the door shut, locking it for good measure. Her father would make everything right.

#

The janitor was swabbing down the floors of the room 'Amm Ahmad shared with seven other patients when he woke. At first the clatter of cleaning and the smell of kerosene took him back to his mother's house in the village; Saturday had been for house cleaning. But as soon as he woke, he knew his mind had played a cruel trick on him. His hand ached with raw pain and he reached to rub it with his other hand, meeting nothing but crusty bandages. Slowly he recalled his last memories: Washing that old white Mercedes and then sudden pain and shock.

"What happened to me?" he asked of no one in particular.

"It could be worse," the painfully thin man in the next bed offered. "You only lost a hand. It's enough to make people feel sorry for you, but not enough to keep you in bed. You'll haul in plenty on the streets with the other hand ... I know a good street corner. I guess I won't be seeing it again." He gestured to his wasted body. "If the cars don't get you, disease will."

A street corner? Was that his fate? He had always made an honest living ... nothing fancy, but honorable. How would he be able to live with himself as a beggar? "But who did this? Isn't there some penalty for them to pay?" he demanded.

"They'll have settled with the hospital ... unless someone got their name, you'll never see them again."

#

The nurse bundled up his medicine in a small plastic bag, "Make sure you stop by the accounts department before you leave. Don't want to leave a bill unpaid, do you?" Before 'Amm Ahmad had even left the room, she had forgotten him and gone on to straighten the bed for the next patient.

Standing in front of the accountant's desk, 'Amm Ahmad's stomach churned. What if there was a bill to pay? He rubbed the short curly hair on his head as the accountant lifted binder after binder. "How many days did you say you'd been here?" he asked without looking up.

"I don't know. I was in an accident. I don't know."

"Well, what day did you come in?" he asked impatiently.

"It was Wednesday. The basha goes out early on Wednesday and I was polishing his car."

"Ah, here it is. She was quite a pretty thing that hit you," he gave 'Amm Ahmad a knowing leer.

"I never saw her."

The accountant looked 'Amm Ahmad up and down. "You don't have any family with you, or what?"

"No. No one."

The accountant gave a great hacking cough, spitting a wad into the corner behind his desk. This one didn't have any money to be had. "The girl left enough to cover your expenses ... at least almost. The hospital will take care of the rest ... sometimes the administration does a good deed or two."

"But what was her name? Why wasn't a report made to the police?"

"Oh, you'll never find her again; her father was a big shot. Best to forget her." The clerk nodded knowingly to himself, suppressing the smile that those 500 pounds had put on his face. They'd taken care of all his expenses and let him put a bit away too.

With a nod, 'Amm Ahmad turned and shuffled out of the hospital, nothing but a plastic bag in his hand. The bright light of day framed his weary body in the doorway.

#

Blinking rapidly, 'Amm Ahmad stood on the street corner trying to figure out where he was and how he was to get home without a pound in his pocket. He greeted a man standing at a bus stop, shelling sunflower seeds with his teeth and dropping them like so many bits of confetti to lie at his feet. He was just about to ask for directions, when the man fished in his pocket for a 50-piaster note, turning resolutely away from 'Amm Ahmad as soon as he had thrust the bill into his hand.

Tears welled in 'Amm Ahmad's eyes. "I'm not a beggar, just unfortunate. I was asking for directions," he spoke to the man's back, never receiving a response. The tattered galabiyya that the hospital had kindly furnished him with coupled with his severed hand spoke louder than his voice. In shame, he turned away from the bus stop and wandered down the street, thrusting the money into his pocket. If he were ever to return home, he'd need some money.

#

'Amm Ahmad wandered for an hour, too proud to ask again for directions, but unable to spot anything that would identify the district, more than once cursing his illiteracy, before his exhaustion overtook him. At last, he sank to the ground next to a building. With his good hand, he covered his face, trying to rub away his reality. He drifted in and out of sleep for what must have been an hour. When he woke, he found several fluttering bills in his lap. To his dismay, he had been transformed into a beggar unawares.

"Hey, what are you doing here?" a haggard old woman poked at him with her bony fingers. "This is my place. I've been sitting here for three years. You can't just come and sit here. You'll have to find your own corner to work."

Still sleep-dazed, 'Amm Ahmad stood. "I'm sorry. I just wanted to rest. Can you tell me where I am?"

The little old woman squinted up at him quizzically, "You really don't know? You look like you really are straight out of the hospital. You're in Sayyida Zeinab."

"Thank you, may God bless you," he turned away. At least now he knew which direction his wandering should take.

#

'Amm Ahmad finally managed to leap onto a big red city bus after losing his grip several times. His plastic bag of medicine, clutched firmly in his good hand, almost cost him his life when he first tried to ascend the steep staircase as the bus pulled away from the crowded bus stop. Without a second hand, he had nothing to hold on with. Finally, he lodged it firmly under his armpit and rode the tide of passengers that pushed him up into the next overcrowded bus. Within the confines of the packed bus, he felt people trying to pull away from him even though there was nowhere to go. As he swayed with the bouncing bus, he tried to make himself as small as he possibly could.

With great relief, he began to recognize landmarks that heralded his arrival home. At last he could go back to his old life, his old work, his old friends.

As he emerged from the musty interior of the bus, the cold breeze that met him refreshed him and offered hope.

He built up speed as he crossed to the building, his building where he had made his life, such that it was. His first stop, he thought, would be the coffee house; forgetting the picture he would present to his old acquaintances. The dusty, gray buildings looming overhead offered the protection of familiarity. Then his eye caught his corner. The small black figure huddled on his cardboard was completely unfamiliar, at least in this setting. As he drew near, the figure resolved itself into two separate bodies, huddled together sharing in the meager protection that the thin layer of cardboard offered them from the persistent dank.

The two large innocent eyes that fixed immediately upon his stump of a hand belonged to his brother's only child, his only living blood relative. "Ya 'Ammo, Uncle, your hand … what happened to your hand?" the five-year-old whispered.

"Oh my God! How could such a disaster befall us?" his brother's widow shrieked. "My brother! God has given you a harsh fate." She fell back against the building wall in a swoon.

The crisis spurred 'Amm Ahmad into motion. He dashed across the street to the little sidewalk café, "Ya Tarek, a glass of water, may God protect you!"

It was only after he had woven through the closely spaced tables up to the waiter's station that he realized what he must look like. His galabiyya had always been in good repair even though it was a far cry from being new; but now he was wearing a tattered, bloodstained one. The nurse had washed it out before she'd given it to him, but not very conscientiously. His beard had grown long over the course of his hospitalization. And of course, his stump waved insanely in the air, no fingers attached to express his violent emotions.

He felt the eyes of all the café patrons firmly fix on his arm. Suddenly, there was nothing familiar about the place. The friendly young waiter handed him a cup of water, "'Amm Ahmad, thank God for your safety!"

As he wove his way out of the café, silent, dazed, one of the more well-to-do patrons fished in his pocket for a bit of change. But 'Amm Ahmad had yet to develop a knack for palming alms, and he simply brushed past without noticing the offering.

#

"So, you're getting married? Well, congratulations. No one could hold it against you; you're still young and have your whole life ahead of you," 'Amm Ahmad squatted opposite Zeinab, his brother's widow.

She pulled her black veil across her mouth, a sign of embarrassment or discomfort. "Thank you, ya hagg. I knew you'd understand. But what I wanted to talk to you about was the boy. Could you take care of him, just until the honeymoon is over?"

Youssef's dark eyes turned to him, too young to understand, but old enough to dread a life without his mother for even a few days.

#

The rattling of the ful cart as the peddler pushed it into position for the morning's business woke 'Amm Ahmad. Youssef was cradled in his arms, as he had been for a month. At least it was warmer than sleeping alone on the sidewalk. 'Amm Ahmad eased him down onto the sidewalk, wrapping the blanket closely around him. His daily routine had lost some of its flavor. Somehow people turned away too quickly, pity reflected in their eyes.

As he finished wiping down the white Mercedes, the owner emerged. "Good morning, ya 'Amm Ahmad," the older man tried for a hearty tone to wish the poor man a good morning. He cleared his throat, turned and spat on the ground. "I was thinking ... since your accident, it's too much to ask you to clean the car. Starting tomorrow, you don't have to do it anymore. But don't worry; I'll give you your money every month. Just as if you were working."

'Amm Ahmad lowered his head. He almost turned away, but then he raised his head and said, "I'd really rather work. It's not too hard for me. I don't like to take charity. There are people who deserve it more than me."

But the Mercedes owner wasn't listening. He'd turned away mentally, even if he still faced the man in front of him, "Well then, you just come by every month, just like you always have." With that, he got into his car and drove off.

#

One after another, each of 'Amm Ahmad's customers delivered the same speech. And for a few months, 'Amm Ahmad managed to make the rounds and collect the offered sums. But somehow his monthly rounds had become heavy on his heart. In years past, there had always been jokes, inquiries about his health, comments about the weather. But now he only rapped on the door and then stepped back quickly, gazing silently at the floor. Whoever opened the door would always understand that he'd come for his monthly handout.

Finally, he stopped making the rounds. Instead the car owners would find him on the street sometime during the month and thrust the money into his hand, turning quickly away from him.

Eventually, the money stopped coming in regularly. And Youssef's dark eyes grew hungrier and hungrier. Then one morning, 'Amm Ahmad was sitting on his cardboard bed a bit later than usual and the change started making its way into his hand. Without meaning to, he joined the legions of beggars in the teeming city of millions. He never attempted to emulate the guile of his fellows; the endless ruses that others used to elicit people's sympathy never appealed to him. He never played the weeping unfortunate next to a broken carton of eggs spilled on the asphalt or a few broken water jars fallen off a cart. He never needed to. His situation spoke eloquently enough to people—religion mandated charity—and at the same time a bit of alms-giving was often a salve to the soul when one had just spent far too much on frivolity.

From that day forward, he never had to worry about feeding Youssef again. His life had never been easy, but suddenly it was a lot easier than it had been when he was working. He managed to build a little shelter between the buildings, and the authorities ignored it—they knew he was a cripple after all. He even managed to get a school uniform and books and notebooks for Youssef.

One dreary year dragged after another. Youssef's mother never came to get him. The two grew to love each other, and 'Amm Ahmad thought of him as the son he would never have.

#

The little shack wasn't much—just some wooden struts with odds and ends of plastic and cloth stretched between them. But the two boys met there every day to study and talk. Youssef's upper lip had sprouted a mustache, and his friend Tamer's voice cracked at every third word. They were both the sons of urban poverty.

As they shelled the green fava beans, popping them into their mouths, they pondered their futures. "What do you think you'll do after we finish all this studying?" Youssef asked.

"I'm going to work as a barber; my uncle is going to start letting me work in his shop this year after school. He says the boys that work for him make good tips," Tamer dreamed. "I can't wait to have some money to spend."

"Me either," Youssef dreamed with him. "But how on earth am I going to make any? Maybe I'll have to cut off one of my feet to get some."

Just as Youssef came up with his plan, 'Amm Ahmad was pulling back the plastic sheet that served as a door. Youssef's words sliced through his fog of humiliation.

Silently, he turned away from the shack and sat with his back against the wall of the building. All these years he had endured being a beggar for the two of them. But now something had to change. He pulled the money he had collected out of his pocket and counted the ragged bills, swearing he'd taken his last bit of charity. Then he called out to Youssef.

"Yes, Uncle?"

"Follow me."

With the money, 'Amm Ahmad bought a large burlap sack of lemons and some plastic bags. He filled each bag, but when he came to tie them, he couldn't one-handed. He turned to his nephew and bellowed, "Help me, ya Youssef!"

Then he went to stand on his customary street corner. It wasn't easy to get people to stop giving him charity. So often they'd offer a bit of change and decline the lemons. But 'Amm Ahmad stopped accepting money unless they bought something, and eventually, his customers came just for his lemons. He never brought home as much as he had when he was begging, but he could finally enjoy his wages again. Slowly, he added other wares, some lettuce and parsley, dill and coriander. But he would always remain known as "'Amm Ahmad, the Lemon Man."

#

MOMENTUM

From: Aida Nasr
To: Fatima ElKalay
Subject: Your message
Sent: Mar 9, 2008 at 5:00 PM

Dear Fatima,

Thanks so much for your e-mail and comments on my story … they are all very helpful and I was so glad that the main themes came across. Yay! Your timing was perfect, giving me a much-needed boost to continue writing. I'm considering this the beginning of a "birthday year" and am very energized to dream big this year. I really believe the 3 of us can create a lovely book. Thanks also for your message on my birthday! I had a really lovely day with a tea party for my friends ... wish you were there! …

Love and hugs,

Aida

From: Fatima ElKalay
To: Aida Nasr
Subject: RE: Your message
Sent: Mar 11, 2008 at 7:38 AM

Dear Aida,

It was lovely to hear all your news, and I am thrilled to see you are up and running with creative ideas … How is Mariam these days? I chat with her infrequently on MSN, and she seems a bit better about what's going on with Sarah.

On Valentine's day we all went to Medina for a couple of days and that was wonderful, and much needed. I had been hitting a really bad low point in my life, struggling with self-image amidst domestic pressures of all kinds. Nothing totally out of the blue, but just my inability to cope with things, coupled with tremendous guilt at not being able to cope.

Well, going to Medina made a huge difference. I don't know if you've ever been, but it is the most beautiful place in the whole world, and everyone I've ever known who's been feels as if she or he is going home there ... I am fine now. Pressures are still around me, but I am learning to handle them. It really is all about attitude ... Anyway, need to go!

Please write soon. I want to share part of another story I'm writing. Actually, I am not sure where it goes from here and was wondering if you could think of something with me!

Lots of love,

Fatima

From: Fatima ElKalay
To: Aida Nasr, Mariam Shouman
Subject: Re: PMS story comments
Sent: July 27, 2008 at 2:07 AM

Hi!

Looking forward to meeting you in a few hours' time, Aida (don't ask why I'm still awake!). Mariam, wish you were here. Thanks for the feedback on my story. I know it's not a perfect fit at the moment. I had long gaps in between writing, and that doesn't work much for a short story. I think you have to get most if it down within a short time or your mind wanders.

I like your comments a lot, Aida, especially how to make it work as a marriage gone bad ...

I like stories that have not much going on but are rich in underlying themes and implied plots. They are more challenging to write, though.

Anyway, will talk more in the morning, Aida. See you at Greco!

Love,

Fatima

From: Mariam Shouman
To: Aida Nasr, Fatima ElKalay
Subject: RE: PMS story comments
Sent: Aug 2, 2008 at 5:01 PM

Hi girls!

I'm so jealous that you've seen each other! How did it go??? How is everyone's progress? I'm kind of exploring options here, but it will take a while. Big news! We've decided to stay for the year [in the US] and see how things go and make sure we've gotten all the evaluations, etc., that we need for Sarah. Life is very very chaotic here, but I'll be back in touch when I can!

Take care!

Mariam

From: Mariam Shouman
To: Fatima ElKalay, Aida Nasr
Subject: Hi+ Mannequin and Brussels feedback
Sent: Aug 18, 2008 at 9:49 PM

Hey girls,

… I can hardly believe that we've made this momentous decision, but now that we have, it feels right. Cairo was exhausting me. Of course, the kids are having a hard time … and in some ways so am I, but I think things will settle down. And I am absolutely interested in our project and making a move on it. I'll be looking into ways to get published from here as soon as I get moved into our new house.

The only thing I'm missing about Cairo so far is my friends :(I miss our outings, Aida! Are you coming back to Cairo, Fatima? I hope no one minds this threesome email thing, because it makes keeping in touch easier.

I don't have any groundbreaking thoughts on our project because my brain is full to overflowing right at the moment ... but keep going! Let's say the week after the Eid we have a reassessment and maybe everyone compile their latest editions of each story and send them out to all of us so we can look at what we have....

Love ya all!

Mariam

From: Mariam Shouman
To: Aida Nasr, Fatima ElKalay
Subject: Happy Holidays
Sent: Oct 3, 2008 at 1:15 AM

Hey girls,

Sorry to have dropped off the face of the earth ... it's been a hard month. We got Sarah's diagnosis on Sept. 2nd—she's got Angelman Syndrome, which is pretty serious in terms of impairment. But after a few weeks of grieving, I'm starting to see how lucky I am to have such a pretty happy little girl who loves everyone around her so much. I can't even begin to put into words what the last period of time has been like, so I won't try in this brief email.

I just wanted to wish you both a happy Eid and Fatima, a happy late birthday. I can't remember the last time I missed it! Sorry about that. Where have we gotten in terms of work? What's our plan, girls? Mohamed is here until the 14th, and then I'm going to start kicking butt :)

Take care both of you and love to your families!

Mariam

From: Aida Nasr
To: Mariam Shouman, Fatima ElKalay
Subject: RE: Happy Holidays
Sent: Oct 4, 2008 at 6:33 PM

Dear girls,

I've been thinking of you both. Happy Eid to all. Mariam , I'm sending you my hugs and prayers as you adjust to Sarah's diagnosis. Sarah is such a sweet, precious little girl, and she is lucky to have you as her mother. Words seem inadequate here, but I know God will send you as much faith, love and inspiration as you need for this journey.

… Girls, I agree let's get back to writing! I've gotten down detailed notes for my next one, "The Scent of Lilacs" and will send you the finished draft when I've got it, insha' Allah soon …Take care girls and miss you.

Love,

Aida

From: Fatima ElKalay
To: Aida Nasr, Mariam Shouman
Subject: Your message
Sent: Oct 21, 2008 at 3:57 PM

Hi girls,

Great as ever to hear from you … Mariam and I caught up with each other's news on MSN two days back, and we did our best to motivate each other! …

Aida, I dreamt of you a while back. Dreamt you were moving to the US to be with your sister for a while because she'd had a baby. I even saw the baby, a blue-eyed cute little thing! I was really sad though because

I was going back to Egypt not to find you or Mariam. Wonder what that means.

Anyway, take care girls and be inspired!

Love and hugs

Fatima

From: Aida Nasr
To Mariam Shouman, Fatima ElKalay
Subject: Deadline for FINISHED stories
Sent: May 31, 2009 at 8:34 PM

Hi girls,

Sounds great. So our deadline is AUGUST 1 to have at least 4 stories each, finalized and polished. NO EXCUSES!!! We have to make the time for our writing, period, whatever it takes. This is a life goal for all of us and will benefit our loved ones tremendously if we are happy and fulfilled as PUBLISHED WRITERS. Let's do it, girls!

I volunteer to go to London in October to find us a literary agent. Let's all start visualizing our finished book in our hands; this is apparently a very powerful way to get things to happen …

Love,

Aida

From: Mariam Shouman
To: Fatima ElKalay and Aida Nasr
Subject: RE: Update
Sent: Feb 9, 2012 at 5:16 PM

I love that "Goals are dreams with deadlines." That's exactly how I feel! A deadline is essential! … I hope you guys have a successful meeting! Wish I was there! And stay safe!

Love you both!

Mariam

SHELL-WHISPERING

by Fatima ElKalay

A part of me has already died. What I have lost, I don't quite know, but I can never be myself again. I will surely go mad before I find out. I have learned what it means to feel truly alone, cut off from everyone and everything. Even as I stand in all the noise, I see and feel nothing. My own deep loneliness and isolation are the only things that embrace me—

She tore the sheet out of her journal and stuffed it in her pocket, wishing she had the courage to keep it. But she couldn't.

The clock struck one. The autumn sun faltered amidst thick clouds. She needed groceries. And a present for Gigi. A little "Masha' Allah" with a turquoise stone frame. She'd seen it pinned on the velvet tray in the window of the gold shop near the market. She looked at herself in the hallway mirror. The scar through her eyebrow was hardly visible with the penciled-in kohl. She brushed her curls to one side to cover the stitch-marks near her temple, as if hiding them could help her forget.

"It's okay my child. Time heals the wounds of body and soul."

Nine stitches and partial blindness for a month. A desperate stay with Mama, vowing never to return.

"Dil ragel wala dil hayta."

In all her years growing up she had always loathed this proverb. Maybe because it was a lie? The chances of a wall collapsing and fatally injuring you were far less than those of a man crushing you with all kinds of abuse. Walls were more protective, and infinitely more predictable. But she returned. She returned because she always did, so the girls could have a father, and because—as Mama pointed out—she couldn't leave her marriage nest, however thorny, for another bird to squat in. She returned because it was the respectable thing to do, and because there were no other walls to enclose her.

She slipped on a pair of practical shoes, gave one last pat to her hair. It wasn't windy out, so hopefully the curls would stay in place until she got into the car. It was the time of day when she was unlikely to run into neighbors—men who greeted her with cold scorn, their wives nodding with embarrassed pity. Of course, the bawab and his wife and children would be clustered outside the building. Not that they didn't know. Like everyone else, they heard things. But she didn't like the way their eyes searched her face for new cuts and bruises, as if they were following updates of breaking news.

"Assalamu 'alaikum." She tossed off the greeting to the bawab's family and walked briskly to her car at the corner of the road. The bawab's middle son followed her with his dust cloth to polish her windscreen. Leave it grubby, don't clean it, she mumbled to herself. He was the kindest of the children, but he never did a good job, and she didn't want the rest of his family joining him to peer at her while she revved her engine.

She opened the window slightly and looked at the boy.

"Madam Azza, I'll do it nicely …"

"It's fine, Hassan, I'm in a hurry." She moved the car forward and he made way for her as she swerved out of the parking space and out of sight. Beyond her street, it didn't matter. She rolled down the windows and let the rush of air toss her hair where it would. It felt nice to speed. She only wished she had somewhere far away to go, so she could keep driving with an aim in mind. But the supermarket wasn't far enough, nor the gold shop. And what use would it be? She would still have to be home by four in time for her children.

She busied her mind with immediate thoughts. Gigi's present. For lunch, she needed potatoes to go with the chicken. Then cheese triangles and strawberry yogurt, the children's favorites for breakfast and supper. Finally, some cream and chocolate for Gigi's cake. She always baked a two-tier chocolate cake for Gigi when there was a celebration. Deep in her thoughts, she almost missed a perfect parking space right outside the gold shop. It was rare to find a place to park on this busy road, let alone one exactly at her destination. A small thing, but it felt like a great stroke of luck.

A young assistant was polishing the inside of the shop window with a yellow dust cloth and doing a much better job than the porter's son ever did with her car windscreen. The little Masha' Allah was there, gleaming on the tray, encircled in the bright blue gems that Gigi loved so much. Perfect. She looked at her watch, 12:20 PM. It would be an easy lunch today, chicken and potatoes, thrown into one dish and left for the oven to do the rest. That way she would have time to make her rich chocolate cake and allow the sponge to cool. Then she would whip up the chocolate cream icing to decorate it, and by seven it would be ready for when Gigi came. What a surprise! A cake and a gift to celebrate!

Amidst her reverie, the sky darkened and a shadow fell across her face. More autumn clouds? She looked up and saw to her horror an obscure figure dressed in black, towering above her, almost blocking the sun. She could not make out the features. Then the figure moved closer, bringing their lips uncomfortably near to her face, and spoke.

"Washwishy ..."

It was a woman. Her voice was low and raspy, her breath wafting the sourness of pickled lemons. Azza shuddered. Hastily, she pushed the shop door open and the bell chimed a panicked little jingle as she hurried in. The assistant who had been polishing the window was now standing behind the counter.

"Who is that woman?"

Azza turned to point, but there was no one there. The young man looked out of his spotless window, then back at her inquiringly.

"Someone dressed in black, with a dark face ..."

"Perhaps you saw a beggar, Madam."

"More like a djinn."

The young man shrugged and bared his teeth in a disinterested smile.

"Whoever she was, she's gone now. How may I help you?"

"I want the framed Masha' Allah in the window tray please, on the left."

People came in and browsed, sauntering from shelf to shelf, cooing at heavy gold pendants and gem-studded bracelets. The assistant glared at Azza as she picked out the Masha' Allah. Maybe he found it inappropriate that she knew what she wanted and had no wish to stop and admire the elaborate craftsmanship of his more expensive pieces. Or maybe, she thought, his glare had something to do with her scar. She wished it didn't bother her so much what people made of her face.

He weighed the piece and punched in some digits on his calculator. It was within budget.

"Please polish it."

He seemed insulted, perhaps because polishing was part of his job description. He stomped off into the recess and emerged a few minutes later cradling the pendant in a soft cloth like a newborn baby.

"A nice pouch, please, preferably blue, to match the stones."

"We only have red."

"Fine."

He wrapped the trinket in silvery tissue and slipped it into the pouch. Azza paid and made for the door. Then she remembered the woman outside. Was she still there? She wanted to ask the assistant if he could check, but he was already busy with a tray of diamond rings and another customer. Outside, there was no one. She walked to her car. Then out of nowhere the woman appeared. She had been waiting.

"Washwishy ..."

The woman commanded her to whisper.

"What do you want?"

"It's what you want that matters."

The woman brought a tightly clenched fist up to Azza's face in a gesture she knew too well. Azza flinched, but the woman wasn't going to hurt her. Instead, she unfurled her hand. In her palm were shells, five, maybe six, unremarkable, yellow-white, like dirty teeth. The woman held her gaze; Azza noticed that her eyes were yellow, too, sunken, and very darkly smeared with kohl.

"I-I have no time for this." Azza tried to sound disinterested. The woman leaned in and gave a guttural laugh.

"You have time for nothing else."

Azza tugged at the strap of her handbag. For all she knew this woman could be a thief. Perhaps she ought to scream for help.

"What do you mean?"

"Things can change. I can help, I can make the pain go away ..."

Azza's lip trembled. The woman had seen her scar.

"I don't need help. You know nothing. Only God can help."

"Praise Him! I never said otherwise, but in His Glorious name, some of us are His tools on Earth. Some of us have the window to the future."

"What are you saying? No one knows the future!"

Azza knew she ought to slip behind the steering wheel and just go. But what if this was something she had to hear? The woman smiled and pulled something out of her pocket.

"See this cloth?"

It was an unremarkable cotton rag, yellowed with age and frayed at the edges.

"It's just a handkerchief," said Azza.

"Watch, child."

The woman made a hollow in the cloth and threw in a pinch of sandy dust from the street. Then she arranged the shells and knotted the cloth into a tiny bundle. Lowering her lips, she breathed heavily and whispered to the bundle. Azza couldn't make out what she was saying. They didn't sound like words at all. After a moment, she untied the cloth and pointed.

"Look, just look!"

Azza looked. The dust had gone.

"Now do you believe? Where has the dust gone? Someone has given you the evil eye, my child. I can help you, but only if you whisper!"

Azza brought her lips to the shells, but realized she had no idea what to say.

"Ask them your heart's desires."

For a moment, she felt confused. She didn't believe in fortune tellers. She didn't want to be drawn into this, but it was as if she were a shell herself, sitting there in the woman's dark palm.

"Washwishy! The shells want to hear your whisper!"

Azza whispered. It was a wish, not a question. A small wish, made of only a few words. She wasn't even sure it was what she wanted. Then the woman rolled her eyes for a moment so the dark irises disappeared, and all Azza could see were the yellowed whites.

#

Gigi came just after seven that evening.

"It's a gorgeous gift, Azza!" Gigi held the pendant in her palm and smiled at it with genuine approval.

"But the cake—"

"Sshh! It tastes great. Who cares what it looks like? Your girls have devoured half of it already!"

Azza knew the girls had eaten so much cake because she hadn't cooked lunch for them after all, not because it was irresistible. She hadn't been able to go to the supermarket to get missing groceries after her encounter with the shell whisperer. At home, she was too drained to put together a proper meal and had made the cake without fresh cream or chocolate.

"You do understand that she is just a silly gypsy woman." Azza was staring at the remains of her crumbling cake, but Gigi knew what she was thinking about.

"You know, I was stopped by a small band of them once downtown. It was a while back, when things were a lot safer. They had tattoos on their cheeks and chins and wore flowing, black head veils. They were dark and creepy. A street vendor shooed them away, and they flurried off like crows. He said they were from Sinai—or maybe it was the Western Desert—and came all the way to Cairo to con people with their silly predictions. Now what did she even predict for you? Nothing."

Azza thought about it. The woman hadn't said anything remarkable. Gigi put on a deep, austere voice, "'Await changes, for they will find you and they will find your loved ones', isn't that all she said? You and I know that change is about the only thing that's certain to happen!"

Gigi strung her new Masha' Allah next to the letter "G" around her neck as she spoke.

"Let's face it, it's just another form of begging, Azza. She'd have left you alone for a couple of pounds. I hope you didn't give her too much."

Azza bit her lip and thought of her last moments with the fortune teller.

"Pay me, child, pay me now, generously—you have much money in your purse. We will meet again. We will meet again when change comes."

Without thought, Azza had dipped her hand into her bag and pulled out two crisp twenty-pound notes. She folded them and placed them in the gypsy's cold palm. It was the same palm she had whispered into, but there were no shells now. She didn't want Gigi to think she was foolish, so she didn't tell her. But Gigi already knew.

"You believed her, didn't you?"

"She said she could help me. She said things would change. Maybe she knew. What about the dust . . . where did it disappear to?"

Gigi looked disappointed.

"Oh Azza, please, it was probably a trick. Maybe the cloth had holes or something, I don't know! But the point is, it wasn't real!"

Gigi realized her tone had been too harsh. She opened her arms and let her best friend fall into them. A moment later, Azza was sobbing.

"It's okay, Zooza," Gigi said in a whisper, using Azza's favorite childhood nickname. She wiped a bead of sweat from Azza's brow and ran a finger along the scar above her eye. Azza gave a tiny wince.

"You know, you could get rid of this with laser once it's healed."

"What's the point? There will be more where it came from."

"Maybe not. Maybe he'll see the light and improve or seek help. Maybe—"

"—Maybe I'll leave?"

The question was old but awkward. She would have left already if she knew how. But the years within this marriage had piled up and walled her in, crushing not just her body, but her spirit. The teen bride was now a woman of thirty, broken, resigned, but mostly just terrified.

Gigi placed a kiss on her best friend's brow. It eased the tension. The Masha' Allah swung gently on the thin, gold chain around her neck. It was indeed beautiful, thought Azza; she had chosen well. A Masha' Allah—who didn't have one? A phrase to keep away the evil of jealous eyes, crafted into swirling Arabic calligraphy. She reached up to touch it, and suddenly realized what the words actually meant. She said them aloud.

"What God wills."

Azza found herself reciting part of a prayer she had learned as a child:

"Masha' Allah kan, we ma lam yasha' lam yakon"

What God wills, will be; what He does not will, will not be.

Gigi smiled.

"Exactly. You said it yourself. A gypsy woman cannot change what God has willed."

Azza suddenly felt guilty.

"But I whispered into the shells. I made a wish."

Gigi pecked her brow again.

"Don't think about it too much."

Gigi didn't leave until after nine. It was a rare treat that she could stay so long, made possible only because Azza's husband was on duty for two nights. She helped Azza bathe the children and put them to bed. She would have stayed longer but had her own grumbling angry baby waiting with the nurse for her to bathe and feed him: Siddique, her father.

"Drive carefully Gigi. Don't take any back roads."

Gigi laughed.

"Seriously, Gigi. It's dangerous these days."

Don't worry about me; I can wrestle a gorilla. I'm not the one dishing out money to a creepy gypsy! I'll call you when I am home. Stay safe, lock up tight."

Azza was alone now with the night. She turned on the TV, flipped from channel to channel and back again: news, drama, talk show, news. She made herself a mug of mint tea and wandered into the study.

Solemn volumes stood in rank behind the thick wooden desk; not her territory, nor her interest. She turned instead to the squat shelf near the window, her fingers flitting across the titles: *The Poetry of May Ziada;* Youssef Idris's *Masterpieces; Othello Translated; A Short Introduction to Cake Decoration.* Then she came across the thick dark album at the end. She flinched to its touch, as if it was an instrument of torture. There was a gold inscription in English on the spine: the letters AA, for Azza and Adel; a date, and the words: Ajmal el-Zikrayat—The Most Beautiful Memories. Slowly she tugged it out. How heavy it seemed, heavier than pots and babies and furniture. The first page was pasted with a sheet of parchment, inscribed with that familiar verse from the Quran:

"And one of His signs is that He created for you from your selves spouses that you may find rest in them, and He created between you love and mercy …"

"Love and mercy …" she echoed.

Staring at her from the next page was a lanky boy with heavyset eyebrows and a sharp-jawed, expressionless face, his hands deep in his pockets. It was hard to tell where he was, as the background was blurred, but he always claimed he was on board a ship. The picture beneath was a smiling young Azza, with shining eyes and braided hair. She was standing on the sun-drenched roof of a country dwelling, surrounded by palm trees, a little woodpigeon snugly nestled in her chubby hands. Gigi with pigtails was looking at the pigeon over her shoulder. Azza loved this picture, taken at Gigi's country house when they were children. It was funny, but Azza was always grateful that Gigi was with her in the picture, as if it somehow scared her to be alone with the lanky boy on the same page.

She turned the page; there she was, a young girl in a woman's dress, her pinch-toed heels peeping out beneath the hem, her hair taut under a short, puffed-out veil. Azza hated everything about herself in these pictures, how padded the dress was, her leaf-green eyeshadow, her circular-rouged cheeks. The attempt to make her a woman only turned her into a moulid doll, flounced and garishly painted.

The heavy-browed boy with no expression was now the man standing next to her, his eyebrows now almost a mono-brow, his sharp-jawed face still blank in every single frame. Even with the lights dimmed for the first dance, or amidst his cheering pals or close family, the face was as unchanged as a stone. But Azza saw something else, something she had failed to recognize back then—a tension in the sharp jawline, like a spring held back, waiting to uncoil. She shuddered and turned to the next frame. It was her mother smiling triumphantly, her face plump and polished, one big shoulder tilted to the camera.

Next there was a picture of Gigi and her parents. Gigi's dad had one hand clamped heavily on his daughter's shoulder, while Gigi's frail mother stood half a step behind them. Azza moved on from frame to frame: the exchange of rings, the towering white cake and blood-red sherbet in tall frosted glasses, the famished guests tucking into the wedding feast.

The final picture was of her and Adel outside the Police Club where the wedding was held, lights glittering, flag caught in motion, a blur of faces definitely happier than the new couple whose union they were celebrating.

The phone rang. Azza jerked, and the album bumped to the floor.

"Did I wake you?"

Gigi was whispering.

"Huh? No, no. Did you just get home?"

"Of course not ... Aisha left when I arrived. He just slept. Babbling like a baby, swearing at me mostly."

Gigi gave a whimper-like chuckle.

Azza's mind went to Uncle Siddique. Growing up there was everything to fear about this giant, rubicund man—his hands, his bellow, his perpetual frown. She thought of the last time she had seen him some months earlier, thin and pale, shriveled in an oversized bathrobe, the fire drained from his cheeks. Gigi had just finished bathing him with motherly patience.

"God bless you, Gigi, you really are an angel."

"Nah. You're the angel."

"Then maybe we both are."

"I'd better get some rest. I have a presentation first thing. Aisha will be back tomorrow to give him his midday injection. I'll call you in the lunch break. Tisbahee 'ala kheir."

Gigi hung up.

"Tisbahee 'ala kheir." Azza murmured the words to herself. It seemed an odd greeting. May you wake to good things. When was the last time that had happened? She knelt to pick up the album, then stayed there, head down, eyes closed, the dust of a thousand memories unsettled in her mind. Words came to her, words meant for her journal:

I wish I could go back again, not to weep and relive the pain, but to save the girl that was me. But she is locked there, and I cannot help her—

Cannot help her. The face of the gypsy woman suddenly appeared before her. Azza shook the image away and jerked to her feet to return the album to its proper place on the shelf.

She didn't sleep well. All night she wrestled with troubled dreams and outbreaks of sweat and daughters who alternately needed to pee. She rose for dawn prayers, then sat on her prayer rug in quiet meditation. The clock on the dresser ticked like heartbeats. Six AM. She would wake the girls in a half hour and prepare them for school. The calendar showed it was Wednesday. Adel would be home tonight. The thought made a knot in her stomach, like a familiar little punch. She would cook a nice meal and give the apartment a good cleaning, so he wouldn't complain about thin gray dust on the dark wood of tables and chairs. She worried most about polishing his desk. The slightest shift in a pen holder or notepad and the whites of his eyes would turn very red and his jaw would tighten. And of course she would need to dress in a way to keep the peace. Not too casual or he'd consider her sloppy; not too much detail or he would accuse her of being inappropriate while he was away.

The alarm went off and she rose to wake the girls. The morning routine never varied: wash, dress, breakfast, bye-bye, bus.

By 8 AM the house was empty. Azza made coffee and began her morning chores. She picked up a dust cloth to polish the surfaces.

"Where has the dust gone—now do you believe?"

She repeated the gypsy's words out loud. Where had the dust gone? She wished she'd asked. It bothered her that she was still thinking about the woman. She pushed the thoughts away. There were other things to plan: she would grill yesterday's chicken without potatoes; she'd make rice with fried vermicelli and cook a pot of garlicky, green molokhiyya, doubling the quantities for when Adel arrived that evening. She had leftover cooked mince that she'd use to make a rokak; its crumbly, buttery pastry was one of Adel's favorites.

With robotic precision, she put the meal in order and was done by midday. Exhausted, she flopped down in a kitchen chair to catch a moment's rest. She had enough time for a quick shower before Gigi's lunch break call, but somehow, she didn't have the energy. She reached out and opened the closet where she kept a sack of rice and other provisions. Digging deep into the sack she pulled out a little book, wrapped in plastic: her latest journal. Gigi always marveled at the places she devised to hide her writing: the detachable base of a decorative pedestal, behind the flower box on the window ledge, inside an unused china cauldron in the dining room cabinet. She would, of course, be caught from time to time, and the journal would be confiscated. Her husband knew how criminal minds worked, and like all criminals, she would be punished. Here amidst the grains of rice her words had been safe, so far. She opened the journal at an earlier entry, one she had not torn out:

Is it so hard to love me? Am I a creature so repulsive, so unworthy of the touch of a gentle hand?

She looked down at the words. Such a sad plea for love. She liked to imagine it would move his heart to read them, but she couldn't fool herself. He would tear the page and her hair out in a flash.

She remembered the time when he once read a journal entry, how his features had seemed to soften, so that his eyes looked like those of a gentler man, as he mouthed the words she had written:

I am mystified: what is this soul who says one thing, does another, whose eyes erupt fire, even as his lips curl in smile? Which part of a man's face is a woman to trust?

She had been pregnant at the time. The fleeting hint of compassion quickly vanished, his eyes erupted their fire, his lips curled in a sneer, and she had learnt that there was no part of a man—not his face, nor his hands nor his feet—that she could trust.

She had lost the baby, the first of many.

Azza shivered at the memory. She clutched at the notebook and crumpled its pages. Why did she keep writing when it brought her so much trouble? She had no answer to that, except that she could not stop writing. Something inside her survived on these scribbles. She brought her mind back to the present, turned to an empty page, and in a feverish moment wrote:

My soul is weary, ancient, the age of rocks and trees and sandbanks along the Nile. How can change come to one so old, so dried out, and what would change mean? A slap, a spit, a broken wrist, a splinter of glass embedded somewhere unreachable ... scars go deeper than the skin. No Mama, time doesn't always heal the wounds of the soul. Gypsy woman, what would I do with change if it knocked on my door?

A clock somewhere struck the half hour. The muezzin made the call to afternoon prayers.

That meant it was three-thirty. Why had Gigi not phoned? The children would be home soon.

Azza picked up the phone and dialed Gigi's mobile.

The number you have dialed cannot be reached at this time ...

It wasn't like Gigi not to call; it wasn't like her to turn off her phone. Maybe her battery had died. Azza wondered if this had anything to do with Gigi's dad. He was becoming more and more frail with each passing day. Azza worried every time she called Gigi that she would hear bad news about the old man. She tucked away her journal in the rice sack. Only a quarter of an hour to wash away the scent of garlic and onion and change into a fresh dress before her daughters came home.

She rose and made her way to the bathroom but was stopped by a shuffle on the stairs. Then the doorbell rang. Azza hadn't heard the familiar grinding brakes of the school bus. If it wasn't the children, it had to be Adel, home early. But Adel never rang the doorbell. He only ever turned the key and slammed the door. She peeped through the eyehole: sure enough, Adel was there in uniform, only he looked strange. He was shorter, and his face seemed rounder, the features softer. The illusion surprised Azza, until she realized it wasn't Adel; It was another man in uniform. Her stomach tightened. She took a breath and opened the door.

"Madam Azza, Colonel Adel Helmy's wife?"

"Yes?"

Azza realized that the man was older than her husband, too.

"I am General Abdul Hamid Hafez. I have something I need to share with you."

Azza recognized the name.

"My husband isn't home."

"I know, Madam."

The man looked at her with apologetic eyes.

"Madam, do you need to sit down?"

Azza convinced herself it was a meaningless question, but something frightening edged closer in her mind, a distant rumble before the first clap of thunder.

"Sir, please tell me why you are here."

"Madam, I can find no other way to say this. I regret to inform you that your husband has been killed. He was shot earlier this afternoon by armed baltagiyya in Matariya. I'm so sorry to share this news. To spare you the heartache, we are attending to the paperwork, which should be ready in time for the burial early tomorrow. You should be proud of your husband. He died in the line of duty, a brave man and a true martyr."

He went on to say they were sorry to lose him, that his superiors had insisted on posting an obituary in the newspaper and booking a hall at the Police Mosque for the condolences.

What was she hearing? It didn't make sense. Adel dead? Why would he be dead? Azza stared emptily ahead of her. A ray of sunlight fell across the stairway, a thousand particles of dust suspended in it.

"Madam?"

If Adel was dead, who would eat all that molokhiyya? There was certainly too much for the girls. And they didn't like her buttery rokak.

"Madam, are you okay? Is there anything I can do? Is there anyone I can call?"

"I'll-I'll call Gigi."

The officer was still talking when she closed the apartment door.

Adel dead?

The school bus bellowed up the road and ground to a halt in front of the building. The bubbly chatter of her little girls filtered through the front window. The porter unlocked the gate, and they clambered up the stairs, laughing.

Mama, I'm hungry; I grazed my knee; you have to sign this; I got chocolate milk on my shirt …

Azza walked away. She needed Gigi.

The number you have dialed cannot be reached at this time …

Where had Gigi disappeared to all day? It was almost five.

She served her daughters their dinner and put their soiled school clothes in the washing machine. She emptied their schoolbags, washed their lunchboxes, laid their books on their desks. Then she went to shower, washing away the day's sweat and cooking and confusion.

Adel is dead. That meant he wouldn't be coming home. Ever. A man knocks on her door and tells her that her husband is dead and now she is a widow.

Azza crouched down on her knees in the shower and began to cry.

"Mama, Mama, phone!"

She wrapped herself in a towel and hurried out of the bathroom; it must be Gigi, calling now that her phone was charged.

"Gigi, Gigi, where have you been? "

"Madam Azza."

Azza recognized the worried voice. It belonged to Aisha, Gigi's trusted nurse. Why would she be calling? The old man must have died. Oh God! Both men in one day!

"Aisha, what's the matter? Has something happened to Uncle Siddique?"

"No, Madam Azza, no, Siddique Bey is fine."

"What's the matter then? Where's Gigi? Her phone has been off all day."

"I was hoping you knew where she was, Ma'am."

"What do you mean? She went to work early, for a presentation. She-she should have called me at lunchtime. She didn't."

"Oh Madam, she didn't call to confirm the Bey's injection this morning, so I thought maybe she was working from home today. I called her mobile; it was off. I tried calling home; no reply. The Bey never answers the phone, but Miss Gigi always does. I got worried. I took the bus across town and arrived at 2:30 PM. Siddique Bey was alone and angry. He hadn't had lunch or taken his medication, so I gave him both. Miss Gigi's phone was still off. Then the office called on the landline and asked why she hadn't come in. They'd been trying to get in touch with her all day. I thought-I thought she would be with you."

Azza could no longer hear what the nurse was saying. She was trying to find a place to stand or sit that was not collapsing.

#

She comes to me in dreams, the woman with a face as dark as coffee beans. It is always the same: I am looking into a pool of turquoise blue, still and somber, and from its depth the dark face emerges, eyes closed. Then she opens them wide, and in a haunting murmur commands me to whisper to her shells. I whisper. She rolls her eyes and mouths the words "await changes." Then I scream and awaken. The room is dark. No one stills my pounding heart or grabs my wrist as I reach my hand across to the pillow next to me. Then I remember I am alone.

Azza no longer tore pages from her journal. She kept it under her pillow now, not in rice sacks or china cauldrons. Sometimes she awoke in the night and wrote. She wrote to heal herself. It was the only time she felt whole.

 Adel had been buried. More people showed up at the mosque to pay condolences than Azza expected. Long faces exchanged glances and nodded sadly at the young widow and mother of little girls. But Azza's mind was stuck on one thought: Where was Gigi? When she asked the police, they nodded mechanically and said they were doing their rounds, asking questions. It was a difficult time, they said; keeping up with crime was impossible. Azza wondered ironically if Adel would have helped with the investigations if he were alive. He had been a good police officer, so he probably would have.

Moments passed, and became the hours of long, empty days. Alone, Azza polished surfaces and wrote in her journal. She cooked, but never made cakes. She often looked at her scar in the mirror as if this—not her daughters—were her only legacy from Adel. She waited for the phone to ring, and watched the door, craving a gentle knock or an angry slam. From her wedding album, she peeled the childhood picture of her and Gigi on the sunny country roof and propped it up against her bedside lamp. It was the first time in nearly twenty years that the lanky boy would be alone on the page. It was the first time in her life that Gigi had been away for so long.

Azza's mother called often, to warn her that it was now dangerous and unacceptable to live alone in a house with two small children. It was time, she said, to abandon her nest and move in with her old mother. Azza held the phone to her ear while her mother recited the same terse message every time, sometimes not even noticing when the old woman had hung up.

Aisha stayed on with Gigi's father, but Azza could not bring herself to visit without Gigi there. Instead, she called Aisha daily to ask about the old man. He'd been told Gigi was on a business trip, which infuriated him. How dare she leave without informing him? Aisha said he swore himself to sleep every evening, cursing his daughter for abandoning him.

The days soon became weeks. By now, Azza could hardly bear the seclusion of her four walls. Sometimes walls can crush worse than a man. Out of the house, she wandered more and more, to buy groceries to pay bills, to look for someone.

She sped with her car far away, along highways, without caring whether it was safe or not. She shuffled through crowded markets, and walked along canals, where cars and donkeys often skidded on the mud banks and slipped under the water's surface. What did she expect to find?

Then one day she saw a crouched figure, head down, dark hands. It was not Gigi, but the moment she saw the woman she realized that she had been looking for her, too.

It was the gypsy. She was dressed differently, in a bright blue peasant's smock and a floral headscarf. She was busy arranging lemons and bunches of mint leaves in a straw basket. "Won't you have some lemons?" She said, her head still down.

Azza's heart skipped a beat at the raspy voice.

"You!"

The woman looked up at her with surprised, kohl-smeared eyes.

"What happened to shell-whispering?"

"Ah ... We have met?"

"You whispered into shells, made dust disappear; I made a wish, you made a prediction."

Azza's voice trailed away.

"Did my prediction come true?"

Azza's eyes twitched with impending tears. She said nothing.

The woman shifted closer.

"What did you wish for?"

"I wished to be alone."

"And are you?"

"I am."

"So, are you happy?"

The tears spilled from Azza's eyes.

"Where is Gigi? Why did you upend my life?"

"Who is Gigi? I did nothing. Things often happen because you believe they'll happen, but it is God's will that moves the universe."

The woman dipped her hand in her pocket and took out a shell, turning it over in her palm.

"How can this fragile little thing change anything?"

She threw the shell up in the air, and it landed on the roadside, yellow and small, hardly visible amidst Cairo's dust. It was as Gigi had said; the gypsy woman was a fraud, a beggar posing as someone with a trade.

"You're right, gypsy woman; you and your shells know nothing. You don't even scare me."

She turned her back to the gypsy and wiped away her tears. It was time to go home to her daughters. As she left she took a last look at the shell, surrounded by dust. Then she stepped on it, grinding it to nothing beneath the heel of her shoe.

\#

DESSERT FOR THREE

by Aida Nasr

"Three desserts for the guilt of one," said Farida, who always ordered the chocolate cake. She cut it with quick, broad slashes, leaving three, squashed, chocolatey mounds on the gleaming white plate. Amina had already cut her apple tart. Heba carefully sliced her cheesecake into three.

"It doesn't have to be perfect." Farida said breezily. "It's only dessert, and anyway, if there's a bigger piece, it's mine."

"I have to go to a wedding next week," said Heba, taking her first bite.

"That's nice," said Amina tentatively. She knew Heba sometimes found weddings tiresome.

Heba fiddled with one delicate, dangly earring. Its tiny rhinestones glinted in the dim light of the café. "I don't know. It's going to be the same as every other wedding. And everyone's going to be saying, 'Hope you're next.'"

"Just smile at everyone and relax," said Farida. "Make a plan with your parents to leave right after the buffet."

Heba looked around at the people drinking their lattes and cappuccinos, eating their sandwiches and cakes at polished wooden tables. Many looked to her like university students, people she now thought of as "kids." Most people our age are at home with a husband and children on the weekend, she thought, but then corrected herself. Not most. Half her friends weren't married. Lately it was all she thought about.

"And I have nothing to wear," she added.

"Nothing to wear? Heba, I would have thought you had enough dresses in your wardrobe for all three of us," said Farida. Heba had a penchant for pretty things.

"No, I need a new one. Will you come with me to buy the fabric?"

"Only because you're my friend, and I love you. Shopping with you is enough to drive anyone mad. Remember, it's only a dress. Your life doesn't depend on choosing exactly the right fabric," answered Farida.

Each woman had finished a portion of the dessert in front of her, and simultaneously, as if passing off batons in a relay, they handed their plates to the friend on their right.

Farida savored a piece of apple tart and told them about a manipulative colleague. "He's convinced my boss that he's a star, but he's inventing problems, constantly barging into my office with one made-up crisis after another."

"Well, you're very good at your job, Farida. Maybe he feels threatened," said Amina.

"His inferiority complex is his problem," said Farida with a sniff.

When the plates made their final round, Amina had the chocolate cake. She was just lifting a forkful to her mouth when Heba asked, "How's Neda?"

Amina's daughter had spent every Friday with her father, Amina's ex-husband, since the divorce a year ago, and she felt a rare and pleasant lightness to be out on the weekend alone with her friends. But she also pictured her daughter, bouncy and chatty, and felt a twinge of guilt about enjoying this time without her.

"She's fine, at her father's today," she answered vaguely. "I feel bad, but it's really fun to be out with you two, with no interruptions from a six-year-old."

"Why should you feel bad, Amina? You deserve to enjoy yourself. Anyway, you're a fantastic mother," said Farida.

Amina didn't reply.

"Did you know that Osman Hassan recently had a baby? I think it's their third," said Heba. Osman was the boy she had had a crush on all through university, and she still followed his news.

"That's nice," said Farida, but she wondered how Heba really felt. She knew that, of all the boys they had gone to university with, Osman was the one Heba would have liked to marry. Amina was silently wondering if Osman was happy with his wife and children. Life turned out so differently than you expected somehow.

They had finished their desserts, and soon it was time to go. They left the sounds of jazz and pop music and the din of animated conversation and stepped out into a blare of car horns, traffic, and the dust of Cairo's streets.

#

"Madam, come take a look at what we have."

Heba and Farida got out of a taxi at Wekalat el-Balah and walked past wooden carts piled high with ladies' underwear and children's fluffy toys to reach the inner streets of the fabric market.

Every few steps, a merchant called out, making Heba want to dart away like a frightened cat, while in front of her, Farida strode forward in a manner that got people out of the way. They had to walk single-file, with one shoulder forward, to navigate the crush of people and carts on the narrow, dusty streets.

Heba wanted to touch the bolts of fabric everywhere and admire their colors. Apple green, watermelon pink, lemon yellow. But she only took quick, sidelong glances, afraid that if she showed any real interest, she'd never escape the pestering salesmen.

She was the director of public relations at a luxury hotel, and it was strange to her that she could deal with people successfully all day in her air-conditioned office and at elegant receptions in the ballroom but felt flustered in places like this. Here, she didn't know how to get what she wanted or avoid what she didn't.

"Madam, what are you looking for?" someone called from a shop.

I'm not "madam," she thought. Just a few years ago, they called her mademoiselle. Now she was in her thirties, they all assumed she was married. The title of "madam" reminded Heba of her mother and aunts. She had a job she enjoyed and was actually quite happy in the company of her girlfriends, but lately she found herself wanting to do what society thought she should do: get married. And leave home.

What she really wanted was an apartment, children … and china. She thought of a fat teapot with hand-painted flowers, a table dressed in beige linen with glinting purple glasses next to each shiny white plate, and friends for dinner, laughing over pasta.

Obviously, there were china and glasses and tablecloths at her parents' apartment, but what Heba really longed for was a life that was her own. One chosen by her, not one that fit within the perimeters of her family. What her husband should look or act like was somewhat vaguer in her mind except that he would be sweet, considerate, and hopefully, tall. The truth was, she couldn't envision him at all, and that scared her. How was she going to find him then?

They had reached a shop known for its evening-dress fabrics. Farida was along for her impressive bargaining skills. "If you see something you like, let me do the talking," she said.

A salesman started pulling down bolt after bolt of fabric, which he unfurled with a long flourish, trying to convince them that everything was "very chic." Heba couldn't see the colors clearly in the dim, fluorescent light of the shop, and being bombarded like this made her hesitant. She felt irritation rising like gently foaming milk threatening to overflow as she heated it for tea in the morning.

"Let her take her time," Farida ordered.

In the end, Heba chose a light purple fabric that she hoped would look elegant. Farida looked the salesman in the eye and offered less than half his asking price. After a few minutes, they walked out with four meters neatly folded in a bag at the price they wanted.

Heba got home exhausted, hot, and headachy, but triumphant about her purchase. She shook out the fabric and wrapped it around her body, turning in front of her bedroom mirror. Then she called the seamstress and told her she needed a dress in a rush.

#

"We have a problem," he said urgently.

Farida was only half-listening as her colleague blathered on about what she knew was nothing. She stared at the numbers on the paper in front of her. It was the third time she had looked at them, shifting uncomfortably in her suit. The first day after the weekend was always the hardest.

"—and if we don't do something now, this will be a real crisis," he was saying.

She was thinking of all the things she enjoyed with her salary. Lovely perfumes, dinners with her friends. Trips to Paris and London. Stylish clothes, although finding the right size was increasingly difficult. Could she do without it all?

Banking was all she knew. It was a career that won high approval from her parents and relatives, most people she met, actually. It was a predictable, understandable job, prestigious, stolid like sensible shoes, and most of all, secure. People expected her to stay at this bank until she retired.

And yet she couldn't get an image out of her head. It kept wafting through her mind like the gentle breeze that whispers off the Nile on summer nights. The image of a café. She saw wooden window frames and layer cakes covered in swirls of thick frosting sitting on old-fashioned cake stands lined up on a wooden counter. Cakes like no one had ever tasted before and the best coffee in town, both espresso and Turkish. She would put a tempting square of Turkish delight on each tiny saucer. She'd develop new cake recipes, chat with all her regulars, whom she'd know by name. She'd wear jeans and her favorite big hoop earrings, her hair curly instead of styled straight at the salon every week. She'd be enthusiastic about her life instead of just existing in it ...

"—and we'll need to solve this before the meeting tomorrow," her colleague was saying. He just wouldn't stop talking.

"Do you understand I don't have time for your emergencies every day?" she told him. "I have a whole department to run here. I'll handle it this time, but in the future, if you see this as a problem, solve it yourself."

He glared at her. She smiled at him thinly. After he left and before she picked up the telephone to sort things out, Farida opened her desk drawer and reached for a chocolate.

#

"Mama, do you know what I did?"

Amina opened her apartment door after work to find her daughter waiting for her in her school uniform. It was always the same, with Neda jumping up to tell her everything that had happened at school before Amina had even put down her keys. She gave Neda a hello hug and said goodbye to their housekeeper.

Neda trailed after her mother into the kitchen, telling an elaborate story that Amina couldn't quite follow, mainly because she wasn't listening. Neda always had enough energy for ten little girls, and it made Amina smile and wonder where she got all this enthusiasm. It also tired her at the end of her long days at the advertising agency.

"—and Sally made up a new game today. Mama, what are we having for lunch?"

Amina turned slowly. Neda often changed subjects before her mother could catch up. "Chicken, rice and—"

Neda was already telling a new story. As her daughter talked, Amina made a list in her head of all the things she'd love to do, something new, anything new at all. Visit Paris, learn French, take a painting class …

Ever since her marriage had ended, Amina had a heavy feeling, a thick fog pressing around her all the time, that she'd wasted her life, and now she had to catch up. Her idea of marriage had been long conversations with her husband, sharing good meals, and going out on the weekends. The reality that crept up on her eventually shocked her: evenings alone, the silence when he was there, or worse, their arguments and the biting remarks that still curled around her. She had slowly sunk into a dull, confused sadness.

What if she fell into more years of confusion, wasting more time in her tiring job, her endless routine of work and caring for Neda? She felt like she was moving so slowly through life, as if she were walking through molasses. Nothing seemed to have a flavor or a color or a meaning anymore. She wanted to be light and quick, doing everything she had never done before. She wanted to delight in life like it was a fine painting, with all its rich colors and textures.

"—and Sally's handwriting is better than mine, but I draw better," Neda was saying.

Amina wished she wasn't so tired. She wished she was really listening to her daughter instead of just nodding. She wished she felt as totally devoted all the time as people thought a mother should be. She really wanted to just sink into a comfortable chair and close her eyes. Learn to bake a chocolate cake from scratch, a really delicious chocolate cake, one you never wanted to stop eating.

#

The next day, Heba's phone rang at work, and she picked it up casually. The phone had been ringing all day.

"Hi Heba, how are you?" Farida's voice sounded far away. "I have bad news."

Heba's heart thudded, and there was a pause in which everything seemed to stop.

"Osman Hassan died in a car accident this morning."

Farida went on to tell her about the burial and the condolences at the mosque. Heba was barely able to listen or respond. Osman was only thirty-seven, a year older than her and her friends. She thought, if he had married me, I'd be a widow right now. Something had dislodged in Heba's world, like the earth's plates suddenly and silently shifting, creating a large, jagged fault line.

#

"We were all together for the last time on the weekend, at my parents' for Friday lunch." The three friends were sitting next to Osman's sister at the mosque. Her eyes were red-rimmed, and her voice was so low

156

they could barely hear her. "We had such a good time on Friday. Osman joked with everyone. You know how he was ..."

More women arrived to give their condolences. Osman's sister got up to receive them. The friends sat back in silence.

El-baqaa' l'Allah. Indeed only God is everlasting, thought Farida, repeating the phrase that everyone said as a condolence. People sure don't last, she thought. What the hell am I doing with my life?

Amina glanced at Osman's mother, sitting in a grief-stricken daze, and felt a wave of guilt and regret about all the times she hadn't listened to her daughter's stories. What was I thinking; go to Paris, learn French? I want to learn things with my daughter, have adventures together.

Heba looked around the room, filled with women dressed in black, and felt foolish about the importance she had placed on the purple fabric. And that she had assumed a husband would be there when times got difficult. She looked at Osman's wife, a woman younger than she was, a widow with three small children and a tearstained face. Everyone acts as if once you get married, you've got a life. But nothing is ever guaranteed. Ever. I do have a good life, right now.

The Quran reciter paused to take a break, and some people got up to leave. The three friends stayed till the end, till the last recitation was over and the last person left.

#

"Let's join them," said a cousin, taking Heba's hand. They stood in the crowd at the edge of the dance floor, clapping to the loud tambourines and drums of Arabic pop songs and watching the newlyweds dance with their friends. It was strange attending this wedding, just days after Osman Hassan's death. Heba went with her parents, wearing her beautiful purple dress. She felt happy for the bride and groom but also awkward, oddly removed from the celebration, as if she were floating above it. She wondered what the future held for everyone here.

The newlyweds' friends linked arms and danced in circles around the couple. Heba looked at all the women in their long evening dresses, admiring the colors. The next time I go buy fabric, I'll stop and look at everything that catches my eye. Spontaneously, she decided to join the dance herself. The purple dress swayed around her as she danced.

For once, Heba didn't feel bad she wasn't the bride. It wasn't her time yet. Maybe it never would be? No, she decided firmly. There was a time for them all, insha' Allah. She thought of Farida and Amina at the café.

"May it be your turn next," said an aunt, when Heba went back to their table.

"Thank you," she smiled. And genuinely meant it.

#

Farida was sitting in her office thinking about Osman Hassan. She remembered him as someone who added gentle humor to any conversation, always making everyone laugh. He had a natural, easy knack for people, for life ...

The colleague knocked on her door and walked in. He began talking very fast, and as he did, Farida almost had to shake herself to try and bring herself back to her office. Then she realized something. She saw that her patience for this situation was like a box of tissues, the kind you still got in Egypt, where all the sheets were connected to each other with perforations, and when you meant to pull out one tissue, you ended up with three or four in its wake. Sometimes when you plucked out a long string of tissues like this, you realized that the box was empty.

This man, this bank, this career had been pulling and pulling on her patience, until right now, he had just plucked the last shred she had. Farida very calmly realized that the box was empty—totally empty.

"I don't have time for this," she said. He stopped short for a moment and then continued talking rapidly. Farida opened her drawer and took out a pad of paper. I need to do something, she thought. Now.

"Do you understand how critical this is?" her colleague asked.

At first, it seemed he had read her mind. Then she realized he was talking about banking. "No, I don't. Deal with it yourself."

"But—"

158

"And close the door on your way out," she told him pleasantly.

He looked at her in silent surprise and left.

Farida took up a pen and began writing down ideas for her café in quick, broad strokes, visions of layer cakes dancing in her head.

#

"Mama, do you know what I did today?"

Neda was waiting for Amina in her school uniform, same as every other day. As they went to the kitchen Neda was saying, "Sally taught me a new clapping game, Mama."

Amina had promised herself that she'd listen to her daughter's stories. She said, "That sounds like fun. Why don't you show it to me?"

"Okay, Mama! Put your hands like this, and I'll teach you the song."

Amina's heart did a little leap to see how much this excited Neda, and her stomach sank because she realized how much it meant for the girl to get her undivided attention. For the first time in a year, she didn't want to run to catch up with life. She wanted to slow down to a leisurely stroll. As they clapped and sang, she looked at Neda's small pink mouth upturned into a smile. Amina felt lighter, the fog of her sadness lifting. She wanted to suspend this moment in time.

"Neda, after lunch, why don't we get out your paints and paint a picture together."

"Yes, Mama! I'll go get them right now."

#

In the café on Friday night, the three friends talked about Osman Hassan for a while and then lapsed into silence.

"How was the wedding?" Farida said finally.

"All right, actually, better than expected. There was a man who saw me there, a relative of the bride's who wants to meet me. A thirty-nine-year-old doctor," said Heba.

"Well, that's good. You should definitely go," said Farida.

"She's right. You never know," said Amina.

"I've already agreed to meet him," said Heba. She was a bit nervous but also realized that, for the first time, she didn't care how it turned out. She just felt thankful to be sitting here with her friends, these women she had grown up with.

The three got up to look at the glass case holding the desserts. Farida saw a layer cake with thick, white frosting. "That's definitely what I want," she said. "No chocolate cake today?" asked Heba with a raised eyebrow.

"It's time for a change. I'll tell you all about it later."

Heba looked at the cheesecake but realized she didn't want it either. She usually chose it because it was her favorite, a foolproof choice. Should it be that one or that one? she thought, looking into the glass case. Just choose, Heba. It's only dessert, she told herself.

"I'll try that one," she said, pointing to a cake piled high with colorful, glossy slices of mixed fruit. Her friends smiled.

"Well, I'll take the chocolate cake then!" said Amina.

They walked back to their table and settled into the velvet armchairs to chat while they waited for their desserts.

#

BREAD AND SALT

by Mariam Shouman

T he flowered sheet flapped damply against the window. The dank warm air of the summer night was cloying in the lungs; each breath seemed to leave a residue. A haze around the newly installed street lamp prevented night from ever truly coming to the street and illuminated the face of the apartment buildings that stretched from corner to corner without so much as a walkway between them. The walls of each building met the walls of the next, leaning on and supporting each other—if one fell, what would happen to the next and the next?

Splat! Splat! Splat! The girl drew patterns in the dust on the windowsill as the sheet hanging from the upstairs neighbors' clothesline billowed heavily into her apartment. It blocked the slight stirring of a breeze that might have blown cooler air into the stuffy apartment. Why couldn't they fold their wash so that it didn't hang in front of the one window in the apartment? It just wasn't neighborly.

Samia couldn't sleep. She had lain in her bed for what seemed like hours, feeling the hot walls baking her in the small apartment she shared with her parents and two brothers. The curtain that she pulled around her bed at night to give her a minimum of privacy seemed to trap her own breath in the little alcove. It kept the air from the ancient white ceiling fan, as it wobbled through the night, from reaching her. The constant hum from the white, one-door refrigerator next to her bed exacerbated the heat that radiated from it.

When she could no longer tolerate the sweat dripping down her forehead and into the crease of her neck, she gave up on sleep and went to sit next to the only window in the long, narrow room. She had eased open the shutters so that the shimmer from the streetlight now fell across her two sleeping brothers where they sprawled on the traditional cotton-stuffed couches in what served as their bedroom at night but doubled as a sitting room in the daytime. Their limbs askew, they slept in thin pajama pants and undershirts. Samia wondered what it would be like to sleep with such abandon. As long as she could remember, she had always slept in the alcove curled on one side, securely covered with at least a sheet, and as soon as she had started preparatory school, her mother had made a drape to pull around her at night. A girl had to have some privacy, her mother explained, and there was only the one small, windowless room that her parents shared and the tiny, equally windowless kitchen with its eternally damp floor and even damper little bathroom next to it. The heart of the apartment was the hall where the children slept at night and where all activities took place during the day.

#

The dreary pull of sleeplessness made her lay her head on her arms on the sill. Perhaps after the dawn prayer, the coolest time of the day, she'd be able to sleep an hour or so. She'd thought she'd try to study rather than tossing and turning the rest of the night through. Her secondary school exams were approaching, and she had piles of books, sheets, and notes to memorize, and the traffic through the small apartment was overwhelming during the day. There was always some neighbor popping in to share a tidbit of gossip or deposit a toddler while the mother went off to the market. Samia preferred the relative quiet of the night. But tonight, she couldn't manage to gather her thoughts. Her schoolbook lay on the small table, open but unattended. Concentration escaped her. Niggling little thoughts kept sidetracking her … like how inconsiderate it was of her neighbors to hang a sheet down over the apartment's only window.

#

Umm Ossama, the upstairs neighbor, was always asking them for something, "Could you look after Mostafa while I go buy a kilo of tomatoes?" or, "How about a cup of tea, ya Samia?" or even, "Don't you have a calculator to spare for Amira? The teacher has threatened to beat her if she doesn't bring one to class tomorrow, and I just don't have the money." Her list of impositions was impressive, but every time Samia mentioned Umm Ossama's laundry habits and how they cut off light and air to the apartment, her mother would hush her and forbid her from saying anything to Umm Ossama. "We just have to put up with it. You must treat your neighbor well like the Prophet commanded us." Why didn't Umm Ossama have to treat them well too, Samia would have liked to know, but she knew better than to ask. Her mother was the same with all their neighbors, even the ones who dumped their mop water in the street, spattering their freshly washed laundry, or the ones who borrowed things and never brought them back. "We've eaten 'aish wa malh together, ya Samia."

Samia thought to herself that their neighbors had definitely eaten more than just bread and salt, but didn't say. "Nothing that they do now can diminish what we've been through together. You don't remember, ya Samia, but believe me, neighbors are important."

So Samia clamped her lips firmly together every time Umm Ossama came to dump Mostafa, her toddler, at her doorstep for an hour or more, even though the two-year-old was insufferable and always ended up ripping a page out of her notebook or scribbling on one of her books. She obediently made Umm Ossama tea when she came to call and escaped into the kitchen to wash dishes when she thought she couldn't contain herself any longer. She would take a cup of sugar down for Umm Mohammed when she called up the stairwell, begging for some sugar for her tea since Mohammed hadn't managed to go get the sugar rations yet. She even managed a tight smile for Umm Saeed, the mop water dumper. But inside she couldn't smile. Inside, she boiled.

She lifted the hair off her neck and twisted it into a ponytail. Next to the flowered sheet hung a long, narrow pillowcase that swung in the breeze. Peering up at the line, Samia noticed that just two flimsy clothespins held the case … Perhaps if Umm Ossama lost one of her pieces of laundry, she'd take better care of it the next time? Samia could almost hear the conversation.

"Good morning, ya Umm Hossam (Samia's eldest brother's name was Hossam)."

"Ahlan, ya Umm Ossama. How is the world treating you today?"

"Disaster struck last night, ya Umm Hossam!"

"Disaster? May evil keep away from you. What sort of disaster, ya Umm Ossama?"

"I lost a pillowcase from the line. One minute it was there, the next it wasn't."

"What a shame, ya Umm Ossama, what a shame! We, live and learn. Next time make sure and use more clothespins and try not to leave things on the line at night. I hear that thieves like to steal the best items off the clothesline at night."

"I live on the fifth floor, ya Umm Hossam! What thieves? What are you talking about?"

"Well, I've heard stories of thieves with special sticks with hooks on them that they use to snatch whatever they want off your line … maybe they are just stories, but you can never be too sure."

And at this point, Samia would interject smoothly, "There was a breeze last night. I'll bet the pillowcase got blown off the line. Maybe if you folded your wash in half over the line it wouldn't fall so easily, especially long things like sheets and pillowcases." And that would be it. The message would be delivered without any sort of confrontation. As she considered her plan, her heart beat a little faster. It was wrong. But oh, so tempting. She rubbed her jawline and the back of her neck. The sweat hadn't dried. It was so hot. That was what was making her think crazy thoughts. She couldn't do anything so wrong as stealing from her neighbors. But Umm Ossama had more things than most in the neighborhood; she could probably spare a single pillowcase. The fact that the pillowcase and sheet were still on the line at night were proof of that; her mother always had to wash the sheets first thing in the morning so that they'd be dry by night or else they'd have nothing to sleep on.

Samia left the window and crept silently to the bathroom to wash her face and rinse away the sweat. In a minute, the terrible plan would seem just as impossible as she knew it was. She couldn't steal from her neighbor, no matter how awfully that neighbor treated her. But when she came back to her perch by the window, the pillowcase flapped even more temptingly in front of her. She'd only have to reach up to tug it down. She crept quietly through the apartment again, this time stopping in front of her parents' door to listen to the snoring that emerged from within. From the sound of it, they were both asleep and deeply so. She snuck past her brothers' makeshift beds. They were sleeping an exhausted sleep after long hours in the carpentry workshop where they both worked.

Samia seated herself once more in front of the window. This time she looked down at the street. It was never quiet, but this was the quietest time of the night. Even the coffee shops had closed for a few hours before dawn. Surreptitiously, she pulled one shutter closed and then swung the other perpendicular to the window to block any inquiring eyes and, with one backward glance at her brothers, she reached up and gave the pillowcase a swift tug. The pins gave with a crisp snap, and it came loose in her hand. Just as she was pulling her hand into the window, the startling voice of the muezzin coughed over the loudspeaker from the nearby mosque in preparation for the dawn call to prayer, and Samia lost her grasp on the bit of cloth. She watched it tumble to the street, failing to catch on the other clotheslines below, spiraling down to lie in a puddle of mud. Her heart pounding, she slammed the other shutter closed—more carelessly than she had wanted—with an alarming bang. As she latched the shutters, she heard her brother's sleepy voice, "What are you doing, ya Samia? What time is it?"

"Just getting a breath of air, ya Hossam. It is time for the dawn prayer. I'm going to pray, and then I'll go back to sleep."

She shuffled to the bathroom, her feet unwilling to lift themselves off the floor, and splashed water on her face and arms, but she couldn't get herself to pray. Her heart pounded for hours as she lay in her alcove, thankful for the curtain that sheltered her from everyone's eyes.

She was just drifting off to sleep when her mother pulled the curtain aside and poked her head in, "Aren't you going to go get us bread, ya

Samia? Your brothers need to go to work! The line is getting longer as you sleep!"

#

Samia rolled out of her bed. It was already hot. The cotton mattress was hot and the cotton pillow even hotter. She made her way to the bathroom after a glance at her still sleeping brothers. At one time, they had gone for bread, too, but now that they'd started working at the carpentry workshop, the duty had fallen to her, and she hated it. The line would be long, the people rude, and the sun hot. She turned the faucet and waited in vain. Not a drip this morning. There would be water downstairs at the neighbors' because they had installed an illegal pump, so they always had water. With a resigned sigh, she lifted the heavy water can and poured a measure into the metal cup that hung on a hook in the bathroom. She rinsed her face and mouth and splashed some water on her neck, back and front, winning momentary relief from the sticky sweat that plastered her hair to her neck. She pulled her dark blue abaya over her nightgown. She'd have to hurry to be able to get back before her brothers had to go to work. As she banged open the apartment door, snatching her headscarf off the nail next to the door, she remembered the pillowcase and felt a flash of guilt, but then she heard Umm Ossama calling from upstairs, "Ya Samia! Get us half a pound's worth of bread while you're there! I'll pay your mother back later in the afternoon!"

Muttering under her breath, Samia called back a short, "Okay," and went back into the apartment to get an extra half a pound from her mother. She was none too happy as there was a limit to how much bread she was allowed to get. To get more, she'd have to cajole the man in charge of doling out the bread, and she might even have to return with only enough for breakfast and have to go again at noon.

As she left the building and walked down the broken sidewalk, her guilty feet led her straight to the heap that had once been Umm Ossama's clean, flowered pillowcase. It had fallen in a puddle of water around a drainpipe and Samia thought to kick it aside to conceal it from view, but then decided to tread upon it instead. Her heel ground the cloth further into the muddy water, and she felt a tiny thrill of satisfaction. Even if Umm Ossama took the trouble to find the pillowcase, it would never again be clean and fresh. She nudged it a little closer to the wall of the building with her foot.

#

The city was just beginning to wake up. Shop boys were busy swiping dirty water out of the shops with long, rubber wipers under the close scrutiny of the shopkeepers. A crowd had gathered around each of the ful carts for a quick breakfast on their way to work. The vendors dipped huge ladles into the gigantic pots that had cooked on a slow flame all night long, slopping the beans into a metal bowl or half a loaf of baladi bread, depending upon the preference of the customer, with a sprinkling of salad and pickles to go with it. Samia's stomach growled as she hurried past the vendors. As she came in sight of the bread kiosk, she realized she'd have quite a wait. There was already a clump of children, teens, and women clustered around, waiting for their turn. Some bread had just come out of the oven and all the waiting customers had their hands thrust onto the counter, clutching their money, in the hope that it would be their turn. The bread seemed to disappear in an instant, with patrons snapping it up and then moving a few feet away to air it on rough wicker trays. One woman protested loudly, "I have been here all morning; she just got here!" pointing an accusing finger at one of the women who was quickly snatching up her bread. The vendor waved an indiscriminate hand at her and turned back to his oven. Unless there were actual punches being thrown, it was hard to attract his attention. Samia found a bit of wall to lean against in the shade and waited until the next batch emerged from the oven, joining the others in their rush to proffer their money. When she finally got her turn, she asked for a pound and a half's worth of bread, but the vendor shook his head, counting out 20 loaves and returning her fifty piasters to her, saying, "One-pound limit." He was too busy for cajoling, so Samia took her bread and after airing it for a few minutes, made her way back home.

#

Instead of taking any bread upstairs for Umm Ossama, Samia threw open the door of her own house, pulling her headscarf off and hanging it on its hook, and put the bread on the counter in the kitchen. Her mother was just laying out the breakfast on the big metal tray from which the family would eat; aluminum dishes of ful and chopped salad as well as a dish of soft white cheese and a plate of scrambled eggs swimming in ghee. "You got Umm Ossama's bread for her, ya Samia?" she asked.

"No, ya Mama," Samia shook her head. "He wouldn't give me more than a pound. You should tell Umm Ossama that she should get her own bread."

"Take ten loaves up to her, and maybe she'll go at noon." Her mother's tone left no room for argument.

"But, ya Mama, she's so lazy. Why doesn't she go herself?" Samia argued anyway.

"It's not for you to judge her. You have to be a good neighbor, ya Samia, or you won't find anyone to stand by you when you are in need. Now go." Her mother ended the conversation by heading back to the kitchen for the tea.

Grudging Umm Ossama every step, Samia climbed the stairs to the fifth floor, pounded summarily on her door, and thrust the loaves into Ossama's hand when he opened the door. Without a word, she turned and raced down the steps.

All day, she waited for the visit from Umm Ossama during which they would enact her imaginary conversation, but she only appeared for a moment to hand Samia's mother a stack of hot bread around noon.

#

The next Monday, washday, was even hotter and stickier. Sometime in the dark of the night, Samia woke to thoughts of more drastic action. She tiptoed from her bed to the window, easing the shutters open and peering up at the clothesline. With a shock, she realized that Umm Ossama had taken in her wash before going to bed. Umm Ossama had a bit of a reputation for being a sloppy housewife, as demonstrated by her habit of leaving her wash on the line all night long to soak up the bad, nighttime vapors. Good housewives always took great care to be the first to hang their wash out to dry and to gather it in before nightfall, but Umm Ossama had never been a good housewife. Perhaps she'd gotten the message after all? But why didn't Samia feel any satisfaction?

She went back to bed, sweating and disgruntled. As she lay stewing in her bed, she heard the sound of running feet in the apartment above. What on earth was Mostafa up to now? Or maybe it was Ossama or Basma or Fayza or Amira. It could even be Umm Ossama pounding garlic for all she knew; the woman had no respect for the needs of her neighbors. Samia's own mother was always taking the neighbors into account. Every time she made a pot of mahshi, she sent a plate down to Umm Mohammed, the old woman who lived with her grown-up son in the apartment below them. She always said that Umm Mohammed had grown too old to make her own stuffed cabbage or vine leaves, so she wanted to give Mohammed a treat. She said she didn't like the idea of him smelling the mahshi cooking and wishing for some. How Samia hated always having to think about what everyone else needed. Didn't they have enough trouble already just getting through the day? Even though her mother always made a huge pot full of mahshi, the idea that some of it went to Mohammed rather than to her and her brothers rankled.

#

Bang! Bang! Bang! The noise from the apartment upstairs was insufferable. She had dealt with the problem of the wash, but how would she retaliate for the endless noise? She almost wished that Umm

Ossama's wash had been hanging in front of the window so that she could have taken something else—but something valuable this time, something to keep rather than let fall into the dirt of the street. She'd get her chance.

As she stared down at the street, puzzling over how to get back at Umm Ossama for something she'd stopped doing, her eyes focused on the apartment below her … the neighbors had left their shutters open, and she could see straight into the apartment. The streetlight fell on Mohammed's desk, illuminating his books and papers. He was a funny sort; he'd finished high school and university but hadn't given up studying even after he'd gotten a job. Mohammed was the only person Samia had ever known who had done so well at university that he'd been given a job there. He was a quiet young man who hardly spoke, always seeming distracted by thoughts of what he had to do. He hardly seemed to recognize Samia when he saw her on the stairs or when she brought a piping hot plate of mahshi to him; he just nodded absently and bid her good day. Suddenly, Samia was seized by anger at the endless plates of mahshi that her mother had provided him, with no thanks or appreciation. If she couldn't punish Umm Ossama today, maybe Mohammed was within her reach. The pristine, white pages filled with the rows and columns of numbers called to her. Wouldn't it be a lovely moment for Umm Saeed to dump her dirty mop water? Of course, Umm Saeed would be sound asleep at this hour. But she was sure to get the blame for any water cascading down from above because the whole building knew that she had the nasty habit of dumping water out of the window, and it had been the cause of many a fight in the stairwell. Even a well-aimed cupful of water would wreak a little havoc with stuck-up Mohammed and his mother who was always looking for handouts. As she sat gazing down at the open window, the owners' transgressions multiplied in her mind until she was burning up with righteous anger.

In something of a daze of adrenaline, she went into the bathroom and took down the tin cup from its hook on the wall and filled it with water. As she looked down into the cup, stirring it with her finger, she thought it seemed too pure, too pristine. What good was a cup of clear water in repaying the neighbors' transgressions? After pouring it into the sink, she tiptoed to the kitchen and bent down in front of the sink. The plastic bucket under the leaky drainpipe was half full of murky, smelly water. Gingerly, Samia dipped the metal cup into the bucket and then carefully carried it to the window. Leaning out into the stifling night, Samia took aim at the window and flung the contents at it. Immediately, she pulled her head in and slipped into her bed. After an endless half hour measured out in the ticking of the wall clock, Samia snuck out of her alcove bed to peer down at the lit window. A satisfying blur of literary wreckage sat exposed to the night. With a tiny sigh, Samia slunk back into her bed, pulled the sheet up over her shoulders and slept the sleep of complete comfort, in spite of the sticky sweat that plastered her hair to her brow and trickled down her nose.

#

The morning dawned to the whining recriminations of the old woman downstairs directed at Umm Saeed. As soon as Samia woke to the old woman's voice, she leapt from her bed, pulling her nightgown down around her knees, and went to listen at the door. "Shame on you, ya Umm Saeed! Shame on you!" Umm Mohammed couldn't seem to think of anything else to say because she kept repeating the same phrase over and over again, while the low-voiced Mohammed hushed her repeatedly. From above, a woman's voice muttered, "Crazy old woman," and the door slammed firmly on the allegations.

From behind Samia, her mother commented, "You shouldn't be eavesdropping, ya Samia."

Smoothly, she whipped her scarf off the nail and rushed into the bathroom, "I'm just getting ready to get the bread, ya Mama." In record time, she was ready to dash down the stairs, hoping that Umm Mohammed would still be at the door, shaking her fist at the stairs leading up to Umm Saeed's apartment. This time when she opened the door, she took care to do it quietly and close it equally gently.

Soundlessly, she slipped down the stairs. Mohammed had managed to cajole his elderly mother inside by the time she reached the third-floor landing, so she ran the rest of the way down. Just as she was leaving the door of the building, she heard Umm Ossama calling, "Ya Samia? Ya Samia? Are you going for bread?" But she was on the ground floor and out the door before the neighbor could call a second time.

Happily, Samia rushed down the street to the interminable queue for bread. This morning, the time seemed to fly as she planned her future revenge on the rest of her neighbors, and as the weeks passed, Umm Ossama suffered from trashcans ostensibly tipped over by cats and rarely seemed to be able to catch Samia on her way to get bread. Umm Saeed endured a flurry of pumpkin seed shells and an occasional cup of dirty water. The next-door neighbors were bothered by predawn tapping and scratching on the walls and sporadically found the dregs of a sugary cup of tea flung against their door.

#

Her secondary school exams came and went. Then dawned the day of the results. Samia dressed carefully in her best skirt and blouse—she'd be seeing all her colleagues clustered around the school gate. She could barely stomach the cup of tea with milk that her mother pressed upon her. She knew it had been hard for her mother and father to send her to school, and if she failed this year, she doubted that she'd have the chance to try again next year. Both her brothers had dropped out during secondary school, so if she managed to pass, she'd be the first in her family to get a secondary school certificate.

"May God be with you, ya Samia!" her parents called after her as she left the apartment. And much to her surprise, she heard doors opening throughout the building and the voices of all her neighbors echoing her parents' sentiment. "God be with you!" they all called.

#

They were all waiting for her to come back, too. But none appeared until they heard Samia's mother's zaghareet. The shrill, ululating cries signaled success and brought a flock of neighbors down upon the small apartment. With the appearance of the first neighbor, Samia's mother thrust money into Samia's hand and told her to go buy the sharbat. The red, sugary drink meant celebration, and although Samia resented the fact that she had to go buy it herself, she flew down the stairs to get it. The shopkeeper greeted her with a hearty smile and genuine congratulations as soon as he heard her request. "You squeaked through, ya Samia? Mabrouk!"

"I did better than squeak through, ya 'Amm Farouk. I got eighty percent!" Samia declared proudly.

"Mabrouk! Mabrouk!"

All day, the door of the small apartment hardly seemed to close for all the well-wishers. At the end of the day, Samia felt flushed with pride and served sharbat without a twinge of possessiveness. As she closed the door on the last guest, her mother said, "I wonder where Umm Ossama is today. She didn't come to congratulate you. She never neglects her social obligations."

"She never neglects a chance to drink a glass of sharbat at someone else's expense, you mean," Samia muttered under her breath, making sure her back was turned so that her mother couldn't hear. As she brought the last tray of cups into the kitchen, a smart rap came at the door.

Her mother swung open the door to find Umm Ossama beaming on the doorstep, carrying a white box tied with a pink ribbon bearing the name of the local dessert shop. She and her whole brood—Mostafa, Ossama, Basma, Fayza and Amira—swept into the room. Basma and Fayza, the two eldest girls, were leading a tall, slim young man who seemed to be in the throes of acute embarrassment. He clutched in his hand a bouquet of fragrant, pink roses. Umm Ossama engulfed Samia in a sweaty embrace, kissing her moistly on either cheek. "Mabrouk, ya habibti! You've made us proud, my dear," she exclaimed. "My nephew Omar was here visiting, and when he heard that you'd passed, he insisted on coming to congratulate you." She grasped the young man by his arm and thrust him forward to shake Samia's hand. He proffered his flowers with his handshake, keeping his eyes firmly downcast. "Mabrouk, Miss Samia." Samia was speechless. She had never been given flowers before. She knew instinctively that this was her first 'areess ... a potential bridegroom come to look her over. Her friends had already had them by the dozen, but her mother had always said that she should wait until she finished school. She couldn't believe her luck ... this young man didn't look like anyone she had expected Umm Ossama to be related to.

In a flurry of visits back and forth, gifts given, gifts received, Samia and Omar got to know each other and agreed to marry. For Samia, Omar was a catch; he was educated, owned his own apartment, held a job, and wasn't asking for anything much from the bride's parents. He was certainly a much better prospective husband than either of her brothers, which was the usual standard by which one judged a 'arees. And to top it all off, Samia genuinely liked him; he was a mature twenty-four to her eighteen years. He treated her like a princess and brought gifts and small tokens of affection every time he came to call. And he always seemed to feel when he might be on the edge of imposing and would swerve to avoid potential pitfalls: jumping up at the noon-time call to prayer to avoid being invited to lunch; never answering her calls on his mobile, rejecting them and calling her back to avoid costing her money; and even insisting on paying her bus fare when they parted ways after a day together. Slowly, the poison that had eaten away at Samia seemed to drain out of her. She stopped punishing Umm Ossama for her transgressions as soon as she became engaged to Omar and even began to forget about her grievances against Umm Saeed and Umm Mohammed.

#

The evening of her henna party found Samia glowing and hospitable, greeting her guests with grace and genuine pleasure. Her family had erected a colorful tent in the street and set up a sound system to provide the atmosphere for the bride's party the night before the wedding. The beat of popular Arabic music echoed against the endless stretch of buildings on either side of the narrow road. Some young men had set themselves up as ushers at the beginning of the street and were herding cars down a side street. Samia's youngest, prettiest aunt had tied a scarf around her hips to fashion a low-slung belly dancer belt over her purple and gold galabiyya and carried on her head a dish of henna and karkaday mixed into a fine red paste. She handed out globs of it to any of the women who wanted to rub it into their palms. The younger girls were busily drawing patterns on their hands and feet with the stylish new henna that they had purchased and which could be applied in finer detail. Some were better than others at achieving a pretty, flowery pattern that would last for weeks. Samia had had the intricate designs applied on her legs and arms and even her belly earlier in the day in preparation for the wedding night. Her stomach fluttered and her cheeks flushed as she surveyed her party … all these people had come to celebrate with her.

Endless bottles of Coca-Cola and orange Mirinda circulated among the noisy crowd. Everyone seemed to be laughing and dancing. Samia was surrounded by her girlfriends and they were dancing like they never would again; once a girl was married, more decorum was expected from her, but tonight Samia could dance to her heart's content. She whirled and whirled around the tent with one of her friends, only stopping when they bumped into a table at which Umm Saeed was seated. Samia was just about to apologize to a beaming Umm Saeed for her clumsiness when Umm Mohammed stumbled up to the table and leaned over to put her face into Umm Saeed's. "Not going to spoil the night with a bucket of mop water? Or maybe you'll wait until you've drunk their sharbat before you sneak away to pour your filth upon us."

Umm Saeed pushed her chair away from the table, knocking it over. She looked around the tent and spotted Mohammed just outside, looking too aghast for words. "Come help your crazy mother home, ya Mohammed. You should know better than to bring her out in public."

At that, she whirled away from Umm Mohammed and went to seek out friendlier company. Samia was horrified by the display of rancor at her party, but Mohammed stepped in smoothly and escorted his mother out of the tent; she muttered and staggered through the crowd.

Samia's mother had come through the press of people as soon as she heard the murmurs of discontent, but she was too late to smooth over any of the unpleasantness. Instead, Samia grabbed her by the arm and hissed, "Can you believe that old woman? Why would she make such a scene at my henna?"

Samia's mother shook her head, "Be more charitable, ya Samia. She hasn't been right since Mohammed's work was spoiled. She blames it all on Umm Saeed and her mop water."

"What's the big fuss about? Couldn't he just copy it over and be done with it? Just a few pieces of paper," Samia dismissed the old woman.

"It wasn't his work. He had sent his research to some big center to do something called statistics. It cost a lot of money—all that Umm Mohammed had saved up. The information they sent him was so badly damaged that he couldn't read it, and he will have to have it done again. She doesn't have the money to pay for it, and she blames Umm Saeed for the whole thing," her mother explained.

For a second, Samia felt a twinge of regret. But then her circle of friends came and engulfed her again in the swirl of celebration.

#

The strings of colored lights hanging down the building façade lent the apartment a carnival aspect. The blinking lights and the high-pitched hum of the generator marked the building as the bride's house. Samia sat in front of a mirror held by one of her friends as another one arranged her veil. She was almost ready to make her triumphant march down the stairwell of the building to meet her husband and start her new life. Another friend helped her put the final touches on her makeup to the sound of Samia's mother's zaghareet, which were echoed throughout the building by the neighbors. Samia could hardly believe how the world rang with her joy as she gazed in wonder at her reflection in the mirror. She had never felt so elated, knowing that all her friends, relatives, and neighbors were waiting for her to make her descent through the wonderland atmosphere of the blinking lights, punctuated by the joyful sound of ululations.

She stood up and turned in front of the mirror, smoothing her white, frothy dress and primping her flowing veil. "The groom is here!" A chorus announced Omar's arrival at the door of the building. After a final touch-up to her makeup and a last pat to her hair, Samia's mother escorted her to the door of the apartment. Her brothers, father, and all her relations had crowded onto the narrow landing to wish her well. Samia, dressed as a bride, but still a young girl at heart, could not resist the temptation to peer down the stairwell at her husband – just as she had always done when shouting down to a girlfriend or up to a neighbor. There in the well of the stairs, stood the handsome man she could now call her husband. She could hardly suppress her grin of delight. Just as she was turning away from the balustrade, she heard a scream that immediately silenced the zaghareet in the house. One of her aunts grabbed her by the arm and pulled her back into the apartment while her brothers sprinted down the stairs.

After a long painful moment of waiting, the news came up the stairs. Umm Saeed had met Umm Mohammed in front of her door and as she tried to hurry past her, the old woman had grabbed her arm. When Umm Saeed whirled out of her grasp, Umm Mohammed had tumbled down the steep stairs. Samia rushed to the stairwell, peering down again to see her brothers escorting a weeping Umm Saeed up the stairs that had been cleared for Samia's triumphant descent. She heard someone behind her say, "The poor woman. She can't possibly survive that fall." And then the exodus began. All the women seemed to be rushing down to see what had happened to Umm Mohammed or to help Umm Saeed. A voice was shouting that a doctor had to be found. The whole building was in a flurry of activity. But Samia was more still than she had ever been in her life. Her moment of glory gone, she could not help grasping for it. "Mother, what about me? What about the wedding?"

A scream rose from the apartment downstairs.

Samia's mother said, "I'm afraid the poor woman is gone. Poor Mohammed."

"Poor Mohammed! What about poor me? My wedding has been ruined!"

"We can't have a wedding with a death in the house. Omar will understand. It's just not done. It would be so inconsiderate, ya Samia. I have to go see about Umm Mohammed." She swept down the stairs, leaving Samia to her friends in an island of silence, the carnival lights still blinking in counterpoint to the screams of death.

#

TURBULENCE

From: Mariam Shouman
To: Fatima ElKalay, Aida Nasr
Subject:
Sent: Oct 7, 2012 at 10:41 PM
Dearest Fatima and Aida,

I'm so sorry it's been so long since I've written and now I'm writing with bad news. Please excuse any errors as I'm typing from Sarah's iPad.

On Wednesday I was diagnosed with a brain tumor. The radiologist is hopeful that it is benign and it is largely asymptomatic, but I am of course worried. I am waiting for a neurosurgery appointment as they say it must be removed. Please pray for me. I love you both.

In terms of our project, I would really like to see this book in print. A friend of mine has published two of his own books through his own company and Amazon and is interested in helping us … What do you guys think? I want to see it in print!

Hope you both are well. Hugs and love!

Mariam

From: Fatima ElKalay
To: Mariam Shouman, Aida Nasr
Subject: Re:
Sent: Oct 7, 2012 at 10:55 PM

Mariam habibti,

I'm so sorry I was jovial on FB. Insha' Allah it will be fine. We will be praying for you hard. How are you feeling at the moment? Insha' Allah kheir ya Rab.

I think your health is the most important issue right now, but if you feel you want to go ahead with the project publication, let's see what

Aida thinks. We will need to do some revision, perhaps, and then move ahead.

When must you operate? Alf alf alf salama. I will be praying for you … I love you too, take care of yourself habibti.

Love,

Fatima xxx

From: Aida Nasr
To: Mariam Shouman, Fatima ElKalay
Subject: Re:
Sent: Oct 7, 2012 at 5:28 AM

Dearest Mariam,

I am so sorry to hear about this. Kheir insha' Allah. We love you and are praying for you …

About our project, I am willing to consider self-publishing if you both want to. I agree with Fatima that your health is the most important thing right now, but if you want to proceed, I think we each just need to do any final revisions that we want on our stories and then unify all the Arabic words according to the system you sent. So, we are really almost there. Just let me know how you want to move forward.

Love and hugs,

Aida

From: Fatima ElKalay
To: Aida Nasr
Subject: Re: Video for Mariam
Sent: Nov 14, 2012 at 6:39 PM

Dearest Aida,

I am sorry I have been out of touch. You're right; Mariam's news has been overwhelming. I can't stop thinking about her. I am sorry I haven't sent the list of words yet; I need to just go over them one last time to make sure I have everything down. I just haven't been able to do that lately. It isn't that I have given up on the stories. I think I needed a small break, and now I will resume.

On the other hand, I am trying to think of something beautiful to make Mariam. I am thinking perhaps an artistic calendar for 2013, or a note book/planner. Would either of these be too painful or too insensitive … If she felt it was specially made for her, would that make a difference? I don't know. The one thing no one has been able to convey is what Mariam is feeling inside. She hasn't talked about that, and no one has asked or can ask. It is so heartbreaking …

Lots of love,

Fatima xxxx

From: Aida Nasr
To: Fatima ElKalay
Subject: Mariam
Sent: Nov 14, 2012 at 8:52 PM

Dear Fatima,

So good to hear from you. And now we have Trish's latest e-mail, and I find myself wondering: why is this happening? There must be a reason and there must be good that's going to come out of this, insha' Allah. We just don't know what it is yet. I think it was the smartest thing for Mariam to tell all her friends and put them on one e-mail list. It has created a powerful web of prayers and love. Connected us all somehow, and I feel like each one of us has been blessed and will be positively affected by the whole situation. Today I was walking home from an appointment and was grateful just to be able to walk. You're right, we don't know what is in Mariam's heart at this time. I was thinking when I got your e-mail that maybe it's a blessing Mariam is not fully awake yet. Maybe this is God's way of helping her deal with this emotionally, by letting her wake up gradually and have brief periods of clarity when she faces her situation little by little, until she is stronger.

… Don't worry about the Arabic word list. Finish it when you're ready. We're making good progress. I have great faith we'll get this published at the right time, when it's meant to be.

Love,

Aida xxx

From: Fatima ElKalay
To: Aida Nasr
Subject: Short stories
Sent: January 2, 2013 at 1:13 PM

Dear Aida,

Thanks so much for the motivational email! I have been promising myself that I won't let this year pass by without utilizing my time and energy more productively, and I'm working one day at a time, but it's hard staying motivated! Why is that? I'm sure it is not a unique thing, which is why writers should stick together, to prop each other up, and infect each other with their inspiration …

I finally wrote to Trish on the side and told her to tell Mariam we are working on putting together a manuscript and seeking agents. I am sure Trish will get back to me with Mariam's reactions. Okay, let's meet soon, insha' Allah, and please do keep writing! There are stories to be told!

Love,

Fatima xxxx

From: Aida Nasr
To: Fatima ElKalay
Subject: Re: feedback for your stories
Sent: Mar 20, 2013 at 02:50 PM

Dear Fatima,

Thank you very much for these. Your comments are very helpful and I will start right away working on revisions. It's so nice to get your opinion on my stories—it gives me a wider perspective of them. Thanks for taking the time to give me such detailed comments. I'm sorry you have been tired lately. I hope you feel better.

I am so glad I was able to get these two stories done, although I am stuck on the next one. I've started it, but it's not really going anywhere just yet, so I may alter or abandon it for something altogether new.

I was so glad to hear of Mariam's walking progress from Trish and also that she has been on Facebook. That is wonderful. I've had a backache these past 2 days, and it's made me realize how much we take for granted in terms of mobility. I really feel for Mariam with her long road to recovery …

Love,

Aida Nasr xxxx

From: Fatima ElKalay
To: Aida Nasr
Subject: Re: Feedback for your stories
Sent: Mar 20, 2013 at 11:56 AM

Dearest Aida,

Salamtek, please look after yourself! I hope you are getting the right kind of rest for your back pain. By that I mean lying/sitting in a position that will make things better.

Love and hugs xxx

From: Aida Nasr
To: Fatima ElKalay
Subject: Re: Feedback for your stories
Sent: Mar 20, 2013 at 1:04 PM

Dear Fatima,

Thank you, the pain is a bit better today, so I think it will just take its time to go away insha' Allah. I am trying to be careful about positions, yes.

Take care, love,

Aida xxx

I DON'T DESERVE A DURRA

by Fatima ElKalay

The apartment building overlooks a small, square garden, wild with weeds and sprawling basil and rosebushes with more thorns than roses. A long hose, like a green serpent, sleeps in the soggy mud and dribbles water into the grass shoots. The dirty water slithers all the way to the entrance and threatens to stain every pair of shoes that dares to cross the threshold. On the front steps of the building, the bawab's daughter lounges, casually picking nits from a toddler's head. The bawab himself dozes behind her, his head lolling to one side, his snores resounding in the early evening air. The young woman sits up reluctantly when she sees us coming, perhaps irritated that she is required to interrupt her nit-picking to see who is entering the building.

"Assalamu 'alaikum," we say.

She peers at us as we approach, suspicious of me, a stranger to this place. To him, she gives a nod of recognition before returning the greeting.

"Wa 'alaikum assalam."

I don't take his hand on the way up. One hand holds the gift, silver-wrapped and slippery; the other hand, the one that holds the memory of the slap I gave him a year ago, clutches the wooden banister. It is rough and splintered, not like the fine alabaster of my own banister, so I touch it with caution or the splinters will hurt my hand and snag my satin shirtsleeve. From the corner of his eye, he watches me and smiles.

"You see? I didn't choose a better home for her."

We stand outside her door, dark wood, fortified with a curling barrier of wrought iron. He puts his hand on my shoulder.

"Ready?"

Is a woman ever? Suspicion, clues, the ugly confrontation, the rage and empty threats, the numb resignation, and I am still not ready for this moment.

I look him in the eye and nod.

"Of course I'm ready."

He presses the doorbell three times slowly, followed by twice in quick succession. A new tune for a new life. To me it is a hollow sound, haunting and mournful. Then he stands in full view of the door, not politely to one side, the custom when visiting a stranger.

Only this is no stranger.

In a moment comes a clatter of heels across a bare wooden floor.

And there she is.

She gives a toothy smile that swallows up a small, pointy face. It is a face weighed down by the burden of a large, boney nose. Much darker than I expected. Her hair is pulled back and oiled, in a poor attempt to disguise kinks. Nothing remarkable there, except perhaps the eyes. Twinkling amber. Thick lashes. Smooth eyebrows penciled with kohl. My eyes glance quickly at the rest of her before returning to the face: heavy bust, made heavier by a short, tight-fitting shirt that ties to one side like a kimono; thighs, round and bulging, stuffed into stretchy black pants that end abruptly above ridiculously skinny ankles. It is a repulsive sight, like seeing giant chicken drumsticks in leggings. Is this what I have been fighting all these years?

But she smells nice. My taste in French perfume, probably bought by him.

"Ya ahlan," she says, stepping aside to let us in.

The least polite way of saying welcome!

We walk down a passage with brown walls, so dark it could be underground. Nothing like my own shades of brown—not warm chestnut, or bronze, or the many threads of gold and copper in a fine sirma tapestry. This is an unclean brown. Like a stain in a toilet bowl. Even the protruding appliqués give off murky light. It could be the entrance to a dungeon.

I have the sudden urge to run out screaming. What am I doing here when I am number one?

First on his wish list. First on paper. First in bed. Mother of sons. And daughters. I make perfect syrupy bassbousa and creamy béchamel sauce. I roll my vine leaves thinner than my little finger. I'm not clumsy with words. I can keep a conversation going for as long as it takes to oven-roast a turkey. Most importantly, I'm beautiful. I have chiseled cheekbones and pale ivory skin. I look elegant in shimmering burgundy and blue. I have perfectly aligned teeth. My hair is naturally straight, like tumbling silk. You can't put a hairpin in it and expect it to stay in place for more than three minutes. Friends tell me I am too slender to have mothered four. I have no stretch marks, no spider veins, no wrinkles. No flab.

But number two came along anyway. The durra steals the show. And just look at her, with her rabbit-like overbite and her drumstick thighs. Look how dark and frizzy she is, overweight and overrated, and oh, so much older than I expected!

Now I am standing in her salon, and in a moment, she will offer me tea.

I hand her the present and her toothy smile gets bigger.

" A gift! Oh, you shouldn't have, really, really shouldn't—"

"It's nothing actually…"

That is both true and untrue. It's worth at least five hundred pounds, but I didn't buy it; it was a hideous gift from an old aunt, all twisted and gnarly, rather like Auntie's knuckles. Not my style.

"I chose it myself."

She rips at the wrapping paper, slowly at first, then faster, like an excited child.

"Ah! A candelabra! Now won't you tell me where to put it? Won't you please?"

I can think of a very nice place for it, but it wouldn't be polite to say.

"I would say the dining table if there isn't much going on over there."

I glance at the table. Indeed, there is a great deal going on. The legs and chair backs are a monstrosity of carved ghouls and gargoyles, entangled so severely that you can hardly tell whether they are in battle or procreating. I think of my own dining table, smooth rosewood, straight-backed chairs. What a blessing it is to have good taste.

Her tabletop is partially covered with a sequined, sandy-beige cloth, purposely crumpled in many places to form a strange array of dunes and valleys. In the center, a huge crystal bowl spills dusty plastic ivy onto the table. Around it sit three small ceramic dishes, filled with shriveled nuts and dried fruit.

"I will make room for it!" She clatters excitedly across the wooden floor and clears the crystal bowl out of the way. It scrapes harshly across the surface.

"Careful, dear."

Careful, dear. Is that the best he can do? How ridiculous! She has probably damaged the wood. He rubs his nose with his forefinger and it turns pink, then opens his mouth to say something else, but nothing comes out.

What a change from the man who was such an expert at putting me down. Like the time I pronounced esophagus wrong in front of his colleagues. Or the time I tripped with the teapot when we had friends over. Never mind being scalded by tea, or the embarrassment of landing in a pile on the floor, or the broken china, I had to get a proper lecture. Everyone left in a hurry. Even while I stood in front of a mirror wiping away the muck of mascara and tears spattered down my cheeks, he wouldn't stop.

"You're the clumsiest creature I've ever seen. A woman should be graceful with her movements. She should glide as though on ice and dodge every obstacle."

The things I put up with. And just look at him now, lowering his standards to accommodate someone who clatters around like an angry flamenco dancer and moves objects with the grace of an elephant. To think I was nervous coming here. Now I just feel insulted having to be on equal footing with this woman.

"You may have scarred your fine wooden table dragging that crystal bowl across it."

The comment is mine. I look toward him; he is shifting uneasily in his chair. Then he throws in a suggestion.

"My dear, aren't you going to offer us anything to drink?"

She leaves the candelabra lopsided amidst the folds of fabric and looks awkwardly from him to me.

"Would you like some tea?"

I need tea. I briefly wonder if she might try to poison me.

"I'd love some, as long as you have fresh mint," I say.

And hold the arsenic, please.

She pats her hair and throws her hands in the air.

"No mint, I'm afraid."

"That's very odd. Samy can't possibly drink his tea without mint, can you, habibi?"

Samy's nose is now as red as raw saucisse.

"Tea is great with mint, but I can do without. How about a few cardamom pods, Gulf-style, ladies?"

Gulf-style? Now that's new. Very new, and very unlike my Samy. Ten years of marriage, one year as his fiancée, and three as his next-door neighbor, and he only ever drank tea with mint.

"Oh, plenty of cardamom pods in this household."

She lets off a high-pitched laugh that sounds like a police siren.

"What's a chicken without cardamom?" she asks with a shrug. "That's what my mother says, but I wouldn't know."

I gasp in exaggerated shock.

"What! You don't cook?"

Samy gets out of his seat and walks to the dining table to fiddle with the candelabra. He tries to find it a more elegant position. It almost comes crashing down onto the ceramic dishes, but he catches it in time.

She looks at me with genuine surprise.

"I work. I'm a doctor, remember. I have no time for the kitchen."

"You should learn. This is Egypt. Your husband is Egyptian. A woman without culinary talents is not worth much in the eyes of her husband. And in society she has little esteem. She is as worthless as … a chicken without cardamom."

I sound more like a mother-in-law than a durra.

She rolls her eyes and points her boney nose upwards, as if balancing a circus ball.

"Oh, I had no idea you were so old-fashioned! Times have changed, habibti. I don't suppose you know much about this, but when I was in Oxford, I did none of that. You just don't waste time in the kitchen. Of course, I can't expect a typical Egyptian housewife to understand."

Damn her! Of course she would have to bring up Oxford. Samy always complained that it took me forever to get a commerce diploma from a second-rate Egyptian institute that taught everything in Arabic. Worthless, he called it. He always resented the fact that I didn't speak much English, as if the language you spoke made you more or less of a woman.

"How does being an Oxford graduate prevent you from making a good home-cooked meal for your husband?"

I already know what her answer will be, but it is my hope that she will dig herself a hole and topple into it.

"Habibti, I don't know what you know about doctors. We're professionals who have no time for the humiliation of frying onions and stuffing peppers. Our talents are out there in operating theaters, saving lives, and we are extremely well paid for it. We can afford the best cooks and restaurants Egypt has to offer. The finest cuisine minus the eggplant stains on the fingertips or the stink of garlic."

She smiles lovingly at her fingers.

"Then I suppose you eat alone? Samy is very health conscious and won't eat any of that precooked, chicken-cube-enriched rubbish they offer in restaurants, and he never touches food made by the cook. It has to be lovingly made by his wife. No wonder he's shed so much weight since the wedding!"

Now let's see her beat that one!

"Actually, Samy has lost weight because he's been working out! He needs to stay fit, to keep up with me, isn't that so, Simsim darling?"

Simsim doesn't answer because he is halfway to the kitchen. He mutters something about making his own tea. She follows him with a clack-clack, and an exchange of low-toned, stressed syllables soon dribbles into the hall.

Should I offer a hand? Probably not. Whether I like it or not, this is a private moment between a husband and wife. In a few minutes he returns, flops down in the armchair next to me, and picks at his nails. I do not ask him what the matter is. When he says nothing, I ask about something else.

"What's this cumbersome furniture, darling? For an Oxford grad she has incredibly ugly taste."

He swings round to face me, his eyes moist, perhaps with sweat, or maybe tears? It's hard to tell with men since they don't wear mascara. It's strangely satisfying to see him look so helpless.

"Darling, please! What's wrong with you! Did you come here to insult her? I thought you were calling for a truce, a chance to become friends, since you now have something in common. Isn't that why you agreed to meet her?"

"Something in common?" I sneer, "People in offices share cubicles and hate each other's guts, Simsim."

I stand up and walk toward the corridor that leads to the inner rooms.

"I'm not a cubicle. Besides, even though you do share me, you each get a generous portion on your own, don't you? Habibti, I've told you endlessly that a man is different; he can love more than one woman in one breath."

"Then he loves neither. He loves only himself and how these women feed his ego. Habibi, I've told you endlessly, this is all a very selfish quest. It's not about love. And it's not as though you wanted to give an old spinster a better life. If you really wanted to do this as an act of charity, why didn't you pick a poor widow with a trail of hungry orphans who need a daddy? You could have contacted your local mosque for one if you wanted."

He sighs.

"Yes, yes, I know the old widow argument, but no one ever actually marries a second or a third for … humanitarian reasons. You know full well my dear that men aren't too fond of extra responsibility."

"Yes, I know—just overly fond of abusing their license for polygamy and twisting religion to suit their whims."

I glance into the kitchen before walking across the corridor. She is standing in front of the electric kettle, engrossed in the simple task of boiling water, and does not see us. I pause before my next words, wondering if there is any point in repeating what he must be tired of hearing.

"Samy, this can't be about finding your soul mate. You said I was that from day one. I completed you, remember?"

I clutch the soft folds of my shirtsleeve.

"There should be no need to add another woman then."

The corridor here is even darker than the entrance.

"You know what I think? I think having a second wife is a pleasing pastime for a man, like an evening of backgammon with a few rounds of coffee and a hookah. It's just a bit of entertainment, not even a serious one."

He doesn't like the things I'm saying. Or the fact that I am about to explore their apartment. But he doesn't try to stop me. He follows me down the narrow corridor and resumes rubbing his nose. He speaks in angry whispers.

"We are not here to psychoanalyze me. The point is you aren't being nice to her. I will not allow you to mock my wife this way! She is very upset!"

We have reached a square, dimly lit room with stodgy blue-black sofas and a sprawling ebony bookcase with an ancient TV set and DVD player from his old clinic. The bookcase is stuffed with a jumble of volumes and crumpled magazines next to dirty statues of glum angels behind a glass panel. Refugees from her mother's house, no doubt.

"Your wife? How perfect! Then who the hell am I? And shouldn't I be a little, just a little pissed off that she stole my husband? Showing off with her stupid Oxford degree, as if that makes it okay. What an obnoxious bitch!"

In the kitchen, I hear her muttering and rummaging for things. There is the sound of toppling plates and cutlery.

"Don't you ever call her that! She's not showing off; she's just incredibly nervous and you're intimidating her. You don't understand that in many ways she is in a weaker position."

He softens his eyes, his features overcome with familiar tenderness. He reaches out to pat my hand.

"You are habibti, as dear to me as a first-born. She's just a new recruit. She hardly knows her way around. Think how hard it must be for her. And as for stealing me, she didn't do that. I'm still here, right?"

He grabs me by the waist and draws me to him. His hands are clammy, and I worry that they'll crumple my shirt.

"Baby, please try to understand, though I know you never will. Men are mysterious creatures. We can't stand alone. We need more than one woman to feel … complete. I mean, take that teapot she's having problems with in there. What use would it be without cups? It wouldn't be much of a tea set if it didn't have enough cups. That's what we men are, teapots looking for our cups. It's a torturous thing, really, a curse sometimes, but that's the way God made us."

Teapots … teacups. What a stupid analogy! I wriggle loose from his clutch and wander further down the hall to a small empty room with grubby windows. It overlooks a squat building with a roof boasting a great convolution of antennas, television wires, and satellite dishes. A dark-gold rooster is hopping carefully in the empty spaces, trying to reach a run-down, plywood coop in the far corner. The hens inside cluck fitfully, awaiting his return.

"Am I supposed to feel better now? Tell me this, dear Simsim, how does that thing in there, struggling to make us a pot of tea and trotting her noisy hooves all over the place, make you feel complete? I can see nothing, nothing in her that makes her worth breaking my heart. She's certainly not a matching piece to your tea set, is she?"

He doesn't reply.

"Did you just need a salty pickle to make you appreciate your sweet cake? Or is it that I've put up with too much and been just too damn perfect that you've taken me for granted? You know, and I know, that I don't deserve a durra."

He chuckles. I know that chuckle. He's letting me know he doesn't agree with me, but I'm not sure with which part. Maybe that she's a salty pickle. Or that I'm a sweet cake. Or that she has not, in some way, completed him. Our eyes meet and I see that he isn't angry. His nose isn't red. He won't drown me beneath a deluge of insults.

A small bathroom is across from the empty room. It is, as expected, a pompous display of bulbous gold faucets, and overdone decor. An old mirror has a gothic frame. A shelf is cluttered with an assortment of shriveled soaps in many shapes and colors. There are shells and petrified crabs and little beach pebbles on a plastic tray on the bathroom floor. An upright basket stands next to the toilet bowl, holding magazines and a cordless phone. A towel rack is in one corner and a huge plastic fern in another. There really isn't much room to maneuver in this bathroom; one false move and you are sure to crash into something. Not designed for the clumsy.

Further down the hall, we reach the final room in the house. It must be their bedroom. He seems reluctant to let me in.

"What have you got to hide in there? More ugly furniture, or did you forget to put away your underwear? Open up and let me see."

I give him a playful push. He moves aside, and I fling the door open. I am taken aback. It is a massive room, bigger than the salon and dining area put together. French windows take up most of the left wall, their curtains like gossamer. A bed, almost semi-circular, curls against the back wall, its bedspread a giant satin lily with pink-white petals. But it is not just the size that is shocking. There is something else. The atmosphere is mesmerizing, like a fairytale. Tiny heart-shaped candles flicker in every corner. The room smells of Arabian jasmine. The wallpaper shimmers with the changing moods of opal: fiery-white, jade-blue, purple-pink. A white chaise longue sits beneath one French window, a dressing table on tapered legs to its side. The rest of the space is bare, save for a plump white Angora rug, stretched across a floor so polished, it reflects the room with the quiet stillness of the Nile in a nineteenth-century painting.

"My, this is … impressive."

I can't think of anything to say, which is a good thing, for any words I might try to say would probably get stuck in my throat. I am stunned. It is like being in a different house, belonging to someone with very different taste. It is perhaps little wonder that he only chuckled when I tried to make my point about being a sweet cake. I won't let him know how hurt I feel at this moment.

"Come on, let's get back. She must have finished making the tea by now."

I walk unsteadily and think over my moves these past years. Why is it I put up with all this in the first place?

Love.

I love him in ways that make me ache. A boy from another world who became the boy next door. Tumbling bronze hair, a flirty glint in his eyes. Ambitious, but modest, bilingual, well-to-do. He was an impossible dream, so I could not believe my luck when his mother crossed the eight slabs of pavement between his building and ours and had a quiet cup of coffee with my mother one afternoon. Everything else fell magically into place, like a fairytale. Perhaps the children came too many too soon. Or perhaps it was my ignorance of languages. I wasn't stupid. I just didn't care much for formal education. But I was sophisticated and shrewd and certainly no social embarrassment. And I was everything to look at.

For a while, it seemed enough. But there was a growing agitation in his movements, like someone who had lost something, and would never be at peace until he found it. And he never let go of the little slips, things spilling or breaking, a stain on a tie or a loose button on a shirt. It's okay, I thought. He's just stressed. It's just work.

But all along I felt I was living on borrowed time. The fairytale was evaporating.

"You didn't make me a room like that."

"Like what? Oh, the bedroom. You never asked for one. Do you like it? I think it's a bit silly."

"No, you don't. You love it. You love everything about it. There's you in that room, and her. Both of you. Both of you are in that room, and you both love it."

She is suddenly standing in front of me, armed with a massive silver tray balanced on her protruding chest. I didn't hear her coming. I look down at her feet and see that she has taken off her noisy shoes and is wriggling darkly painted toes against the carpet pile. She looks so much shorter and fatter without heels.

"You sneaked up on us."

Slowly, she settles the tray on the coffee table and straightens, blinking.

"I wouldn't do that—that would be rude! I only took off my shoes because I was worried I would trip with this heavy tray. Samy, you must get me a trolley for when I have guests."

I sneer.

"You can always invite them out to all the fine restaurants in Cairo, as you mentioned. I'm sure you don't want to waste time and energy struggling to make a cup of tea and then risk tripping over a trolley and breaking your neck."

"Of course. I invite all my important guests out to dinner, but from time to time, insignificant people drop by, and I think a trolley is a lot easier to handle, and more presentable."

She pours the tea into china cups and searches the tray with her eyes for a teaspoon for the sugar bowl. She knows so little about being a hostess! Samy gets up to help. He stirs in the sugar and arranges dainty cream cakes in little serving plates.

"Then you can always buy your own trolley like a proper housewife. Samy has no time to go shopping for such trivialities. You know how busy he is."

"Ah yes, of course. I remember when we worked together at the same hospital. We were always so busy. Even our weekends were full.

It was … exhausting! But being with Samy made time fly, a little too quickly."

She attempts a lusty sigh. All I hear is a snort. Has she no shame, slithering into his life, intoxicating him with her cheap venom! The anger boils in my veins. I don't know who is in a weaker position right now, but I do know I'm not leaving this place without breaking her fangs.

"I know about that, my dear. Everybody knows! You were practically glued to my husband even though ophthalmology and cardiology have no business together. It stank all over the hospital. A girl has nothing if not a good reputation, after all. Didn't your mother teach you the proper etiquette for catching a man? You don't throw your hook for someone else's fish. You know what's being said, don't you? That Samy here is so noble for saving your name. Isn't that what this marriage is all about? Restoring your dignity? But for future reference, madam, the first person to turn against a girl with a compromised name is her noble knight. Don't delude yourself with promises of eternal love. Just wait until you hit a raw nerve with your beloved Simsim; he will shred you. And one last thing: this whole marriage is just a whim for my Samy. What else did you think? My husband would never leave me for a woman without charm or grace or physical beauty. You might be an Oxford grad, but your degrees and fancy job won't count for much once my Samy's done with you. Want to know why? Because you are a salty pickle, and Samy loves sweet cream cakes. Soft, white, and pleasing to the eye. And the palate. Unfortunately, habibti, you are none of these things."

She shrieks. A teacup slips from her hand and hits the edge of the coffee table, spilling scalding hot tea onto the carpet. It's a good thing the carpet has a dark pattern or the spill would have left a visible stain. The teacup handle has broken. It lies like a jagged tusk on the floor beside her foot. Samy's eyes pelt fury and confusion at me. She flops down on the carpet, weeping. Her feet are facing me, and I am relieved that the heels are smooth and without cracks.

Samy mops at the spilled tea and examines the broken teacup handle. Surprisingly, he leaves her to weep without consoling her. I get up and open the door to the apartment. He makes no move to follow me.

"That's right, cry. Cry as I have done for endless nights. You have a lot of catching up to do. You should have known what you were up against before you started."

I slam the door shut behind me and run down the stairs, catching the splinters of the banister in my palms, and snagging the whole length of my sleeve. From behind the closed door of the apartment, I can hear him calling out someone's name, but I can't make out whether it's hers or mine; the rooster from the neighbor's rooftop is crowing loudly amidst his clucking hens, and Samy's words are drowned to a whimper. I am crying now, my eyes a muddy blur of mascara and tears. But I don't fall, and I don't break any bones, and I don't die.

I reach the garden and stumble on the soggy hose in the grass. Muddy water spurts out onto my shoes and ankles and drenches the porter's daughter on the doorstep. She has finished picking nits from the toddler's sun-bleached hair and huffs at me, wiping off the dirt. I hurry away from this unclean place without tossing them an apology or a second glance or the handful of loose change that the poor expect from those who have everything.

#

She has no idea how hard this is for me. I did not choose to love a man who had a life—and a wife—of his own, but these things happen. When you are together for endless hours, the face across a desk becomes your mirror, where your deepest thoughts and feelings are reflected lovingly, honestly, and—ultimately—passionately. It is true she had him first, but what do I do if my heart did its rounds and finally settled on a married man? In the eyes of society coming second makes me less worthy. If only the world could see how I love him, perhaps they would give me a chance.

I sneaked her pictures from his wallet. Am I less attractive? He insists I'm not. There are other things besides fair skin and silky hair that make a woman irresistible, he says. He tells me that my eyes have a rare spark, enough to set a man's soul on fire. My laughter is bewitching, my wisdom intriguing. He tells me that I understand him in ways that scare him, as if I am more him than himself. He tells me that my insight and feeling are precious gems that no physical beauty can replace.

He says, "I see you with my heart and that gives you worth."

My eyes tear over, and I am conquered.

When we are together, he cannot take his eyes off me. He forgets to breathe.

"You make me feel complete," he says.

I plan for the visit carefully, but I am no grand hostess. I dress simply. Nothing extravagant. She has to know that he fell in love with a real person, not a dressed-up puppet. I do not go overboard with fancy canapés and gateaux. Simple cream cakes to reflect my taste and priorities. My greatest priority was to be the wife of the only man I could ever love. I wonder if she realizes the sacrifices I've made to be here, living on borrowed time, trying to build with my love for him, the foundations she has laid with years of marriage and the advantage of four children. She will never guess that this apartment was a rushed affair, the things I bought cheap from an uncle, hand-me down sofas re-stuffed, wooden pieces refurbished to look like decent seconds for the second wife. I made Samy promise not to tell, lest she think I was desperate. Well I was, in a way. Desperate that he might change his mind. Desperate that she would find out too soon and nip my dream in the bud. At least I have the room, our room, made with the love we have for each other. That is all we had time for. If she were to see it, she would know, instantly, that the bond that ties us is straight out of a fairytale, even if I am the frog and he the savior whose kiss turned me into a princess.

I look again at her pictures—the fairness of her skin, the long tumbling tresses, the slender figure. There is one with her in shimmering burgundy, at some sort of formal dinner. She is looking at him with adoration. He has his arm awkwardly around her. His elbow juts out stiffly. Perhaps he doesn't want to crease her dress. Or perhaps it's because they don't fit together, somehow. Yes, that's it. He didn't even want to have his picture taken with her.

I remember his words again, "You complete me." I am the missing piece of his being that she can never understand. Or adequately replace.

The clock ticks the minutes closer to their arrival. Their arrival together. Why is it they come as a couple to visit me, alone? Is that an omen? She will say things. Things to unnerve me and make me sound ridiculous. But that doesn't scare me. I am more experienced, more educated, while all she has ever learned from life is how to change diapers and cook molokhiyya and pose for the camera in the arms of a man who needs more. It's not fair, I don't deserve to be his second choice, when I am the one who completes what she, with all her physical beauty, has failed to do in all their years together.

I don't deserve a durra.

I hear his car pull up. I'm sure I have too much lipstick on. Perhaps my clothes are too sloppy. She will be hurtful, I know it. How rude should I be? Tit for tat, I suppose. But I must make sure she sees the bedroom—that will be the biggest slap. The doorbell rings. His special jingle.

But today it is a hollow sound, haunting and mournful.

#

BUTTERFLIES

by Aida Nasr

D olly's real name is Dawlet, and the grown-ups had something to say about that. "Dawlet is such an old-fashioned name for such a little girl," said one of the old ladies who came to tea. "We like it because it was her grandmother's name," answered Mama.

Dolly was glad Mama was there to explain. She wondered what made a name old or new and why it mattered.

"Mabrouk," said the ladies to Karim. They had brought a big box of chocolates to congratulate him on passing his exams. After the summer, he was going to university. "How you've grown!" one of the ladies told him. "You're old enough to be a groom now. Soon a girl will come and snatch you away."

Dolly's big brother smiled. His eyes were smiling too, but he looked like he wanted to roll them.

These ladies had a lot to say. That Dolly was so much younger than her brother; they seemed surprised she was there at all. That she looked so different from her brother. His hair and skin were the color of caramel candies. Dolly had loose black curls framing a pale face the color of Mama's china teacups on the silver tray.

Dolly's big brown eyes widened as they said these things right in front of her. She pretended to be busy with her coloring book. One lady asked how old she was. "Six," she answered, and they oohed and ahhed and talked to her in loud baby voices. They seemed to think she was stupid. She decided they must be stupid and went back to her coloring.

The ladies peered at the silver frames on the table in the salon, saying something about each one. Didn't Mama and Baba look really young in their wedding photo? Didn't Karim look just like his father?

Dolly wanted these ladies to leave. But she liked the way Mama looked right now in her pretty skirt and high heels as she served the ladies a fancy cake with whipped cream curls that she had brought home in a shiny red box. Dolly also loved it when Mama's real friends came over, and Mama wore blue jeans and shoes that looked like a ballerina's. Those friends laughed on the fat couches in the living room. They drank out of chunky mugs and ate sandwiches and the cake Mama baked that tasted like oranges. Mama never said silly things about people's names or hair.

As the old ladies chattered, Dolly decided that her favorite things in the world were Mama and Baba and Karim, her dolls, coloring, vinegar-flavored potato chips, and butterflies. She loved butterflies because of the necklace Mama always wore, a small, gold butterfly with lacy, sparkly wings. Attached to each wing was a thin, gold chain that went around Mama's neck.

Dolly didn't know much about real butterflies, but when she asked Karim, he showed her pictures in his schoolbook. Their beautiful wings reminded Dolly of Mama's pretty skirts and the dresses in Dolly's own wardrobe that she wore on special occasions. She wouldn't tell these ladies, though. They'd ask too many questions.

When the ladies finally left, Mama kicked off her shoes.

Then Karim said, "Come on, Nunu." Dolly's other family nickname meant "something very small." "I'll take you to get something from 'Amm Sayed."

He took her hand, and they walked down their street in Zamalek. She had to skip-run to keep up with his long, athletic strides. Going to 'Amm Sayed's with her brother was another of her favorite things, she decided. They reached the little kiosk shaded by a tree.

"Welcome, Lady Dawlet," said 'Amm Sayed, whose mouth didn't smile, although his eyes often did. He was wearing his usual gray galabiyya and a small white cap over his gray hair.

Dolly was immediately drawn to the shelf lined with boxes of small, colorful packets. Cookies, cakes, wafers. It seemed to her that 'Amm Sayed lived in a shiny, sugary wonderland. She knew she was allowed two things. (Mama's rule. Karim would buy her anything she wanted.) She chose potato chips and was standing on tip-toe deciding on something sweet, when out of the corner of her eye, Dolly noticed Karim smiling so his dimples showed. He was talking to someone.

She turned to see a girl in a tight t-shirt and jeans with dark, wavy hair running down her back. Who was this girl? Dolly could feel her cheeks getting hot and her throat tightening. Then a thought jumped into her head. Was Karim going to marry this girl? She knew he was twelve years older because people always said so. Did that make him big enough to marry? The tea ladies said he'd grown into a groom. She tried to imagine Karim and this girl in a wedding photo like her parents. Then she tried to imagine Karim wearing a suit like Baba's and leaving for work in the morning. What would he eat if he married this girl? Dolly doubted she could make macarona bel béchamel. She thought of Mama at her stove stirring thick, white sauce and pouring it on top of macaroni in a pan.

Dolly glanced at the girl talking in hushed tones to her brother. She'd probably only know how to make cheese sandwiches. If he married the wavy-haired girl, Karim would have to live on cheese sandwiches, Dolly decided, and he'd be in a bad mood. This girl wouldn't know how to say things to make him laugh when he was tired, like Mama did for Baba.

No, Dolly didn't like this one little bit. Choosing a random packet, she handed it to her brother with the potato chips.

"Yalla, ya Keemo! Let's go!" She used the nickname that embarrassed him in public. Maybe that would get rid of this girl. But no, her brother just smiled widely and reached into his back pocket to pay 'Amm Sayed.

Back at their apartment, Dolly was still worried. "I want to color in your room," she announced at her brother's door. Karim was sprawled on his bed listening to music with tiny headphones in his ears. He smiled and moved his feet over so she could sit at the end of his bed. As she colored, Dolly thought of the girl at the kiosk. She looked like a doll that Uncle Amr had given her, with big brown hair and pursed pink lips that were almost smiling. She'd have to find Karim someone else to marry. But how?

Dolly knew how her parents had met. "Baba's aunt invited us over for tea so we could get to know each other and see if we liked each other," Mama had explained.

"Did you like each other?" asked Dolly.

A pause. "After we met a few more times, we did," said Mama.

Dolly looked at her brother listening to his music. Which girl could she invite for tea? She couldn't think of anyone nice enough to marry him. She felt a slow panic rising and wondered what to do.

#

That evening Uncle Amr visited to talk to Baba. Her uncle seemed mad about something and was talking a little too loudly to Baba when Dolly heard him say, "—constant fighting and arguing … a bad atmosphere for everyone. I'm thinking of a divorce."

After he left, Mama said, "I can't believe it. They were so happy when they first met. Where's he going to go if he moves out?"

"He's looking for a place of his own," said Baba.

Dolly was quietly coloring, listening to her parents and watching them out of the corner of her eye.

Both parents went back to reading, and then Mama said suddenly, "Youssef, don't you think it's strange that we met in your aunt's salon, and we're still married while all these people who married for love are getting divorced?"

He looked at Mama over his newspaper like she was very far away. Dolly could suddenly see his dimples. They did make him look a lot like Karim.

"So, you're saying we don't love each other?" he said in a teasing voice that also reminded Dolly of her brother.

"Youssef! We love each other now. You know what I'm trying to say."

"No, I don't, because this isn't the cinema, habibti. It's real life. Sometimes love isn't enough. Amr's always been difficult and demanding like my father. He should have married a woman like my mother, who's good-natured and smart. Someone who's patient and strong. Not a woman who argues and complains all the time like Mayssa."

Dolly thought of her uncle's wife and her sugary, soft voice that almost whispered and her eyes that never smiled.

"But can you honestly say you were totally sure we were a good match before we got married?" asked Mama, in English.

To Dolly, "match" sounded like when she chose her clothes in the morning so they looked good together. Maybe the English was so she wouldn't understand? She did, mostly. From her cartoons, school, and listening to Karim and his friends, she understood English very well.

"Yes, because I saw in you a good, kind person who would be a good wife and mother. And we do get along pretty well, or don't you think so?" said Baba. His voice was gentle, but the way he said it meant, this talk is over. He went back to his newspaper.

"Yes, of course I think so," sighed Mama, picking up her book.

#

Tante Basma took a sip from her steaming mug in their living room. Dolly was serving her dolls imaginary tea from her dainty toy tea set.

Mama was saying, "Amr came over yesterday. He's thinking of a divorce. Isn't it strange how people who married for love don't stay happy?"

"Maybe they needed more than love," said Mama's best friend.

"Youssef said the same thing. It's strange how you two always have the same reaction to anything I tell you. But I hated the idea of a traditional marriage and being introduced to each other with our mothers there. Can you believe I almost didn't want to meet him again? I was so silly. I didn't like what he was wearing. And he talked and talked about himself."

Dolly thought this didn't sound like Baba at all. He wore really nice suits and never talked and talked.

Tante Basma laughed. "And you agreed to see him again because you really liked his mother. Good thing, too, since you lived here with her."

Dolly's ears perked up. This was who she was named after. She knew that her own bedroom used to be her grandmother's. It still had Teta Dawlet's fancy wardrobe, but Dolly's small, child's bed.

"And after a while, I really liked his sense of humor. And that he's a real man, capable of carrying the responsibility of a family."

When Mama said, "sense of humor," Dolly thought of Baba's dimples. She could understand why that would make her like him.

"It scares me to think I almost didn't go meet him, or see him again," said Mama, echoing Dolly's thoughts exactly.

"Well, you did, because it was meant to be," said Tante Basma very seriously. Then just as quickly, she became her usual self again. "Now where are those sandwiches of yours? I'm hungry."

When Mama went to the kitchen, Dolly asked, "Tante Basma, where did you meet Uncle Hassan?"

Tante Basma's eyebrows shot up. "At university, sweetie."

"When did you like him?"

"Pretty much right away," laughed Tante Basma.

"Why?"

"He was good looking and the funniest person I had ever met," she smiled. Tante Basma was the only person Dolly knew besides Karim who always smiled with both her mouth and her eyes.

Dolly thought about this. When Tante Basma and Uncle Hassan came over for dinner with her parents and she was supposed to be asleep, she could hear their laughter all the way from her bedroom.

"Is it good to be funny?" she asked.

"Definitely, habibti. You don't want to spend your life with someone damou sim". Dolly agreed that someone whose blood is poison wouldn't be funny at all.

#

Karim asked Dolly if she wanted to go to the kiosk again. She felt panicky inside. Would the girl be there? But Dolly coolly said yes. She had decided to give her another chance. Maybe she was really nice and funny under all that hair.

The girl stood with a little purse under her arm. As she talked to Karim, she seemed to be trying very hard to do something, Dolly couldn't figure out what. This girl made Dolly think of the ladies who came to tea. Not the way they looked, because they were old and had clumpy shoes that matched their big, square handbags. No, there was something about the way this girl smiled at Karim that irritated Dolly, just like the tea ladies made her mad. There was something behind their smiles that she couldn't understand.

When they got home, Dolly went to her room and hugged her doll and cried. She wasn't going to let that girl steal her brother, no way. She left the bag of vinegar potato chips unopened on her bedroom floor.

That evening, Uncle Amr came to talk to Baba again. Dolly had gone to put on her pajamas, and she was padding down the hallway in her pink slippers toward the living room to say good night, when she heard, "—I'm going through with it. I'm getting a divorce. I can't imagine living the rest of my life like this. There must be something better for all of us."

Lying in her bed that night, Dolly was scared. "Divorce" sounded to her like her uncle was going away somewhere—for good. Would Baba go away like Uncle Amr? What if Karim married that girl and she turned out to be a whispery, sugary person who made Karim sad and mad, and then he went away?

#

At the kiosk the following day, Dolly watched her brother talking to the girl and tried to figure out how to get him to leave. She interrupted him. She chose three things instead of two. She got mad on purpose when he said no. But he just gave in and bought them anyway.

Then 'Amm Sayed said, "Did you know, Lady Dawlet, that I knew your grandmother well? She used to bring your father and his brothers here, just like Karim brings you now. They chose your name well. You look just like her."

This last comment surprised Dolly so much that she forgot about the girl completely. Then she remembered her again.

"Yalla, ya Keemo!" she said, taking her brother's hand.

At home, Dolly went to find the black and white photo of Teta Dawlet in the salon. She liked this smiling, young woman in a twirly dress, with dark hair around her shoulders. She wondered what it would be like to wear a dress like that, with her hair down instead of in ponytails. She wondered what Teta Dawlet would do about Karim and that girl. Dolly went to find Baba.

"Baba, do I look like Teta Dawlet?"

"Yes, dear, you do."

"Did she like potato chips?"

Baba looked startled and then smiled so she could see his dimples. "I don't think so, habibti. I never saw her eat potato chips." He went back to the football game on television, but Dolly was still curious.

"What did she like to eat, then?"

He tore his eyes away from the game and thought about this. "She liked a piece of cake with her tea," he finally answered.

"And what did Grandpa like to eat?"

His smile vanished. "I don't know, dear."

"And where is Uncle Amr going?" she asked.

"He's not going anywhere, dear."

"I heard him say he's getting a divorce."

Now she had gotten his attention off the game completely. Baba switched off the television and took her hands. "That means Uncle Amr will go live in another apartment," he said carefully. "Tante Mayssa and the kids will stay in their same apartment. Uncle Amr loves his kids very much, and he'll see them on Fridays."

She put her hands on her hips. "And where are you going?"

"Nowhere, habibti. Your mother and I are very happy together. I love you all very much."

"Good," said Dolly, relieved. And then in her most serious voice, she said, "Because if you go anywhere, I'm not coloring you any more pictures."

She could see Baba's dimples again. "That's a deal, Dolly."

Later, she heard Baba say to Mama, "Dolly asked me about Amr's divorce today. She told me that if I ever go anywhere, she's not coloring me any more pictures."

Mama giggled.

Baba laughed too. "Sometimes I think she runs this house and everyone in it."

#

The next morning, Dolly insisted on wearing a white summer dress from her wardrobe instead of her usual jeans and t-shirt. She wanted to look like Teta Dawlet in the photo.

"Yes, why not?" said Mama, amused.

"Mama, where did you get that necklace?" She touched the gold butterfly as Mama clipped the sides of her hair in barrettes.

"Your Teta Dawlet gave it to me a few months before you were born. She used to wear it all the time."

"What was she like?"

"She was sweet like you and kind and funny like your father." A pause. Then Mama added, "Some ladies are not very nice to their son's wife." Dolly thought of the tea ladies, for some reason. "But Teta Dawlet was always good to me. When you get married, I hope your husband's mother will be as good to you, habibti."

Dolly immediately answered, "When Karim gets married, I hope his wife will be as nice as you, Mama."

Mama looked surprised and then laughed and gave Dolly a kiss. Dolly twirled around in her dress. Every day after that, she wanted to wear one.

#

On Friday, Uncle Amr came over with his three children for lunch, without their mother. The youngest cousin, a girl named Malak, played in Dolly's room.

"Would you like to come to a party at my house?" said Dolly's doll to Malak's doll.

"Oh yes, thank you very much," said Malak, in a high, doll voice. After a while, in her own voice she said, "I'm not going to call him "Papi" anymore. From now on, I'll call him Amr."

"Why?"

"Because he doesn't live with us anymore."

"But he loves you very much," said Dolly, repeating what Baba had told her.

"But he doesn't love Mama anymore, does he?" replied her cousin.

#

Karim took Dolly to the kiosk that afternoon. Her heart was beating fast, but the girl wasn't there. Dolly kept expecting her to show up, but no.

At their apartment, Dolly got up her courage and went to her brother's room.

"Keemo, where was the girl today?" she asked.

"I don't know," he answered casually. He added after a pause, "I'm not really seeing her anymore."

Dolly stared at him for a long time. "So you're not going to marry her?"

"Dawlet!" exploded Karim. "No, I'm not going to marry her. I'm only eighteen years old. I'm not going to marry anyone for a while!'

"When's that going to be then?" she persisted.

"I don't know," he said, exasperated.

"Well, when you do get married, I have to see the girl first. If I don't like her, you can't marry her," said Dolly with her hands on her hips.

"Dawlet, I know this is hard for you to believe, but I'm actually your older brother, twelve years older to be exact."

"I know that," said Dolly importantly.

"So that means that when you get married, I should be the one to approve of your husband, not the other way around."

Dolly thought about this and decided it was fair. "Okay, but I have to 'prove of your wife too. She should be able to make macarona bel béchamel."

"Dawlet! What does macarona have to do with anything?"

"What are you going to eat then, Keemo?"

He smiled and sighed.

"And she has to be funny. You don't want to spend your life with someone whose blood is poison, do you?" said Dolly using Tante Basma's expression.

Karim burst out laughing. "Dolly, where do you get all this stuff?" He did know she wasn't budging, though. "Okay, when I decide to get married, you can meet her and tell me if you approve or not." His voice was teasing.

"I mean it, Keemo! I didn't like that girl. She wasn't funny at all."

He paused in surprise and then had to agree, "No, you're right, Dolly, she wasn't funny. You win, as usual." He shook his head and smiled.

"I'm smaller than you, but I'm smart. Six is the best number!" said Dolly to her brother's laughter.

#

When Tante Basma came to see Mama again, Dolly met her at the door and gave her a kiss on each cheek.

"Nice dress, Dolly. You seem happy today," said Tante Basma.

Dolly skipped off to get one of her dolls and when she came back to the living room, Mama and Tante Basma were talking with mugs in their hands.

As she put a new dress on her doll, Dolly thought that when she grew up, she'd like to be kind and smart like Mama and funny like Tante Basma. She'd wear twirly dresses like Teta Dawlet with pretty shoes like a ballerina's. She'd never carry a little purse under her arm or a big, square one, either.

She'd like to have a living room with big, fat, pink couches and serve her friends orange juice out of mugs and huge bowls of potato chips. Mama could teach her how to make cakes and macarona bel béchamel. She wouldn't marry anyone unless he smiled with both his mouth and his eyes. What would he call her? Dolly, and Dawlet for special occasions, she decided. She wouldn't let him call her Nunu, since she wouldn't be small anymore, would she?

Dolly looked at Mama on the couch next to her friend and the butterfly sitting delicately at her throat. She wondered if Mama would give her the necklace to wear when she grew up. But no, she always wanted to see Mama wearing it. Instead, Dolly would ask her husband to buy her a ring with a sweet, gold butterfly sitting on top. Then he'd put the ring on her finger, and she'd hold out her hand for him to see the beautiful, sparkly butterfly that looked ready to fly away.

#

THE STAINS ON HER LIPS

by Mariam Shouman

The tall, brown girl seemed to swagger through the narrow village streets. Her black shugga wrapped her body, its edge draped over her head. Beneath it, the brilliant pink of her dress peeked through where her upraised arm emerged to balance the basin on her head. The black sheet-like garment accentuated her fine lines and graceful walk. No one could resist the temptation to rest their eyes on her if even just for the barest moment. Even the women were drawn to her, seeming to hunger for a look. A tomato vendor left off bellowing the virtues of his wares to nod at her. A fishwife stopped whisking the flies away from her basket of fish to hail her, smiling and inquiring after her mother's health, "Ya Touta, you light the world with your presence!"

Instinctively, Touta adjusted the burden on her head to keep it balanced. Adding to her perfect grace and charisma, she seemed completely unaware of all the attention, taking it all for good will and neighborliness. With a genuine smile, "May God always bring you light!" she called out to the wizened little woman squatting over her fly-ridden fish.

Her path to the riverside ran through the village and no one who saw her on her way neglected to greet her, if only with their eyes. As she made her way to the river, she sang a song to herself. It was a bright little tune of spring and love, and it lightened her heart and her burden.

The large aluminum tisht on her head was stacked with dirty dishes from the past day's meals and today's breakfast. She was taking them down to the spot on the Nile where the women gathered every day to scrub their pots and exchange gossip to lighten the day's work. She was the only unmarried girl who was assigned the task, but her mother was elderly and sickly, and her sisters all married with their own stacks of dishes to wash, so it fell to her. Her mother ignored no opportunity to bewail her fate, but nothing could change it. The dishes had to be washed, and no one else was going to wash them. Still she fretted over her youngest daughter, the flower of the lot, going down to the river by herself to sit amidst the gossiping crones. The matrons down by the river loved her, Touta assured her mother. But she would not be reassured, "Mind your own business and come straight home. Walk in the light and let no shadow fall upon you."

As she neared the gentle slope where all the women sat to wash their dishes, heads began to turn to greet her. "Morning of light, ya Touta!" they called. "Come sit by me, my dear. There's plenty of room here," one gray-haired woman called out. It was Fathiya. She was a childless woman whose husband had thrown her out, and so she'd gone to work at the Hakim villa. Touta liked her and pitied her plight, so she carefully set her load down next to her, greeting her with a kiss on the head, "How are you, Mother?"

"Yaaa! To be Touta's mother, I'd give my eyes for that!" the woman exclaimed. The Hakims treated Fathiya like one of the family, but she worked hard taking care of their household. They were the richest family in the village, far above Touta's family, but their youngest son had made no secret of his admiration for Touta, and all the women were predicting that young Tarek would marry whomever he wanted. Touta didn't think about it much; she refused to dwell on what she had no power to change.

All the women had cast aside their black outerwear so that they wouldn't get wet. As they scrubbed and scraped, slopped and rinsed, spread over the green hillside like a flock of colorful birds, the women's tongues never stopped. The latest story that had grabbed their attention was the bird flu that had decimated the bird population, impoverished chicken farmers, and stricken a few humans.

"Did you hear about the woman who died in Menoufia? She was sleeping with her chickens so no one would find them!"

"I heard the government knew that there was bird flu here months ago and didn't tell anyone!"

"Ya sheikha! Why would they wait if they were going to kill all the birds anyway?"

"You've probably still got chickens hidden under your bed, too!"

"You know who has some for sure? Amina! She's too poor to slaughter her chickens and throw them away. I won't let my kids play at her house or with her kids."

"I killed all of mine and threw them in the Nile. Can't take any risks."

"Yakhti, they say you poisoned the Nile with your filth! Who would throw dead, sick chickens into the water we drink and wash in?"

"I've seen whole camels floating down the river, a few chickens can't make that much difference."

"But it wasn't just you; it was the whole country. It's disgusting how people use the river as their garbage dump. I buried mine and burned the pen."

"I slaughtered mine and gave them away to any of the neighbors who wanted them. It's a waste to throw away good food!"

"I'd like to know what we are going to do for the Eid. And how are we going to live without the eggs? Are the kids going to live on ful and felafel?"

The talk went round and round with no beginning and no end. The same comments were made by one woman after another, often contradicting opinions they had voiced earlier. A swirl of gossip refusing to run itself out. Without gossip, what would there be but grimy dishes and slimy water?

When Touta finished her stack of pots and pans, she carefully laid them in her tisht, stacking them upside down so that they would finish draining by the time she got home, then she folded a bit of toweling, which she placed on her head to cushion the tisht, and with the help of one of the other women, settled it on her head. Just as she was about to leave, Fathiya crooked her finger at her conspiratorially and whispered loudly, "The mulberries are out. The big tree down on the Hakims' land is full of them, and they are all going to the birds! You know the one I mean? The one in the hollow." She ended with a wink. "I know our little Touta always liked her tout!"

Hameeda spit on the ground next to her, "But you'd better be careful, ya Touta, young Master Tarek wields a heavy stick. But maybe he'd let you take all you want …" she leered at her knowingly.

Fathiya turned on Hameeda, "Your brat was breaking the branches, that's why Master Tarek chased him away."

"I've gotten too old to stand under a tree and pick tout, ya hagga! What would my mother say?" she said with a laugh. With a carefree greeting, Touta left the gossiping women to their scrubbing and strode down the path.

As she walked, Fathiya's comment about the tout, the mulberries that she so adored and that she'd been nicknamed for, swirled in her mind. The tree that Fathiya had talked about lay down the other path, the one that led past the Hakim villa. Both paths would take her home, but her regular route ran through town and was a little quicker. But Fathiya said the tree was loaded with the juiciest mulberries she'd ever seen. Without meaning to, Touta found her feet taking her down the dappled path to the tree. It was a tree like no other; one side produced the tart black mulberries that stained the children's lips and clothes, while the other side bore the fat, juicy white mulberries that looked like swollen caterpillars, but tasted like heaven. Which would she have today? She'd better stick to the white ones or her mother would notice right away.

The prospect of a mid-morning snack at the mulberry tree perked her right up and her feet seemed to fly down the path, the heavy load on her head forgotten. The shaded path was much more comfortable, too, and she wondered why she didn't take the path every day. Relief from the scorching sun could be purchased with a few extra steps. She sang her little tune as she considered the joys of the spring day. While the sun was hot, the air lacked the oppressiveness that it would hold during full summer. The trees had all exchanged their old leaves for new bright green ones and the birds were twittering noisily in the underbrush.

When she reached the old tree, it was indeed raining mulberries. The whole hollow where it stood was littered with ripe fruit. Each shift in the breeze produced a flurry of them. The whole bird population seemed to have taken up residence in the tree and was chattering away, exchanging bird gossip.

Touta's feet flew the last few steps to the tree and then as she looked up at the tempting plump berries from under her oversized burden, her heart sank with dismay. How was she to pick the berries with the tisht on her head? And if she laid it down, she would never be able to restore it to its place on her head by herself. She was just about to turn away from the feast in front of her when a man's voice from behind her said, "Help yourself. Get your share before the birds take it all!"

Startled beyond all reason, Touta whirled around, almost losing control of her dishes, to find Tarek watching her from the path. "I was only taking a look and remembering the days when I was young and would come here to eat berries from your tree. They were sweeter than honey in those days."

"They haven't changed. Go ahead and eat as many as you want. This year God has granted us an ample crop." He walked a few steps closer to her, stepping out of the sun into the dappled light under the tree.

"Walk in the light and let no shadow fall upon you …" that was what her mother had advised her and here she was, bathed in shadow. She took a hurried step toward the path and the sunlight, "I really must be going. My mother is waiting for me and wanting to start lunch." Her mother was probably deep in slumber by now since Touta had given her pain medication right before she left.

Tarek's tall slender form stepped in front of her, "Won't you at least taste them, ya Touta? I know you love them so."

She gave a nervous laugh and said, "I'll have to come back someday when I'm not balancing a tisht on my head! I can't pick berries like this! I can't even reach over my head."

"If that's the problem, then allow me," he said, reaching up and pulling down a supple branch loaded with black berries. He plucked a few of the ripest and handed them to her. "Surely you must have a plate up there that I could put mulberries in." And he reached up over her head and pulled out a white dish.

Touta clutched the berries in her hand, beside herself. What should she do? She couldn't offend him by refusing them, but could she eat them while he watched? Somehow it seemed so intimate, to eat berries that he had picked for her. As she looked down at her hand, she noticed it had been dyed red from the bruised berries and without another thought, popped them into her mouth.

Tarek looked over at her and laughed, "I should have given you white ones, your mouth and lips are stained red just like the little urchins who come to play here."

She put her fingers to her mouth and giggled in spite of herself. "I guess Mama will know I've been eating tout."

"With a name like yours, how could you pass them by?" he smiled and turned back to the tree, busily picking the plumpest berries. "Why don't you put that thing down and help me? Or are you just going to watch?"

She blushed and cast her eyes away. "I won't be able to get it back on my head if I put it down; someone has to help me balance it or the whole thing will come tumbling down."

"That's easy enough. I will help you," Tarek said as he turned toward her, reaching up to take the tisht without waiting for her permission. As he knelt to set it down in the green grass, he looked up at her, face in shadow but her form framed against the sun, "Now that's better. Now get to work picking the tout or we'll be here all day and your mother will come after you with a stick."

With a giggle, Touta stooped and took another plate from the tisht and then turned to the tree and started plucking the sweet white berries, fingers seeking out the swollen ripe ones and leaving the greener ones. Every fourth or fifth one made its way into her mouth. "It seems you're going to eat instead of fill the plate," Tarek smiled at her. She looked at him out of the corner of her eye and then pelted him with a particularly ripe one, missing him intentionally. "Do you have any objections?"

"No, no, bel hana wil shifa." He held his hand to his breast, just like the host of a banquet, wishing his guests bon appétit.

She stared up into the green leaves of the mulberry, "Why do the best berries always seem to be at the top where we can't get them?"

"Which one do you fancy? I'll scamper up there and get it for you, just like we did when we were children," Tarek moved to stand next to her.

She pointed up to a branch a meter or so away. "See that cluster up there, the one with four ripe ones and a little green one? That looks the sweetest to me."

Without another thought, Tarek swung himself up the trunk of the tree. He climbed swiftly and agilely as she watched. "You stay right there under the berries, so I'll be able to hand them down to you." He inched out over the thickest branch he could find. It gave uncomfortably under him, but a glance down at Touta's upturned face spurred him on. "Almost there," he said as he reached up to the plump berries that she wanted. Just as his fingers brushed them, the branch below him gave an unpleasant crack and the whole branch snapped off the tree, taking him down with it. As he hit the ground with a grunt of surprise, he rolled over on his back and took a deep breath. He lay on the grass for a minute looking up at the berries that were now so far out of reach. With a little laugh, he said, "I guess there's a reason I chase those kids off when they start climbing the tree! It's a good thing no one was hurt." With that, he rolled over on his side and started to get up. But the scene in front of him took his breath away. Touta lay crumpled on her side under the branch, which had smacked her full on the forehead. Her plate of mulberries lay spilled on the grass; his had landed right side up and the mulberries still glistened in the white bowl. The tree leaves covered her like a blanket. A little dab of blood marked her head and even though he called to her, she showed no signs of waking.

He crawled over to her on his knees and shook her arm, "Ya Touta, wake up! Oh, please be all right!" he begged, but he got no response. She was breathing but unconscious to the world or the disaster facing them. How would she explain this little mishap to her mother? What was he to do? How could he get her home? If he went and got help, he could be bringing disaster on her head. The tongues of the village gossips would be set in motion. What had they been doing here in this private place? Then he remembered Fathiya; she would help the poor unfortunate girl think up a story to explain the state she was in and help her get home. At the thought, he jumped to his feet and ran down the road to the villa.

As he ran down the path, he failed to notice the tiny pebbles flung at his back by a dirty little urchin hiding in a neighboring tree. The filthy boy of seven slipped down the tree and crept closer to stand over Touta, looking down at her perfect face with the trickle of blood running down her cheek. He stooped and took a few berries from Tarek's plate of mulberries and popped them in his mouth and was just about to take more when he heard laughing voices coming down the path. Without a second's thought, he scampered up another tree, watching as they came into view.

"Where are these mulberries you've been gabbing about all day, ya Fathiya? You've got my mouth watering for them! Between you and my monkey son Ziyad, you'd think there was no other food in the world!" Hameeda's voice rang out loud and made the little boy cringe. No other woman in the world had a voice like his mother's.

"The tree is right over here, as if you hadn't eaten your share from it in years past!" Fathiya called back. "I love the black ones, but the white ones are sweeter than honey. By God, look! Those wild little boys have broken a great big branch. What a shame!" She went to examine the damage and as she looked down at the broken branch and counted the mulberries that would go to waste, she finally noticed Touta lying unconscious under the branch. "May God have mercy! Help me, everyone! Touta's under this!" The women converged on the broken branch and began to pull it off the girl.

"What on earth happened to her, do you suppose," Hameeda exclaimed. Just as she was about to bend down to straighten Touta's clothes, she saw something drop out of a nearby tree. "What was that," she asked no one in particular and walked over to the tree. In the shade of the spreading willow lay a battered old slipper. Without even looking, she knew who she'd find there. She picked up the slipper and flung it into the tree. "You monkey Ziyad! Come down here right now!" He slithered down without a word. "What do you know about all this, ya Ziyad?"

"Nothing," he replied sullenly.

"What do you mean nothing? What happened here?" she demanded, grabbing his ear and twisting him closer to her.

"I was just picking a few mulberries when I heard someone coming down the path. I hid up in that tree—didn't want Master Tarek to take after me with that stick again. When I saw it was just Touta, I was going to climb down, but then he came down the road and they stood and talked forever. I fell asleep for a bit; the sound of the tree branch cracking was like a shot. It woke me up. I saw him get up and he ran on down the path."

"Who? Who got up?" his mother demanded.

"Master Tarek. He's even left his big stick here next to her tisht, see?" he said, pointing at the big gnarled walking stick that Tarek carried when he walked around his father's land.

Fathiya gasped, "That's his stick all right. But why would he run away and leave Touta like this. Carry her into the sun so I can see if she's all right."

As the women tugged at her, dragging her through the grass, Touta groaned and began to stir.

Hameeda grabbed Ziyad's shoulders and shook him, "What were they doing, boy!"

"I don't know!" the boy spluttered, "He was picking tout for her and filling her plate. They were saying silly things. I got bored and went to sleep. I woke up when I heard the branch breaking. I saw him lying next to her in the grass for a minute and then he jumped up and ran down the road."

Hameeda turned to Fathiya, "Looks like Touta wanted to make sure he'd marry her, meeting him here in the shade of a mulberry tree. Her mother will be so disappointed. What a disgrace!"

Fathiya looked up from where she knelt by Touta, "The girl didn't do anything wrong. I'm sure there's an explanation. I told her about the tout and she came to pick a few, that's all. Master Tarek is always walking around the land; he probably thought she was a kid making trouble and came to see what was going on. We'll ask her when she wakes up." She frantically chafed at Touta's wrists, "No one has any water to wake her up?"

At Hameeda's comments, the women began to murmur softly to themselves. What had Touta been doing here in the dark little hollow with a strange man? How did she come to be lying unconscious in the grass? The air was ripe with the scent of scandal. Fathiya could feel the web of gossip being spun in their heads and turned on them, "Shame on you all! Help me wake up the girl so she can explain herself!" Frantic, she slapped Touta on the face, harder than she had intended to. "Wake up, girl!" The slap seemed to bring her around; she opened her eyes and looked up into Fathiya's concerned face. "What happened?" Fathiya demanded.

Touta looked up at the spreading mulberry tree. "I was just picking berries, and something fell on me."

"Was Master Tarek here? Answer me, girl!" Hameeda demanded.

At the sound of Tarek's name, Touta's eyes searched the grass, her cheeks blazing red, matching the smear of mulberry juice on her lips and palms. She remembered how he had plied her with tout and picked the sweet berries for her.

"That's enough answer for me!" Hameeda spat on the grass, scornfully. "Just because a girl is pretty doesn't mean she can do anything she likes! I thought your mother had taught you better than that. I thought you always walked in the light." She whirled around, finding her tisht and balancing it on her head with the help of one of the other women. "Come on! We have to get back to our homes like respectable women." Grabbing her errant son by the ear, she began to pull him home. The other women heeded her call, each balancing her tisht on her head.

Fathiya looked at them, knowing what tale they would bear to the village. She shook her frantically, "Touta, Touta, you must speak now and tell them what happened, or it will be too late."

But Touta had swooned again and no answer was to be had from her.

As the black-clad women glided down the path like so many crows headed for their nests with a juicy tidbit, Fathiya mourned Touta's reputation. "May God grant you and your mother patience."

Fathiya carefully wrapped Touta's shugga around her, covering up the pink dress that seemed so incriminating. She put her head in her hands and began to rock back and forth, keening.

#

As the two women limped through the dusty streets, no one called out to greet them. In fact, no one would meet their eyes. Fathiya brought a still-dazed Touta to her mother's house where the old woman was waiting in the darkened interior. She waited until Fathiya had helped Touta recline on the hard, flat couch, arranging a bolster behind her head. "Thank you, Fathiya for bringing her home. May God be generous to you." The words were perfectly appropriate for thanking someone who had helped her, but no emotion lit them. "Sit down and drink a cup of tea with me," she said, ignoring the plight of her daughter.

"Some other time, ya hagga," Fathiya murmured, ready to turn for the door.

"Even you will refuse my tea? They all refused to drink what I offered when they came to tell this awful tale."

"No, ya hagga, I wouldn't refuse you. I didn't want to tire you, that's all."

"Ya Baheya! Bring a cup of tea for your Aunt Fathiya!"

Fathiya reluctantly perched on the edge of the chair nearest to the door.

"What happened, ya Fathiya? Is it true? Did you see him with her? Why did he hit her?"

"I don't know, ya hagga. She won't talk. I tried to get her to explain before the women came back to the village. She turned the color of her dress when they spoke his name to her. The boy says he saw Master Tarek lying in the grass with her in the shade of the mulberry. But I don't know what happened."

"Shadow has fallen on her and my family."

Fathiya couldn't disagree. Baheya brought a glass of dark-red tea on an aluminum tray and set it next to her on a side table. On her way out, she stopped by the couch where Touta sat and put her hand on her shoulder, "Do you want anything, ya Touta?"

"That's not her name," her mother snapped. "I won't hear that name in this house again. Her name is Sabra. I don't know who thought of that ridiculous name, but we've had quite enough indulgence here. It all comes to no good."

Fathiya took the glass of tea and sipped it in silence, remembering the fat little girl who had sat under the mulberry tree and gorged herself on the sweet fruit before she could even walk. She had given herself the nickname. Fathiya mourned with Touta's mother until she had finished two thirds of her tea. Leaving the last third out of customary politeness, she rose and set the glass on the tray. "Thank you, ya hagga. I have to go now. I'll send your dishes home with the girl at the Hakim's villa."

"May God be generous to you, my daughter."

As Fathiya reached the door, she turned, "It was hassad, you know, that did her in. Everyone always stared at her and envied her beauty. The evil eye fell upon her."

Touta's mother nodded, "But she should have walked in the light. I told her every day. Bad things happen in the shadow."

#

From that day forward, Touta tried to think of herself as Sabra; her name meant "patience" and apparently that was what she needed. Every step she took in the village she felt eyes turning away. The women barely spoke to her if they could help it. The men seemed to have something else behind their eyes; the adoration of a spoiled child had been replaced by something she could only describe as ugly. Her mother longed to lock her inside the house away from the slights and stares, but they had no one to rely upon for the daily chores that Sabra took care of.

So, she continued to buy fruit and vegetables and wash dishes at the riverside, but she always tried to be the first one there and the first one to leave. Her mother had begun economizing with dishes to make sure she didn't have to stay long. When she took down a plate to give one of her sister's children a slice of cake, her mother would snap, "Give it to him in his sister's plate. One less to wash!" In truth, the daily journey to the river was the hardest thing she had to do. Fathiya was always kind to her and came and sat next to her, patting her on the arm and trying to get her to talk, but the rest of the women treated her with cold indifference at best, occasionally directing malicious stares and comments her way.

One day as she sat on the riverbank finishing her dishes, the women arrived in a chattering cluster. Sabra knew from the instant they arrived that their chatter had something to do with her, as much from Fathiya's nervous, pitying glances as from Hameeda's spiteful stare. As they settled their burdens on the green grass and went down to the river to get water, Sabra tried to finish her work so that she could leave. Hameeda took up a position unusually close to Sabra. As she settled on the grass, she called out to Fathiya as if she were 200 meters away rather than five, "So what's this news that we hear, ya Fathiya? Is it true that young Master Tarek has proposed to a young woman?"

Fathiya murmured, "His mother has picked out a girl. They visited her yesterday in her village. Who knows where destiny will lead? Fate is a funny thing. He'll marry the one he's meant to marry."

Sabra felt her face flushing, not because she had believed that he intended to ask her to marry him, but because of the injustice of it all. Why was he able to go on with his life as if nothing had happened, when her life had been so tragically and irrevocably changed? If she posed the question to her mother, she would say, "It's because women have to walk in the light." She vowed that she would forever walk in the light from that point onward. She began to hurriedly stack her dishes in her tisht, her hands flying, racing the tears that threatened to cascade down her cheek.

Fathiya leaned over to her, "Careful, my dear, you'll break something if you don't watch out. This dish needs rinsing." She took the dish and rinsed it with her own supply of water and helped Sabra stack her dishes.

Hameeda crowed in a triumphant voice, "I'm sure the girl is a good one, very well-behaved and from a good family. Rich, too if I know his mother! He's one that nothing is too good for!" She laughed her awful crow's laugh again and cheerfully scrubbed her dishes.

Sabra rose to her feet, almost stumbling as her head spun. Fathiya stood with her and helped her raise the tisht to its place on her head. She kissed Sabra on her cheek and whispered, "Don't take it so hard. Walk carefully on the way home."

She held her shugga close about her, making sure not to brush the cluster of women that had gathered around her for the first time since the accident. As she pushed her way through their little group, she was thankful for the tisht that kept her head held high.

As she reached the top of the grassy hill, out of sight of the gawking women, she looked down the path that led her home. The tall trees lining the path dappled it with shadow. "I will never walk in the shadow again. I want the burning sun." The other path leading to her home led past the infamous mulberry tree and lay even more deeply in shadow. The only other road she could take was the one leading out of the village, the main road to Cairo. The sun beat down upon the broken asphalt, scorching and purifying. Without thinking, her feet started down the path of light.

The hot asphalt burned her feet through her thin sandals, but she accepted every discomfort, welcoming it. She strode down the road as if she knew exactly where she was going. Every step a step in the light. As she walked, she pondered the injustice of her plight. It wasn't that Tarek was to marry. He'd never made her any promises, and she'd never dared to dream that he would marry her. But that he could go on and live his life without a single setback while she had become an outcast, there lay the injustice.

Minute after minute dragged by. Kilometer after kilometer of scorching road seared her feet. The tisht on her head grew heavier, seeming to push her into the pavement. As she grew more and more weary, she embraced the sensation of the world being reduced to one footstep at a time.

When she finally realized that she would not be able to go on much longer and looked around her for a clue as to where she was, she found herself on a long unfamiliar road with no ending and no beginning. No roads met it, and none diverged from it. Rows and rows of cotton surrounded her on either side. The only moving thing she saw was a small, white pickup truck speeding down the road toward her.

As the little truck whipped past her, it was as if the wind from the passing vehicle was too much for her and she crumpled into a heap of black cloth along the roadside, her heavy tisht crashing down, upended in the dirt of the cotton field.

The driver of the little truck brought it quickly to a halt. He had almost stopped as he drew closer to the girl, sensing it was Touta, but had thought better of it. But Tarek could never leave her lying on the side of the road. He jumped out of the truck and ran back to the broken form. He knelt in the dirt and helped her to sit up, bringing a plastic bottle of water to her lips and insisting that she drink.

"What are you doing here, Touta?" he demanded.

"My name isn't Touta. It's Sabra," she murmured. "I'll be going home now. I just have to find a path in the light," she gestured wanly to the broken dishes and the upended tisht, "Mama will be angry. I must get home."

"Come with me and I'll drive you home. You're ten kilometers from your house. What brought you out here in this heat? You could have killed yourself."

"Don't worry about me. I always manage somehow. I don't need your help this time either," her near delirium from dehydration brought the words to her lips.

"I didn't mean to leave you last time, ya Touta. I went to get help, but Fathiya wasn't at the house. By the time I came back you were gone and all that was left was that heavy broken branch. I had wanted to get Fathiya to take you home. But whatever made you bring up my name? Couldn't you have made up an innocent tale? Picking berries and you fell? Anything? You brought disaster upon yourself. I had thought to save you from it by leaving you."

"The boy saw you. He lied to them, and I didn't understand what they thought had happened until it was too late. I thought they were accusing me of speaking to you in private when they were actually accusing me of …" her words trailed off and her eyes fell on his hands around her shoulders. She staggered, trying to stand and distance herself from him.

"Come get in the truck," he grabbed her elbow to steady her.

She pulled her elbow from his grasp, stumbling back a pace or two. "I want to stay in the light. I can't get in that truck—it's too dark and shadowed."

"What are you talking about? The sun is beating down everywhere. You'll feel the sun inside the truck just like you do here on the road."

But she wouldn't be swayed. In the end, she climbed into the back of the truck and sat on the newspaper that he spread for her, leaning her elbow on the tailgate and resting her head on her hand. As the landscape sped past, she had the disorienting sensation that she was living the last moments of her life. What would the village say when it saw her riding in Master Tarek's truck? Perhaps it would have been better to lie down on the side of the road and die. She pulled her headscarf across her face and waited for the tears to come, but they refused. Her eyes followed the scrawny trees as they whipped by, encrusted with dust after the endless days without rain.

When the pickup entered the little village, it seemed strangely deserted, but then she looked up at the sky and realized that the afternoon prayers had come and gone and most of the villagers were having their afternoon nap to escape the worst of the humid heat.

Tarek stopped in front of her building. Once, the apartments had all been filled with her father's brothers, but they had long since left the village for Cairo, and now Sabra and her family lived among strangers. Thankfully, they all seemed to be asleep, with just the shutters on the windows ajar to let in any possible breath of air. Tarek came around to the back of the pickup and lowered the tailgate. "Come on, ya Touta. You are home." She dangled her legs off the tailgate, her only reply, "My name is Sabra."

"Come inside, I think the sun has made you sick," he insisted.

She stared at the shaded entrance to the building. "There's no sun. Even in my father's house. There's no light."

"You've had too much sun, ya Touta. I'll get your mother," Tarek turned his back and dashed up to the building entrance. Without hesitation, he knocked at her father's apartment on the ground floor. With dull eyes, she watched him and thought, "Oh, to be a man and never have to be ashamed of your actions." And then her fevered mind wandered to the dappled entrance to the building, "Dil ragel wala dil hayta?" What would be a better shelter, a man or a wall? Maybe just scorching sun.

Tarek stood talking earnestly for a minute or so and then the door was flung open, and her elderly mother hurried out of the house. She grabbed her daughter's hand and pulled her to her feet, in hushed tones she urged her, "Come into the house, we don't need any more scandals."

Standing at the old woman's elbow, Tarek interjected, "Nothing she has ever done has brought scandal. People envy her for her beauty."

"What business of yours is her beauty?" the old woman whirled upon him. "You have a roaming eye, and in truth, you are the one who has brought the scandals to a respectable house and a decent girl."

"Enough, ya hagga," Tarek hushed her, "we will talk inside. Let your neighbors finish their afternoon naps."

Touta stood at the edge of the sunlight, "Where is the light, Mama?"

"What do you mean? We are standing in the blistering sun; what do you want with light?"

"You told me to walk in the light. Where is the light?"

"God always blesses the shade of your father's house," the old woman tugged on her arm and led her inside. At the door of the dwelling, she stopped and blocked Tarek's path. "We have no men here. It is not right that you enter."

From the dim interior of the house, Touta's father demanded, "Have you forgotten me? I no longer count as a man?"

Tarek called out, "Assalamu 'alaikum, ya hagg," and ducked into the house. As his eyes adjusted to the muted light of the entry hall, he found the old man reclining on a traditional cotton-stuffed couch. He crossed rapidly to him and seized his hand, kissing him soundly on each cheek, "How is your health, ya hagg?"

"Thanks be to God, my son. My health is as good as I can expect. But my mind is just as sharp as it was twenty years ago. Where have you been with my daughter, ya ibn Hakim?"

"I found her on the road, ya hagg. The heat had overcome her. She wouldn't ride in the truck with me, so I put her in the back. There is nothing else to tell. Even the old crones of the village couldn't find anything wrong with what happened."

"Those crones have more potent imaginations than you give them credit for. Ya hagga!" he called to his wife. "Bring us lemon juice to wet our throats."

She had been helping her daughter to her room. Touta seemed to have lost all will of her own. She only followed where her mother led her. When Touta's mother heard her husband's call, her mind rebelled, and she muttered to herself, "Lemon juice! Why should I play host to that son of disaster?" But she replied, "I'll just help Sabra lie down." She removed the girl's black shugga and hung it up behind the door, loosening her clothing. "You need lemon juice, even if that son of Adam outside does not." She piled pillows on the narrow bed and eased Sabra back on to them. She lay with her eyes open, head inches from the door. Her mother fussed around her for a minute more and then bustled out of the room in the direction of the kitchen.

The two men sat in hushed conversation as she walked past them. As much as she hated to sit with this despised creature, she feared the whispered tones of the two men, so she called out to her daughter in the kitchen, "Ya Baheya, make a lemon juice for your sister … and two for your father and his guest," and she settled down across from the hated visitor, tucking her feet underneath her on the high sofa.

Both men stopped talking and glanced guiltily at her, obvious conspirators.

In a louder voice, Sabra's father continued after a pause, "Are you sure this is what you want? If you break your word, it will break my family."

"I am sure, ya hagg. I want to make everything right for her."

"Ya Baheya, bring sharbat, ya Baheya!"

"Sharbat for what?" his wife snapped. "Sharbat is for weddings and births; what do we have to celebrate?"

"Master Tarek wants to sign Sabra's marriage contract on Friday after the prayers."

"And who will allow him to do that?" she retorted.

"I have given him my word."

"You haven't even asked Sabra. God gives her the right to refuse."

"I will ask her," the old man replied simply. He rose from his place and hobbled toward the bedroom. Baheya was standing open-mouthed at the door to the kitchen, holding a tray of lemon juice. "Bring one of those for Sabra," he directed as he went into the still bedroom. She set the tall, cool glass on the table next to the bed and brought a chair for her father. "Close the door. I want to talk to your sister."

As he carefully settled into his chair, he looked at his beautiful daughter, so tortured, not by love but by the evil potency of rumors. "Sit up and have a sip of this, ya Touta." As she drew herself up, he offered her the glass and she took it, drinking carefully.

He would not speak until she had drained it. Once he had taken the glass from her limp hands he began, "Bismillah al-rahman al-raheem." It was a very formal way to begin a speech, but somehow it seemed appropriate.

"My dear daughter, life has not treated you kindly recently. I would never have wished to see you in such a state. But Master Tarek has offered us a way out. He has asked for your hand, and he assures me that it is not out of pity. What do you say? This would cut out the poisonous tongues of those village crows forever."

"What do you think, Baba? What should I do?" she murmured.

"He is a fine man, you could do no better. But I know that the shame has made the choice bitter."

"I want to pray istakhara and put the matter before Allah," she said. As she tried to rise to perform her ritual washing before prayer, she swooned, falling back to the bed.

"Ya Baheya," her father called, "Bring a bowl of fresh water." When she brought the bowl, he instructed her to help her sister with her washing. The cool water splashing her face revived Sabra, but when she made to stand in prayer, her father stopped her with a hand on her arm, "Pray sitting down, you are too ill to rise. God has made everything easy for us. He is great in His leniency. I will wait on the balcony until you have an answer. Do not hurry. You can make him wait all day; it would serve him right."

As the old man hobbled over to the chair on the balcony, Sabra began her prayer. She asked Allah to guide her to what was good and keep her away from evil. As she finished her prayer and sat in contemplation, she imagined herself married, with children, living in a home of her own. And then she imagined herself refusing Tarek. She saw herself holding her sisters' children, watching them play from the balcony, knowing that she would never have any of her own. She saw the sneers of the villagers when she passed, sneers that became habitual rather than easing with time. She knew what she would do. Whether her vision of happiness would come true, only time would tell, but she felt sure that her vision of isolation would be final.

#

CALM

Viber message from Aida Nasr to Fatima ElKalay.
(November 7, 2014)

Thank you so much Fatima. I was up all night in pain, so I prayed and said Quran. I prayed for myself and everyone I love including you.
Mommy slept next to me and held my hand so that was comforting.
Please keep praying. The painkillers I am taking don't seem to be working too well. Thanks Fatima. Appreciate all your support.

**Unsent message to Fatima ElKalay
found posthumously on Aida Nasr's phone.**
(November 8, 2014)

Am trying to be strong although feeling scared. Khair inshallah. If I get closer to God that will be a blessing. I love you too. Please keep praying, that means so much to me.

TANGERINE WOMAN

by Aida Nasr

Ola added a stroke of orange to her canvas and stepped back to view her work. Why couldn't she stop painting this woman? A voluptuous nude, suffused with a radiant light, rising out of tangerine-colored swirls. This tangerine woman definitely did not belong in her exhibit.

The other canvas, the one she was supposed to be working on, sat neatly on its easel: a pretty little girl in a pleated white dress. She had already painted the girl's round face and her dainty lace collar. She had been working on the smooth black hair with the big, white bow when the tangerine woman enticed her again. She didn't have time for this. Her exhibit at the Fine Arts College was in a week. She needed to finish the girl she was painting from a black and white photograph of her great aunt Farida.

"On my birthday, my mother always took me for a photograph at a big studio downtown, and then we went to Groppi to choose my cake for our celebration at home. I always wanted the chocolate," Tante Farida told Ola upon giving her the photograph.

The painting of young Farida was a carefully detailed study of beauty, the type Ola always painted: girls in starched white dresses hugging dolls with fluttery eyelashes. Or serene women in flowing burgundy gowns, clutching bouquets of daisies. Or somber gentlemen in suits and tarbouches, leaning on walking sticks. She was known at the college for these distinguished portraits from a bygone era. For this, they gave her high marks.

And now, her PhD exhibit. She had already painted nine portraits. The young Farida in her white dress was the tenth and final painting.

Ola stopped for a tea break. She looked at the clock in the kitchen. In two hours she'd have to pick up Hamada from his nursery. So little time. Why wouldn't the tangerine woman leave her alone? She poured steaming water over the tea leaves in her glass, tipped in two spoons of sugar. It was a useless painting, certainly not one for the exhibit. She was so close to earning her PhD, to being made assistant professor at the college.

She went back to the small studio, the tiny converted bedroom with paintings stacked against the walls. On the easel, the girl's face rose out of the white canvas like a ghost. The phone rang.

"How is my painting coming along, dear?" It was Tante Farida. She called every day to check on Ola's progress.

"I'm having trouble concentrating, ya Tante. I don't know how I'll finish it in time." She didn't say anything about the tangerine woman.

"What you need, my dear, is to take a break, clear your mind. Why don't you come visit me? I'll tell you a story about the photo. Maybe that will help."

A story? She didn't have time for Tante Farida's stories. But she was desperate.

#

Tante Farida leaned back into the cushions of her slouching sofa with its faded, floral slipcovers. The tea tray sat on a table covered in crochet doilies. Ola readied herself for the same story she had heard before: the posh photographer's studio, the Black Forest cake from Groppi.

"You see, on that day, I met Abbas." Tante Farida's doughy body seemed melded into this sofa where she always sat. Her gray hair was twisted into a bun, her brown eyes sparkled out of a soft, wrinkled face.

"Uncle Abbas? But you were only eight in the photo."

"Yes, I was, my dear. On that day, I posed with my favorite doll and chose my favorite chocolate cake on the way home. At my party in the evening, my mother's friend brought her small son, Abbas, who was ten. His mother joked that I'd make a good bride for him when we grew up. Only she wasn't exactly joking, because I do believe she set her sights on the marriage that day. And that's exactly what happened, my dear."

"And how will this help me finish the painting, ya Tante?"

"What you need to know is that the photo was taken on the most important day of my life, just before I met the most important person in my life. Think of that while you're painting."

Tante Farida was a widow. After a few, short years of a childless marriage, she never married again. For as long as Ola could remember, her great aunt had been sitting on this sofa, weaving her stories while sipping endless cups of tea and Turkish coffee. It had never occurred to her that Abbas, this shadow from the past, could have been the most important person in Tante Farida's life.

Ola had met Marwan at the Fine Arts College when they were students. He had asked to borrow her lecture notes. Was he the most important thing in her life? She doubted it.

#

Late that evening, after Marwan had returned from teaching at the college, he sat in their studio, smoking and painting. Hamada was finally asleep. She could get back to her own work now, although she always found Marwan and his smoke distracting. She wished she had the studio to herself.

"What's this orange woman?" Marwan asked. "You've never painted anything like her before."

"Oh, it's just something I'm experimenting with," she said with a vague wave of her hand, as if dismissing the painting altogether. The woman rose from her orange mist.

Ola forced herself back to the painting of the young Farida. She looked into her painted eyes and back at the photograph propped up on the easel. What was Farida thinking, so solemn in her picture? Did she sense that something would happen on this day to alter the course of her life? No, she was probably thinking of chocolate cake. Reluctantly, Ola picked up her smallest brush and began adding fine strands of black hair amidst Marwan's cigarette smoke.

#

Three days later, the painting of Farida was slowly taking shape. Ola had devised a formula to keep working, a bargain with herself. Paint a portion of Farida, and then, for just a few minutes, paint the tangerine woman.

"I'm on the pleats of the dress now," she told Tante Farida over the phone. "They're quite intricate, but I'm almost finished."

"Excellent, my dear. I knew you could do it."

Every day on the phone, Tante Farida told her snatches of the Abbas story.

"I didn't see him again until my eighteenth birthday when he came to ask my father for my hand. We served him chocolate cake. I'm sure his mother is the one who convinced him I'd make a good wife."

After this conversation, Ola felt the need to put a gold ring on the tangerine woman's plump, white hand.

"After we married, he always took a siesta in the afternoon, and so I began to take one too."

The tangerine woman's lids began to droop, as though she had just woken from her own nap, mysterious and sleepy.

"He'd bring me bags of juicy peaches because he knew I loved them so much."

And the sky behind the tangerine woman became streaked with the color of those peaches, as she rose, Venus-like, from her swirling mist into the sunrise.

#

"This orange woman looks so familiar, like someone I know," said Marwan one evening through his haze of smoke.

"Really? I didn't paint her from a model. She's from my imagination."

"She's not the best painting you've ever done. The composition is off, and that orange color is jarring. You should stick to your other portraits, my dear." Then he went back to his own painting.

He was preparing for his solo show at a chic gallery in Zamalek. He had earned his PhD two years ago, was already a professor at the college. Even though having their baby had slowed down Ola's artistic career, the truth was that she lagged behind her husband on purpose. She knew he needed to be first in everything they did.

She let him experiment with his wild, semi-abstract paintings of shrouded blue figures and lurking gold eyes while she continued to produce her calmly realistic portraits with all their painstaking details— pleats and eyelashes and wisps of hair. Except for the tangerine woman.

He often criticized her work, leaving her to doubt herself, feeling as if the disembodied eyes from his paintings were watching her. She often abandoned whole, almost-finished canvases. She looked at the stack of unfinished paintings against the wall and sighed. She thought of the few canvases she managed to finish despite his comments, the praise they got at the college.

She wasn't abandoning her tangerine Venus, though. Somehow, she needed her.

"I wish I knew who she looks like," said Marwan thoughtfully, brush poised above his canvas.

#

At the opening of the exhibition, Marwan took photos of Ola with her professors against the backdrop of her portraits. Tante Farida came, leaning on her cane, a plump figure swathed all in black except for a beige headscarf fastened with a gold brooch. She posed with Ola next to her painting.

"I'm so proud of you, dear. Congratulations."

"Thank you, ya Tante. Does it look like the photograph?"

"Absolutely, you've done a wonderful job, my dear."

Somehow this bothered Ola. She looked at all her carefully painted canvases and the delicate, constricted brushstrokes that never went astray. She thought of the tangerine woman on her easel.

"What's wrong, my dear?" asked Tante Farida.

"I was just thinking of all this hard work, ya Tante. I only seem to produce one type of painting, these replicas of old photographs. I think I'm getting bored."

"Isn't there another type of painting you want to work on, my dear?"

"Yes, I'm painting one now, something completely different, but Marwan thinks it's awful."

"Does he now? And what is the subject of this painting?" Tante Farida's eyes sparkled.

"It's a young woman at dawn, rising out of a mist." She thought it best to leave out the fact that the woman was nude.

"Sounds lovely, dear. I think you should keep painting it. Something tells me it's important." And because her great aunt was rarely wrong, Ola took this as a sign to finish the tangerine woman rather than stack her up against the wall with all the others.

#

It was noon in the studio, and Ola stared at her painting. Ironically, now that the exhibit was over and she had time to paint her, she couldn't bring herself to do so. She wanted to add a flower in the black hair cascading around the woman's shoulders, but she was afraid.

She went for a tea break. What was it about this woman that was so familiar? Marwan was right. Who was she painting in this mist, against this rising sun, this full-bodied woman with the sleepy smile? The phone rang.

"Dear, how is your new painting coming along, the woman in the dawn?"

"I don't know what to do with her next, ya Tante, and I don't even know why I'm painting her."

"You're painting her because you want to."

"Yes, I do. Shall I put a flower in her hair?"

"Flowers are always lovely, but I see her holding one in her hand. Did I tell you about the time Abbas brought me an enormous bunch of pink roses ...?"

When Ola got off the phone, she painted a voluptuous pink rose in the woman's hand, the kind that grew massive and velvety as its petals unfurled with each passing day. Then she pondered the woman's face, wondering if she should add some color to her soft, round cheeks.

#

"You're still painting that woman?" asked Marwan through his smoke that evening. A disembodied eye stared out of the canvas he was painting.

"I'm almost finished with her."

"I'd start on something else. What are you going to do with that? It's not your style. And I don't want it in our living room."

"Tante Farida thinks it's important for me to finish this painting, and so do I," was the only comeback she could think of.

"What does Tante Farida know about art? You won't get anywhere with that painting. It's quite clichéd, a nude rising out of a mist."

"And my other paintings aren't? I'm bored Marwan, I need a change. Not every painting has to be for an exhibit, or our wall." She felt her anger rising.

"Your other paintings show your technical skill. This shows nothing. And what's that big flower you added?"

"It's a rose."

She went out on the balcony to get away from Marwan and his smoke. The crisp March air was welcome against her face as she looked up at the fingernail of a moon in the black sky between two high-rise buildings. Usually his comments drained her confidence like dishwater swirling down the sink when she did the dishes. But tonight, she saw a glimpse of a new canvas, and on it quick, fluid brushstrokes: a woman dancing barefoot by the light of a new moon. She'd start on it after the tangerine woman.

#

She looked at her finished painting, drying on the easel. A few white swirls, like the creamy underside of a tangerine peel, and she was done. Marwan didn't want this painting in their living room, but he couldn't stop her from putting it up in the studio.

Something compelled her to look through the stack of paintings against the wall, until she found the one of young Farida in her pleated dress and big, white hairbow. Fine technical skill, yes. But aside from the deep brown eyes, there was nothing alive in this painting at all. And yet her tangerine woman was clearly alive. Sensuous curves, sleepy lids, knowing smile. Gold ring on one hand, velvety rose in the other. Slowly, it dawned on her. The strange resemblance between the little girl's chocolate eyes and the tangerine woman's.

The phone rang.

"I've finished my painting, ya Tante."

"Excellent my dear, I knew you could do it. Why don't you bring it over to show me, and I'll tell you a story."

"I'd love to."

#

POSTSCRIPT

**Facebook post by Fatima ElKalay on the page of Aida Nasr
(February 9, 2015)**

Three months yesterday. It feels like eternity, and I have aged within this earthly body. I'm learning this about time since you left. I'm learning that our hearts are lonely timekeepers, and time moves at its own pace within them.

I've also learned that time does not really exist. You are here, I am there, there is continuity in our existence. It is just a matter of perspective and the inconvenience of mortality that separate us. Until we are eternally reunited in our perfect forms, I love you dear friend <3.

Acknowledgements

Fatima ElKalay

So many years have passed since we commenced, and there are countless people worthy of acknowledgement along the journey, a sea of hearts and hands rooting for us down the years, too many to recount here. You all know who you are; thank you all for your support and inspiration.

I must give special thanks to my good friend Sherine Elbanhawy, founder of *Rowayat*, who believed in this project wholeheartedly and never once allowed me to give up, even when I was ready to. Sherine, I would not have had the courage to share this collection with the world if you were not right behind me. Thank you to *Rowayat's* great editor Nevine Henein for her gracious and painstaking feedback, for patiently waiting for my redrafting, and for sifting through fourteen years of correspondence and threading the most relevant through the collection.

Where would this collection be without my fellow writers, Aida Nasr and Mariam Shouman? I am forever grateful to *Mother & Child* Magazine, the hub that brought us all together. Thank you to founder and editor-in-chief, Rania Badreldin, and to Mona Hashem, administrative manager, for introducing me to these remarkable women, all those years ago.

I would like to thank Dr. Aya Samaha who inspired me to pick "Dessert for Three" as the title story. She felt that publishing the book was a sweet treat, a fitting tribute to the three of us and everything that happened on our journey.

All the love and thanks in the world to those who live in my heart, the special people who've kept me going: my beloved late parents, my dear siblings Mo and Knock, my wonderful husband Saher. But the biggest thank you ever is to the best of my blessings, my beautiful children, Yahia, Mostafa, and Youmna, who saw in me and my art what I often failed to see in myself and who taught me so much about self-compassion. To you all, I gift these stories, a little piece of Mama to treasure with your own children and families, present and future.

Above all, and far beyond, I thank God Almighty for the gift of the word. I am nothing without Your grace.

Mariam Shouman

Many thanks to my parents Ahmad and Marjory Shouman, who made me who I am, a woman who values her cultural background and the society she was born into. Thanks also to my children, Ahmad, Ibrahim, Hanna and Sarah. You shaped who I am and are mommy's pride and joy. Thank you to Mohamed El-Sharkawy, my husband and partner in sickness and in health, for better and for worse.

Aida Nasr
(by Fatima ElKalay)

This is the only part in this book where I stumble. I don't know for sure what Aida would have included in her acknowledgements, because we talked about many things, but not this. But after some soul-searching, and from what I know about Aida, I believe she would have been thankful to God, to her mommy, her friends, her sister Nora (who tragically passed away less than two years after her), and to her nephew Adam and niece Yasmine "Mimi" of whom she was immensely proud.

Rest in Peace, Aida.
We did it, darling!

The Authors

Aida Nasr was born in Rochester, New York to Egyptian parents and passed away in Cairo in 2014. She held a BA in English and comparative literature from the American University in Cairo, and a publishing diploma from the University of the Arts in London. She was a writer and editor for several magazines and blogs including *Cairo Today* (later *Egypt Today*), *Business Today*, *Mother & Child*, and *Cairo Art Blog*. Aida also wrote and translated awareness material for breast cancer patients and volunteered with cancer survivors and disabled children. Her stories in *Dessert for Three* are her only published fiction.

Mariam Shouman was born in Las Cruces, New Mexico to an American mother and an Egyptian father. She holds BAs in both history and theatre arts from the University of New Mexico and an MA in Islamic history from the American University in Cairo. Mariam has worked as a teacher and as a freelance writer and editor and was the senior editor of the Egyptian parenting magazine *Mother & Child* for several years. She is the mother of four and lives with her family in Cairo, Egypt.

Fatima ElKalay was born in the United Kingdom to Egyptian parents. She holds an MLitt in creative writing from Central Queensland University. Her poetry has appeared in *Rusted Radishes, Poetry Birmingham Literary Journal*, and the *Shadow and Light Project*, and her fiction in *Anomalous Press, Rowayat,* and *Passionfruit*. She was shortlisted for a flash piece in the *London Independent Story Prize* and in *Arablit Story Prize's* inaugural competition for short fiction in translation. Fatima hops between continents and countries but is based in Cairo, Egypt.

Lightning Source UK Ltd.
Milton Keynes UK
UKHW051630070223
416582UK00004B/308